I0612394

NEVER TOO LATE

JAX BURROWS

By Jax Burrows

The O'Connors

Worth Waiting For
Healing Hearts
Never Too Late
Born to Love

This book is dedicated to paramedics everywhere.
Thank you for everything you do.

Vinci Books

vinci-books.com

Published by Vinci Books Ltd in 2026

1

Copyright © Jax Burrows 2020

The author has asserted their moral right to be identified as the author of
this work in accordance with the Copyright, Designs and Patents Act 1988.
This work is a work of fiction. Names, characters, places and incidents are
the product of the author's imagination or are used fictitiously. Any
resemblance to actual persons, living or dead, places and incidents is
entirely coincidental.
All rights reserved. No part of this publication may be copied, reproduced,
distributed, stored in any retrieval system, or transmitted in any form or by
any means, including photocopying, recording, or other electronic or
mechanical methods, nor used as a source for any form of machine
learning including AI datasets, without the prior written permission of the
publisher.
The publisher and the author have made every effort to obtain permissions
for any third party material used in this book and to comply with copyright
law. Any queries in this respect should be brought to the attention of the
publisher and any omissions will be corrected in future editions.
A CIP catalogue record for this book is available from the British Library.
Paperback ISBN: 9781036708054

The EU GPSR authorised representative is Logos Europe, 9 rue Nicolas
Poussion, 17000 La Rochelle, France
contact@logoseurope.eu

Chapter One

Caitlin had butterflies in her stomach as she got ready. She couldn't quite believe it was finally here. She had been engaged to Brandon for so long, that she had started to forget there was going to be a marriage at the end of it.

Tonight though, was for enjoying herself with her friends, letting her hair down and having fun. Her last night of freedom. Her hen night!

'How do I look?' Caitlin asked.

The theme for the hen night, organised by Sophie, her best friend, was 1950s style of dress. "Polka dots and pretty frocks" for the women and the men could wear whatever they liked as long as it was retro.

Sophie studied Caitlin with her head on one side, then grinned.

'You look great, hon, but you need this.' She rummaged in the bag of goodies she'd brought with her and pulled out a white sash with silver writing that proclaimed, "Bride-to-Be".

'Wonderful,' said Caitlin as she slipped it over her head.

'And these.' Sophie handed over a pair of silver garters and Caitlin put them on, so they just peeped out from the hem of her sleeveless floral cocktail dress. 'Now you look fabulous.'

'I'm really sorry you can't be my matron of honour, but our mothers were determined to have Brandon's nieces and nephews as bridesmaids and page boys.'

'Don't worry about it. Anyway, I had my own sash made to match yours.'

Sophie pulled another sash out of her bag and put it on. It said, "Bride's Best Friend" and looked smart over Sophie's fifties pink polka dot halterneck dress.

They stood side by side and looked at themselves in the mirror. Sophie was plumpish and blonde with a sweet face that belied a mischievous and cunning mind. Caitlin was petite and looked younger than her twenty-eight years. She was dark to Sophie's blonde. They looked like polar opposites, but their friendship was indestructible as they had been through a lot together, including a swish boarding school.

'Happy?' asked Sophie.

'Extremely happy,' said Caitlin. 'Thanks for arranging everything for me.'

'It was a pleasure. Anyhow, what else would a bestie do?'

'I'm really looking forward to tonight,' said Caitlin.

'I think we should go downstairs now to wait for the taxi. It should be here in five minutes and we have to brave your mother, who will doubtless be standing in the hallway to give you a talking to before we leave.'

Caitlin giggled, 'Let's climb out the window and make a run for it.' Even though she was twenty-eight and a qualified paramedic, she always felt about ten years old in her mother's imposing presence.

'You know what she's going to tell you, don't you?'

'Of course, I've been hearing it, or a variation of it, all my life.'

'Okay. Let's go.' Sophie picked up her bag and opened the door for Caitlin.

'What else is in that bag?'

'Never you mind, you'll find out soon enough.'

Nina Hewitt, retired model, and Caitlin's mother was indeed standing in the hallway. She had a glass in her hand which Caitlin knew would contain champagne, her mother's favourite drink.

'Let me look at you,' her mother said.

They both stood to attention for Nina to look them over, but she didn't glance at Sophie.

'Will we do?'

'I don't know why you want to dress in old-fashioned clothes when there are so many modern dresses you could wear. And what have you got on your leg?'

'They're garters, Mrs Hewitt,' said Sophie, 'it's a tradition for the bride-to-be to wear them on her hen night.'

'Ridiculous,' said Nina Hewitt sipping her champagne. 'Now, I don't want to hear any stories about you behaving like a common tramp.'

'What about an upper class one?' muttered Sophie.

'No, Mother.'

'I'm not saying that you can't enjoy yourself but if anything gets back to Brandon about his wife-to-be behaving shamelessly, getting drunk, or making a spectacle of herself in public, he isn't going to be pleased. I know what goes on at these events, especially in *that* part of Leytonsfield.'

'No…nothing will happen.' Caitlin had stopped

listening and was slowly inching her way towards the front door.

'You have our family name to uphold, Caitlin, and if you bring any disgrace on us by raucous behaviour, I'll never forgive you. And neither will your father. And if you get yourself into trouble tonight, don't expect us to come and bail you out.'

'I won't, Mother, I promise. I think I can hear the taxi.'

'I can't hear anything.'

The doorbell rang and Caitlin breathed a sigh of relief.

'Bye, Mother. Don't wait up, I'm staying with Sophie tonight.'

'Goodbye, Mrs Hewitt, I'll look after her, I promise.'

Jay O'Connor lay on his bed staring at the ceiling. He should be getting changed into his party clothes, not that he had any, and combing his hair which was still damp from his shower, but he felt too lethargic to move.

It was the first hen night he'd ever been invited to and he was looking forward to it. The goings-on at these events were notorious. As a paramedic he'd attended to countless young women, falling off their heels and spraining ankles, ending up drunk in a gutter. A group of women together won hands down over a group of men for disgraceful behaviour.

This hen night was going to be different. Caitlin had invited as many of her male friends as her girlfriends. She was calling it a friends' night out and it would probably turn out to be an enjoyable event. Especially as two of Jay's friends—Paul and Matt—were also going.

The reason for his inertia was Caitlin. He had met her

five years ago when she started her paramedic training. Three years of alternating theory and practical. The first time she attended a call-out to a real patient was when they were on shift together. He had liked her then, a lot. Over the years, the liking had changed to something deeper. Now he knew that he loved her. But she was marrying someone else and had no idea of his feelings for her.

Jay got up off the bed and looked in his wardrobe. He didn't know why he bothered as he always ended up wearing the same clothes when he went out. Black jeans and a white shirt worn loose with the sleeves rolled up. There would be dancing, and he was determined that Caitlin was going to dance with him. At the last minute, he swapped the white shirt for a white T-shirt. After all, there was a 1950s theme to the evening, so he could tell people he was channelling his inner James Dean.

Ten minutes later he was ready and left the house to walk to the town centre to meet the others in Mellow, a wine bar on High Street.

The place was buzzing and filled with people wearing 1950s dress. Were they all here for the hen night? Caitlin must have a lot of friends. Paul and Matt were already there, as were two other paramedics he didn't know very well. Paul was wearing a shirt and tie and looked smart. Jay wondered if he should have dressed up too.

'Hey, my man, how're you?'

'Great, Paul, you?'

'I'm alright and looking forward to seeing how the ladies celebrate. My first hen night.'

'Yep, me too.'

Only two people knew about Jay's feelings for Caitlin: his twin sister, Josie, and Paul. He trusted them both to keep his secret.

There were no tables vacant, so they stood around near the bar and waited for Caitlin to arrive.

They didn't have to wait long before a taxi drew up outside and Caitlin emerged with another woman. Jay's heart started racing as he watched her straighten her dress and adjust two garters that she wore on her right leg. She looked absolutely gorgeous and Jay wondered how he was going to get through the night without begging her not to marry Brandon and marry him instead.

'Hi, everyone. This is Sophie.' Caitlin waved to some people and hugged others. Everyone crowded around her, complimenting her on her dress and asking her if she was excited now the day had finally arrived.

They all said hello to Sophie, and Paul went to the bar for another round of drinks. Jay was drinking beer and he intended to alternate it with sparkling water or lemonade. He didn't have a head for alcohol and had decided to stay sober to make sure everyone else got home safely. Especially Caitlin.

'Hi, Caitlin, you look lovely.'

'Thanks, Jay. Glad you could come.'

'Wouldn't miss it for the world. It's kind of you to ask us men.'

'Well, I count you all as close friends. I intend to celebrate with people I care about and that includes you guys.'

'Well said,' said Sally who had just arrived. She was in her forties, Scottish, and had been a paramedic longer than any of them. 'Can I get you a drink, Cait?'

'Thanks, but Paul's at the bar, he's getting the drinks in.'

'Right, I'll go tell him to get mine.'

Once they all had fresh drinks, Sally proposed a toast, 'To Caitlin and Brandon, may they be happy together for the rest of their days.'

'To Caitlin and Brandon,' rang out around the wine bar.

Jay wanted Caitlin to be happy and if this man was the one for her, then he would wish her well. But, from the little she'd told him about Brandon, Jay seriously doubted he was.

'So,' said Sally turning to Caitlin, 'What's the groom doing while you're out on the town? Is he having a stag night?'

'He's having a stag weekend in Monte Carlo. He'll be having the time of his life.'

'Well, good for him,' said Sally.

Jay compared the two. A weekend in a casino in the richest country in the world, where money would be no object, versus a night in Leytonsfield town centre.

'And who have you come as?' Sally asked as she looked Jay up and down.

'James Dean.' He would have done the voice, but he had no idea what James Dean sounded like.

'Aye, I can see the resemblance.'

Sally then came up with one of her famous comments. 'You know what I don't like about all this business of separating the women and the men?'

'No,' said Paul with his arm casually draped across Sally's shoulders, 'give us the benefit of your wisdom, Sal.'

'Men have a stag night, don't they?' Everyone nodded. 'Stags are magnificent animals with strength and grace; those beautiful antlers, you know?' They nodded again. 'And women have hens; little, nondescript birds that scratch about in the soil. How is that fair?'

'Sounds fair enough to me,' said Paul and dodged out of Sally's way as she tried to hit him around the head.

They were all laughing, and Jay watched Caitlin smiling

as Sally chased Paul around the tables, upsetting several punters.

Then three women pushed their way forwards and stood in front of Caitlin and her smile vanished.

'So sorry we're late, darling. We haven't missed anything have we?'

The women laughed and Caitlin looked at Sophie who came to stand next to her.

'Fenella and friends, what a delight. Trouble is, I don't remember inviting you.'

'Oh, you don't need to bother with formalities; we've known each other since school. We weren't going to miss Caitlin's hen night, were we, girls?'

The women said no, and Sophie shrugged. 'We're moving on now anyway, so you've missed the boat.'

'I've got an idea,' said Fenella, 'we'll come with you.'

The women laughed again as if Fenella had said something hilarious.

'Right, everyone. We're moving on to The Late Club, so knock the drinks back and let's go.' Sophie ushered Caitlin out, leaving Fenella and her friends to follow.

Jay wondered who the women were. Nobody Caitlin and Sophie were pleased to see, that was for sure. He wasn't going to bother thinking about them. This was Caitlin's night and she was the only one who mattered.

He couldn't wait to get Caitlin on the dance floor when he'd have the chance to hold her in his arms. Probably the only chance he'd ever have.

Chapter Two

Caitlin had been enjoying herself until Fenella, Bunty and Dido turned up. Three blasts from the past she could have done without on her hen night. It was obvious they had gatecrashed as they were the last people Sophie would have invited.

Caitlin was going to enjoy herself despite their presence. She'd ignore them. They couldn't hurt her now.

She sat in the booth that her friends had claimed and chatted to Sally.

'How do you feel then, Caitlin? Are you excited about the wedding? Next Saturday isn't it?'

'Yes, it is. And yes, I am. Excited and a bit nervous. We've been engaged for a long time and it'll feel strange to be married finally.'

Jay was sitting opposite her and he smiled. Caitlin smiled back.

'Fancy a dance?'

'Okay.' Caitlin got up and Jay took her hand and led her onto the dance floor. It was crowded and there wasn't much room for elaborate moves which was just as well as Caitlin didn't know any. She wasn't much of a dancer and was happy to keep close to Jay and sway from one side to side.

Fenella had dragged some poor man up to dance and was watching her over the man's shoulder. If her intention was to ruin the hen night, then she'd be disappointed. She turned away from her.

Jay took her hands and spun her around a few times and then the music changed to something she couldn't dance to and they sat down again.

'Okay, guys, we're going to play a game,' said Sophie when most of them had returned. 'It's called the shot game.'

Sally said, 'Oh no, I know this game. You're going to get us all to drink as many shots as we can to get us stinking drunk.'

'It's a variation on that, yes, but there's a bit more to it.'

'Okay,' said Sally, 'tell us the rules.'

Sophie explained the game. The shots were lined up on the table in front of everyone. Some of the shots had alcohol in them: tequila, vodka, or gin. Some of the shots, however, only had water, but no one but the barman knew which was which.

They were all listening avidly now, and Sophie continued. 'When I give the signal you drink your shot as fast as you can and the person to finish their drink last is out. I will be the judge.'

'Aren't you playing, Sophie?' Caitlin asked.

'No… for reasons which will become clear in a minute. The person who is the last man, or woman, standing has to spend the rest of the evening handcuffed to Caitlin.'

'Where are the handcuffs?' asked Paul and everyone laughed.

'Here!' Sophie pulled a pair of red, faux fur handcuffs out of her bag and waved them in the air.

'What a fun little game!' cried Fenella 'We'll play, won't we girls?' Dido and Bunty nodded.

Jay stood up and said, 'I'll organise the shots as I know one of the guys working tonight. He'll help us sort them out.'

'You're playing, aren't you, Jay?' Caitlin asked and he winked at her.

'You bet. Wouldn't miss this for the world.'

Jay went to the bar to organise the shots. He explained what he wanted and waited as Dave, the barman, poured alcohol in some shots and water in others. He turned his back so he wouldn't see which shot glass was which. It was tempting to cheat and make sure he got the shot glass with water in it. But Jay was honest and, much as he wanted to be the one shackled to Caitlin for the rest of the night, he was going to play the game fairly. He paid for the drinks and took the tray back to the table.

'Here we go, everyone, gather round.'

'I hope you didn't cheat,' said Paul.

Jay pretended to look hurt and put his hand on his heart. 'Would I do something like that?'

Paul raised his eyebrows but said nothing.

They each had a shot glass in front of them, Sophie stood up so she could see them all better and judge accurately who was the last to drink.

'On your marks… get set… go!'

Everyone except Sophie and Caitlin downed their drink;

some came up spluttering and others pulled a face as there was only water in theirs.

'Sorry, Matt, you were last. Stand up next to me.'

'Oh well, never mind. Ben would have been horrified if I'd lost the key and had to drag Caitlin home with me. No offence, darling.'

'None taken,' said Caitlin.

'Aren't you worried, Caitlin, about who you're going to be handcuffed to?' Fenella asked. 'I mean, it could be one of us.' She waved her hand to include Bunty and Dido.

Caitlin did look worried and Jay hoped Sophie would step in and stop Caitlin's hen night being ruined by the three women. They seemed determined to make mischief.

Jay took the shot glasses back to Dave who was ready with another tray. They swapped and Jay returned to the table.

The next round saw Sally the loser.

'Sorry, Caitlin,' she said and stood next to Matt and Sophie.

They went again, some of them groaning about how much they were drinking.

'Bunty, you're out.' Bunty went quietly.

Then Dido, Paul and several other people Jay didn't know followed. Eventually, there were only two people left; himself and Fenella.

'Right. Last chance. Good luck to you both.'

'On your marks... get set... go!'

Jay downed his shot in a second and everyone cheered.

'I won that round,' said Fenella, petulantly.

'Oh no you didn't,' said Sophie. 'I'm the judge and my word stands.' Sophie lifted Jay's arm as if he was a boxer and said, 'I declare Jay O'Connor the winner!'

They all shouted and cheered until Jay and Caitlin were handcuffed together.

'What now?' Caitlin asked as she leaned into Jay. Although she hadn't had any shots, she had been drinking the wine that her friends insisted on buying for her.

'I'm going to drink water so I can pace myself.' Jay said. He wasn't feeling sober any more, as he'd had several shots of alcohol and the room was spinning.

'And what are you going to do?'

'I'm going to stay right by your side, for the rest of the night.'

'What if I want a wee?'

'Then I'll come with you.'

Caitlin started giggling and Jay longed to kiss her. She had her head on his shoulder and he yearned to put his arm around her. He couldn't because they were handcuffed together but also because he didn't have enough self-control where Caitlin was concerned, and he'd made it his job to look after her, not take advantage of her.

Paul sat opposite them and he was staring at Jay with a smile on his face.

'What?' Jay asked.

'You're looking a bit worse for drink, bro. Had a few shots I take it.'

'I had about half and half.'

'Mine were all booze,' said Paul. 'Well done for winning.'

Jay didn't say anything but dragged Caitlin up for another dance. The dance floor was even busier now, so Jay put his arm around Caitlin's waist and held her other hand, the one that was joined to his.

'Is this alright?' he asked her.

'It's lovely,' said Caitlin, 'you're lovely. Have I told you how lovely your eyes are?'

'No, Caitlin, I don't believe you ever have.'

'Well, they are, you are, perfectly lovely.'

'So are you. I hope your fiancé appreciates you.' Jay knew he was on rocky ground. He wanted to tell Caitlin that Brandon wasn't good enough for her. He really didn't want her to marry the guy. From what he'd heard about him from Caitlin and other sources, the man was a snob and a bore. He had no idea what she saw in him.

'Brandon. We're getting married. We've been getting married for decades.' Then she started laughing and looked up at him. 'Kiss me.'

'Are you sure?' He had to ask, even though he was desperate to kiss her.

'Yep.'

So Jay kissed her, gently, on the lips. He wanted to linger, to deepen the kiss but forced himself to break off.

'Umm, that was nice,' Caitlin said, 'do it again.'

So he did. He kissed her properly, the way he had always dreamed of doing. Her lips were soft and tasted of wine. He pulled her closer to him, then cursed the hand-cuffs that stopped him cupping her face the way he wanted to. So he held her, and kissed her, her mouth opening to his and little moans escaping as he deepened the kiss, their tongues finding each other and Jay not wanting the kiss to ever end but knowing that he shouldn't be doing it.

Jay wanted to say, "I love you". He wanted her to know. Even if she married her fiancé he still wanted the woman he loved to know how he felt. But that wouldn't be fair on Caitlin. She was going to marry someone else and he needed to get over it. Get over her. Forget her and move on with his life.

Just, not tonight. Tonight was for being closer to Caitlin than he could ever have wished for. To be joined, literally, to the woman he loved.

Jay and Caitlin stayed on the dance floor swaying gently as there wasn't the room and Caitlin was too drunk to do anything else.

Sophie and a man who had asked her to dance were nearby and Sophie gave him the thumbs up. He smiled at her and continued swaying.

Then Jay noticed the woman, Fenella, who'd thought she was the winner, dancing with someone nearby. She stared at Jay and then smiled. It wasn't a pleasant smile. It was a haughty look that told him she'd seen the kiss. The illicit kiss that shouldn't have happened. Especially on Caitlin's hen night.

Jay was too drunk to think about it. He'd tell Caitlin later, if he remembered. The evening was drawing to a close and he needed to take Caitlin home. Or was she staying with Sophie?

Jay steered Caitlin back to the booth which was almost empty. They sat down and Caitlin put her head on his shoulder again. Sophie and her new friend were there, whispering together. When he got up to go to the gents, Sophie leaned over and spoke to Jay.

'I don't suppose you'd be willing for Caitlin to stay at yours tonight, it's just that I think Lorenzo will be staying at mine.'

'No problem, but be careful, you've only just met him.'

'Goodness, Jay, you sound like Caitlin's mother.'

'Caitlin's? Not yours?' Jay asked.

'My mother would be up for a threesome,' said Sophie and burst out laughing. 'She's worse than me for taking risks.'

That explained a lot about Sophie, Jay thought. She was outgoing, confident and lots of fun. Caitlin, however, was shy, lacking in self-esteem and was nearly asleep on his shoulder. Did their mothers have so much influence on the adults they had become? An interesting question, but too serious for a hen night.

Sophie stood up as Lorenzo came back. 'You've got the key, haven't you Jay?' She pointed at the handcuffs.

Jay checked his jeans pocket. 'Yep. Got it.'

'Good. Don't lose it or you'll be locked together forever, and it'll be you walking Caitlin up the aisle.'

Jay smiled and nodded. A picture came into his head of him with one of his brothers as best man, standing at the altar. Then, when the music began to play he turned and saw Caitlin in her wedding dress, slowly drifting up the aisle with a smile just for him. The happiest day of their lives.

Jay sighed and buried his face in Caitlin's hair. He wanted to stay like that forever, but people were leaving. The evening was over.

'Come on, sleeping beauty, let's go and find a taxi.'

Chapter Three

Caitlin woke at midday the next morning. Her head was hurting so much she wanted to cry. Her mouth felt like the Sahara desert and her stomach hurt.

She sat up, groaning at how hard and painful that simple manoeuvre was. Some kind person had left a glass of water on the bedside table and she drank it gratefully. There was a pair of handcuffs next to the water. Red, fluffy ones. She vaguely remembered someone wearing them.

She was in a strange bed, in a strange bedroom and therefore, logically, in a stranger's house. A stranger who wore handcuffs. Worrying.

Then Jay appeared in the doorway.

'Oh, thank goodness. I didn't know where I was for a minute.'

'You're at my place, Caitlin. How are you feeling?'

'Awful.'

'Do you remember much about last night?'

Caitlin groaned and tried to think. All she wanted to do

was to go to sleep again, but that would be rude seeing she was in Jay's home. She needed to at least try to be sociable.

'I remember getting ready to go out. With Sophie. Where is she?'

'She left The Late Club with a guy called Lorenzo.'

'Oh, she's always doing that, picking strange men up in clubs. She'll have sent me a text to tell me she's okay.'

Caitlin looked around for her bag which held her phone. Jay picked it up from a chair in the corner, where it was buried underneath her clothes. So, what was she wearing? A T-shirt that smelled of Jay.

'Thanks for this,' she said. Then a thought occurred. 'You didn't have to put it on me, did you?'

'No, don't worry, you were able to undress yourself. Just about.'

'Thanks.' Caitlin looked at her messages. She'd got one this morning at about three with a big thumbs up. That was Sophie's sign that everything was good. 'She's fine.' Caitlin lay back on the pillows and shut her eyes.

'Why don't you have a shower while I make you some breakfast?'

'Okay. In a minute.'

'You could probably use a couple of paracetamols I'm guessing?'

'Yes, please.'

'Right. Come down when you smell the bacon cooking.'

'Oh no, none for me, thanks.' The thought made her stomach heave.

'You're not vegetarian, are you?'

'No, just hungover.'

Jay laughed. 'The best cure for a hangover is vitamins and protein. A large glass of orange juice followed by a full English. Trust me, it works.'

He disappeared and Caitlin lay on the pillow groaning.

With a huge effort, she got herself out of bed and into the bathroom for a shower. By the time she made it downstairs, still wearing Jay's T-shirt, she was beginning to feel a bit better. And, after the paracetamol and juice, she thought that, maybe, she could eat a bit of the breakfast Jay had kindly made.

'Aren't you having any?'

'No, I've already eaten. Been up for a while.'

'Sorry you had to look after me last night, Jay, it was kind of you.'

'It was a pleasure, Caitlin. It was your hen night, so you had every right to let your hair down.'

'Did I wear the handcuffs?'

'We both did.'

'That meant you weren't able to dance with anyone else.'

'I didn't want to dance with anyone else.'

Caitlin looked into Jay's eyes. They were a darker hazel than hers and at that moment, they held depths and secrets that Caitlin wanted to explore.

'Jay? What are you saying?'

'Just that I like you a lot, Caitlin, and wanted to spend time with you. That shots game was an opportunity too good to miss.'

Caitlin didn't know what to say. He must mean as a friend. He'd never mentioned anything before about liking her in any other way. Better change the subject.

'That breakfast was lovely, Jay.'

'Glad you enjoyed it. Are you feeling a bit better now?'

'A lot, actually. Thanks for everything.'

'Do you want to go home yet? I'll take you if you do.'

Did Caitlin want to go home? No, she didn't. Her

mother would be waiting to question her, and she wasn't ready to face her yet.

'Can I stay here for a bit?'

'Of course. Stay as long as you like. In fact, how about we go for a walk as it's such a lovely day?'

'I don't have anything to wear.'

'I can fix that. Josie sometimes leaves stuff here. I'll find you some trainers and jog pants and you can wear my T-shirt. Would that be alright?'

'Perfect.'

Caitlin smiled at Jay. He was being so kind to her. She was sure he must have things to do but he was giving her his precious day off and she appreciated it more than she could express. He was such a gentleman, always thinking of others. Caitlin didn't understand why he didn't have women fighting over him. He was a lovely man and would make a perfect husband.

Caitlin's thoughts turned to Brandon. He rarely did kind things for her. In fact, she was the one who had to sacrifice for him. It was always what Brandon wanted; they only watched the movies he liked, ate at the restaurants he selected, and she couldn't remember the last time they had done a simple thing like go for a walk in the sunshine.

Not for the first time, Caitlin wondered if she was doing the right thing.

———

Caitlin looked unbearably cute dressed in his T-shirt and Josie's jog pants and trainers. She hadn't bothered putting any make-up on and looked young and fresh.

'How about we go to Manor Park?'

'Fine.'

Jay wished he could put the handcuffs back on so they could be tied together again. He wanted to be close to her, to hold her and kiss her, but, instead, he strolled next to her with his hands in the pockets of his chinos.

Manor Park was vibrant with summer foliage. Leaves were thick on the deciduous trees, and daisies dotted the lawns. The flowerbeds were a sea of colour under a blue sky with fluffy white clouds. Families picnicked on the grass, people walked their dogs, and joggers ran past them, sweating and drinking from their water bottles. It was a perfect summer scene.

'Shall we sit?' asked Jay and Caitlin nodded.

'This is so peaceful,' she said.

'I hope the good weather holds for your wedding.'

'Yes, me too.'

Caitlin didn't talk about her wedding as other women did. There was no excitement or sparkling eyes. She seemed very matter of fact about the whole thing.

'Are you having a honeymoon?'

'No, Brandon can't take the time off at present. Our families' businesses are merging and there's a lot for them to organise.'

'Right. Maybe later in the year then?'

'Yes, probably.'

'You don't sound very enthusiastic if you don't mind me saying so.' Jay didn't want to upset Caitlin, but he didn't understand why she wasn't extolling Brandon's virtues and proclaiming to the world that she was madly in love, as he would be if he was marrying Caitlin.

'It's difficult to explain. Brandon and I have known each other since we were children. Our parents have been friends since before we were born. It was assumed that we'd get married and so we are.'

'Do you love him?' Caitlin was frowning and Jay wished he'd kept his mouth shut. The last thing he wanted to do was upset her, but he needed to know that she really loved this guy.

'Yes, of course.'

'And he loves you?'

'Yes, of course, he does. Jay, why are you asking me all these questions?'

'I just want to be sure that you're doing the right thing. As a friend, Caitlin, I really care about you and I'm worried that you don't sound happy.'

'Well, that's sweet of you but, like I say, we've been engaged for so long that I guess the novelty has worn off. Anyway, we're getting married next Saturday and it's too late to back out now.' Caitlin laughed but Jay couldn't join in.

'No, it's not. It's never too late and if you're not sure then you owe it to yourself to do just that.'

Caitlin was quiet and Jay wondered if he'd overstepped the mark.

'I am sure, Jay. I love Brandon and he loves me. Please don't worry about me. I think I'd like to go home now.'

Jay gave Caitlin a lift home on his motorbike. It was his pride and joy, and he savoured the feeling of Caitlin's arms around his waist as she clung to him during the short ride.

When Jay stopped outside Caitlin's parents' house he gazed up at the six-bedroomed mansion and immediately thought of the period dramas his mother devoured on the TV. Something that Jane Austen would have written. It could be filmed here. It put his little two-bedroomed cottage in the shade.

Jay knew that Caitlin's family had money, but it was only now that he considered the implications. Of course, she'd want to marry someone from the same class. Someone who could give her the lifestyle she was used to.

Caitlin jumped off the back of the bike and stood watching Jay as he gazed at her house.

'Do you want to come in?'

'No, thanks anyway. I'm sure you and your family have got stuff to do before the wedding.'

Caitlin just shrugged. 'Thanks Jay for last night. I really enjoyed it.'

'You're welcome. I hope the wedding goes well.'

'Well…bye then.' Caitlin walked towards the front door and then turned when she reached it. She waved and he waved back before turning his bike around and heading for home.

Chapter Four

'Caitlin, sit down, I need to tell you something.'

'What is it?' Caitlin studied her friend's face. She looked worried and her usually cheerful expression had gone, replaced by a frown.

'Sit down, please.' Sophie patted the bed next to her.

Caitlin sat on the edge of the bed and waited. Then she had a thought and jumped up again. 'You're not sick are you? Pregnant? Are you feeling okay? You do look a bit pale.'

'No, I'm fine. It's not me, it's Brandon.'

'Brandon?' Caitlin sat down again. What could be wrong with Brandon? He'd be at home now as she was, getting ready for their big day. The society wedding that their parents had invited half of the Cheshire set to. The wedding her father laughingly referred to as the million-dollar wedding. Caitlin was sure it wasn't costing him that much, even when one factored in the exchange rate to pounds sterling.

'Caitlin?' Sophie brought her back down to earth.

'Sorry? Lost concentration there for a second. I'm nervous about tomorrow, you know. I was thinking of what Jay said about me not being very enthusiastic. Well, it's suddenly hit me. I'm getting married! It's supposed to be the happiest day of a girl's life, isn't it? Not that I'm a girl. In the olden days I would have been an old maid and on the shelf at twenty-eight.' She laughed but Sophie didn't laugh with her. 'Sophie? What is it? You're scaring me now.' Caitlin leaned forward and took Sophie's hands. She was her best friend and Caitlin trusted her with her life.

'I need to tell you this, and you're not going to like it. But please know that I'm doing this for you. If I were getting married and my closest friend knew something about my intended that wasn't good, I would want to know.'

'Sophie. What are you talking about?'

'Brandon is having an affair.'

Caitlin pulled her hands away from Sophie's and stood up.

'What?! Is that supposed to be some kind of a joke? Because it's not funny. We're getting married tomorrow—'

'Caitlin, it's not a joke. I'm so sorry but it's true. I struggled with telling you this, but I feel I have no choice.' Sophie stood up and tried to take Caitlin's hands, but she backed away from her.

'I don't believe you. He wouldn't. He loves me, I know he does. What right have you got to say that, anyway?'

'I've seen them together. Remember that do I went to in Bramhall on Wednesday with my mother? They were checking in and they had hand luggage. They went up in the lift together. You could tell it was a clandestine meeting. I'm so sorry, Caitlin.'

'Who was he with?' Caitlin knew the answer before Sophie spoke.

'Fenella Barton-Brookes.'

Caitlin sat down on the bed and put her face in her hands. His ex-girlfriend. The one he promised he wasn't seeing anymore. The woman who'd gatecrashed her hen night. The woman who was born with a silver spoon in her mouth. Old money, unlike Caitlin's family, the Hewitts, and Brandon's family, the Dodds. They were new money, made by fathers with brilliant business minds and a flair for real estate.

'Caitlin, I'm so sorry but you had to know. I'm on your side. If there's anything I can do.'

It was too much. The excitement of the wedding had knotted her stomach all day but finding out that her groom was a cheating, lying scumbag was more than she could bear. She got up and ran into her en suite bathroom, locking it and slowly lowering herself to the floor with her back to the door. She bent her legs and laid her head on her knees and sobbed.

Caitlin gave in to her grief, pulling the sleeves of her sweatshirt down over her hands and using them to stem the flow of tears. She cried as she had when she was a child; hopelessly and piteously. She could feel the pain in her stomach tighten and twist until there was only one way to release it. She wanted to have a tantrum, kick her heels on the floor and shout and scream as she had done when she was about three.

Instead, Caitlin shouted, No! as loudly as she could, which felt good and eased the pain slightly, until she heard her parents and Sophie outside the bathroom door. They were all talking at once and she could only make out snippets of what they were saying. But she heard enough to want to crawl into a hole and hide.

'Caitlin. I'm sorry, yeah? Please come out and talk to me,' Sophie said.

'Caitlin, whatever is going on?' Her mother's voice was harsh and disapproving.

'Caitlin. I am ordering you to come out now and stop being so childish.' Her father's usual reaction to a woman's tears.

Her father was right. She was being childish, but she couldn't help it. Everything had been going so well. She had a brilliant career that she loved and the best friends and colleagues anyone could wish for. She was marrying a man who had said he loved her, and she loved him.

Now, it had all turned to dust.

Caitlin had stopped crying except for small hiccupping noises and a runny nose. She lifted her head as Sophie spoke again.

'I'm going now, your parents have asked me to leave. Please text me and let me know what is happening. I love you, Cait.'

'Caitlin?' Her mother's voice again. 'You need to come out now and talk to us. We don't have time for this nonsense.'

Then her father's voice again. 'Caitlin. Come out and we'll talk about it.'

Caitlin heard her parents walking down the stairs and then it was blissfully silent. She stood up and stared at herself in the mirror. Blushing bride, what a joke. Her make-up had run, and her hair was a mess, she was pale, and her eyes were red. More Halloween party than June wedding.

She washed her face and brushed her hair which made her look slightly more presentable. Then she left the bathroom and walked slowly down the stairs.

When she got to the lounge where her parents waited, her stomach was in knots again. Caitlin's relationship with her parents, which had always been rocky, had deteriorated further when she had told them she intended to train as a paramedic, but after agreeing to marry Brandon, she had been back in favour again.

'Ah, there she is,' said her mother. 'Come and sit down, Caitlin. That girl had no right to upset you like that, on the day before your wedding. If I were you I'd cut her out of my life altogether. Make it plain that she needs to respect your wishes not to have any more contact.'

'Mother, Sophie was doing me a favour. She saw Brandon and—'

'What exactly did she see? She saw two people who have known each other for decades having a drink together in a hotel. That's all she saw.'

Her mother was drinking champagne and lounging back on the cream sofa. She sat with the studied elegance of the model that she used to be, as if she were posing for a photo. Her make-up was immaculate, and her hair was piled up in an elaborate style that Caitlin couldn't have replicated if her life depended on it.

'God, I need a drink,' said her father as he poured a generous helping of Glenfiddich into a cut-glass tumbler.

'I can't marry him now,' said Caitlin.

'You'll be at that church tomorrow, my girl, if I have to carry you in myself.' Her father was red in the face and close to losing his temper. Her mother waved her hand at him; a gesture that told him to be quiet and he subsided obediently.

'Listen, darling,' her mother said, her voice like honey, 'You can't let the spite of a jealous divorcee ruin your special day. Has Brandon ever given you any reason to doubt him? No, he hasn't,' said her mother before Caitlin had the chance to answer.

'Sophie wouldn't lie, not to me. She's my closest friend. And it isn't her fault she is divorced at twenty-eight. Her husband was a cheating scumbag as well.'

'If she's your friend, as you claim, why would she tell you now, when it's too late to do anything about it? She's a trouble maker and jealous of your happiness, so forget her and her spiteful gossip, okay?' Her mother poured herself another glass of champagne and gestured at Caitlin to ask if she wanted a glass too. Caitlin shook her head.

'I can't just forget something like that. That woman is always hanging around Brandon. What if it's true and they're having an affair? I can't marry him now, not until I know the truth.'

'You can and you bloody well will. I've spent a small fortune on this wedding, and I don't intend to be the laughing stock of Cheshire just because you're having doubts. The Dodds are a highly respected family and I'm not going to let you upset them.'

'Oh, do shut up, Alan,' said her mother, 'you're not helping.'

'I should go around to his and have it out with him. Ask him outright.' Caitlin got up, but her mother stepped in front of her and put her hands on her shoulders, looking her straight in the eye.

'Here's what you're going to do. Have a long soak in the tub to relax. Then you will have an early night and forget everything except tomorrow when you will wake refreshed and ready for the happiest day of your life. Okay?'

Caitlin knew they had won for now, and she obediently went upstairs to do her mother's bidding.

The hot fragrant bath relaxed her, so she put her head back and let her shoulders sink under the water.

Caitlin loved her parents and wanted to please them, especially after the disappointment she had felt from both of them when she had announced her intention to become a paramedic. She was letting the side down. Her father hadn't sent her to a private school so she could waste her education on becoming a common ambulance driver, he had said. She had tried to explain that being a paramedic entailed a lot more than merely driving an ambulance. It was a highly skilled job. A career. But they refused to listen, and Caitlin knew it was futile to even try to explain.

Her parents were all about appearances and letting other people know how rich and successful they were. Things Caitlin used to think were important, too, when she was attending her private school, patronised by daughters of the upper echelons of society. She used to be one of them, but money had never brought her happiness. She had drunk the best champagne and dined at the finest restaurants. She loved Louis Vuitton handbags and Gucci shoes, and the cost of her wedding dress would probably pay off the national debt of a small nation, but since becoming a paramedic her values had changed.

Caitlin's happiest memory was the first time she'd helped deliver a baby. She'd been in the second year of training where some of the time was spent at university, interspersed with time spent partnering a qualified paramedic.

Their patient was seventeen and lived with her mother on the ninth floor of a block of council flats. And the lift didn't work. That day she was partnering Jay and they could hear the young girl screaming in pain all the way up the narrow, dirty, and extremely smelly concrete stairwell.

They'd hurried as best they could, laden down with all their equipment. Needless to say, Jay got there first, but she wasn't too far behind.

The baby was already crowning when they arrived. Jay took charge and Caitlin watched in amazement as the baby made her appearance.

Caitlin remembered the feeling of pride and relief as they watched the young girl and her new daughter getting acquainted. The baby's granny made them a hot drink and they sat together on the couch, sipping tea as if the miracle of new life hadn't just played out in all its wonder.

When they finally got back in the ambulance, after delivering mother and baby to hospital to be checked over, Jay had turned to her and said, 'It doesn't get much better than that.'

The following morning Caitlin woke feeling more like a limp rag than a blushing bride. She had slept fitfully and on several occasions had grabbed her phone with the intention of ringing Brandon and asking him if he was having an affair. She knew, however, that it wasn't something they could discuss on the phone.

Her mother helped her into her dress, fussing around her and organising the bridesmaids and page boys. All Brandon's nieces and nephews. They didn't have much in the way of family. Both her parents were only children and Caitlin didn't have any siblings.

When they got to the church, Caitlin felt sick. There was a crowd of people milling about outside, drawn to the romance of a wedding, hoping to catch a glimpse of the bride. All the guests would be inside the church, waiting for her to make her slow walk down the aisle, smiling radiantly and followed by the entourage of children.

Caitlin looked at her father, but he was taking a nip of whisky from a flask he kept in his inside pocket. He wasn't even looking at her. He hadn't complimented her or given her fatherly advice. He was treating the whole thing as if it were an annoying chore.

Caitlin wished she could talk to Brandon. If he could only reassure her that it was all lies, she'd feel so much better. But it was too late now. She'd have to go through with it and hope that her mother was right, and Sophie was mistaken.

Caitlin walked down the aisle of the church in a daze. She was glad of her father's arm to cling on to or she may have stumbled or fainted. She was aware of the sea of people, some women in brightly coloured dresses and big hats, some in pastel shades, the men in suits. The church was awash with flowers.

As she passed Sophie she turned to her for encouragement. Her friend was looking worried and shook her head slightly. Caitlin clenched her teeth and kept walking.

As they got to the altar, she glanced at Brandon who smiled. Then the vicar began the service.

Caitlin didn't know what made her turn around. Whether it was intuition or the heat from the woman's eyes burning into her back, but the vicar had only just started telling the congregation why they were gathered there, when Caitlin stared into the smug face of Fenella Barton-Brookes, sitting on the front row on the groom's side of the church, and she saw red. She turned back and confronted Brandon.

'Are you having an affair?' Her voice seemed to ring out in the echoing church and some people gasped.

Brandon turned red and laughed in embarrassment. 'What?'

'I said, are you having an affair?'

The vicar was silent, staring from one to the other. The congregation were murmuring but also waiting to hear his answer.

Brandon gave himself away before he had uttered another word. He stared at Fenella Barton-Brookes and his expression was like a little boy in the nativity play who had forgotten his lines.

Caitlin turned back to Fenella and the answer was written all over her triumphant face.

'You bastard!' Caitlin threw the bouquet of flowers with all her might, but Brandon had the sense to duck and the unfortunate vicar took the full force of a bunch of pale pink ranunculus in his bewildered face.

Caitlin heard her name being called and turned to see Sophie standing up and waving a set of car keys. 'Take my car,' she shouted.

Caitlin, who didn't need telling twice, ran down the aisle, grabbed the keys off Sophie, said, 'Thanks, I owe you,' then raced out of the church.

It was only when she was outside that Caitlin realised she didn't know what car Sophie drove. She was in the habit of updating on a regular basis. She clicked the keys and the lights of a Mercedes parked nearby flashed. Without looking back, she got in the car and sped off.

Chapter Five

'Right, I'm off to McDonalds. Want me to get you anything?' Paul locked the ambulance as they both clambered out.

'Thanks mate but I'll buy something from the vending machine,' said Jay.

'Right. See you later then.'

'Ciao.'

Jay made his way to the entrance of Accident and Emergency trying not to think about Caitlin. She'd wanted him to be at the wedding itself, but he couldn't face it, so had only agreed to attend the party in the evening. He knew it was going to be a big, posh affair but he had no idea how long big, posh weddings went on for. She might be Mrs Dodds by now or she might not. Either way, Caitlin would never be Mrs O'Connor.

Jay was deep in thought and nearly missed the little old lady hovering in the doorway. She looked lost and frightened, holding onto the wall with one hand and clutching a walking stick with the other. She caught his eye as he came up to the automatic doors.

'Oh, could you help me, please?'

'Of course, love, what can I do for you?'

'Am I in the right place for Dr O'Connor's clinic?'

She held a letter in her hand and Jay smiled and said, 'Is that your appointment letter? Can I have a look?'

She passed it over to him. The lady was due to attend cardiology outpatients and the consultant in charge was his brother, Riordan. She was already late, and the outpatients was on the other side of the hospital.

'You're on the wrong side, Mrs Bannister. Outpatients is a good walk from here. This is A&E.'

The little lady's face crumpled at the news.

'Oh dear, I'm never going to get there.'

'Yes, you will. Just wait there and I'll fetch a wheelchair. We'll get there in no time.'

Jay gave the letter back to Mrs Bannister and hurried into A&E where the wheelchairs were kept. He grabbed one and hurried back.

'Here we go, just park yourself on this. Hang on tight now.'

Mrs Bannister sat on the wheelchair with her handbag on her lap and held on tight to the arms.

'We'll go around the outside of the hospital. It's quicker and I know a shortcut.'

'It's really kind of you,' said Mrs Bannister.

'It's a pleasure,' said Jay, his stomach rumbling like a blocked drain. He'd have to get a packet of crisps and some chocolate before he went back on duty, or he'd faint from hunger. He didn't think Paul would thank him for that, especially as he'd been such a misery guts all morning. She'd be married by now, he thought.

'Here we are, Mrs Bannister, right on time.'

He helped the lady from the wheelchair and made sure she was comfortable on one of the grey, plastic chairs in the waiting area.

'Oh, thank you. What's your name?'

'My name's Jay and it was nothing, really. It was a pleasure. I'll tell the receptionist you're here.'

'Oh, thank you. I'd have been lost without you. You're a good lad.'

Jay smiled and hurried to the reception desk. 'Mrs Bannister,' he shouted over the heads of the patients standing in line waiting to book into the clinics.

'Okay. Thanks, Jay,' said Bernie, one of the receptionists as he grabbed the wheelchair and left the outpatients department.

He was tempted to leave the wheelchair in outpatients and go and get some lunch but knew how important they were to the A&E department staff, so did the right thing and wheeled it swiftly down the road to the other side of the hospital.

Just as he arrived at the ambulance bays, Paul ran towards him.

'There you are! Come on mate, we've got a call-out.'

'Just a tick.' Jay ran in with the wheelchair then raced out again and clambered up into the front of the ambulance.

'Where've you been anyway, and what's with the wheelchair?'

'Doing a good deed. Don't suppose you've got any of those fries left have you?'

'You suppose right, I've eaten them all. Anyway, you're always poking fun at my fast-food lunches. Haven't you eaten?'

'Didn't have time.'

'Right. Here's a protein bar, that'll keep you going for a bit.'

'Thanks, mate, you're a star.'

It was only after he'd stuffed the protein bar into his mouth that he read the screen on the dashboard with the details of their next patient.

A young woman had crashed her car into a lamp post on a roundabout in the busiest part of Leytonsfield. Query concussion but she was breathing and conscious. The police had called it in.

Jay sat back, still munching, and thinking of the church where Caitlin was getting married. They'd be having their photos taken now. Happy, smiling faces. He didn't think he'd ever be happy again.

'Funny one, not sure what's going on with her.' said Paul.

'Why? It seems straightforward to me.'

'Something the police officer said. The woman was wearing a wedding dress.'

At the mention of a wedding dress, Jay's heart plummeted to his boots. As they raced through the streets, the siren going and the lights flashing, nervous adrenaline rushed through his veins. As soon as they were there and treating the patient, he was usually calm and efficient, cracking silly jokes to put the patient at their ease if it wasn't a life-threatening situation.

This time, however, all he could think of was Caitlin in a blood-stained wedding dress and a smashed-up car. It couldn't be her. This day was getting to him in a way he hadn't anticipated. He'd thought he could reason with himself and get through the day normally. The facts were simple. He loved Caitlin, had done for a long while. The same length of time she had been engaged to another man. Therefore he was the loser and there was nothing he could do about it. He had to wish her well and move on. But he couldn't. Even after admiring the engagement ring she had proudly shown to everyone, a massive rock that probably cost more than his yearly wage, he had still been hopeful that something would happen to prevent the marriage.

'You okay, mate?' said Paul.

'Yes. No... I don't know to be honest.'

'Right, thanks for clearing that up. We're here.'

Paul pulled up about fifty feet from a car with its front concertinaed against a lamp post. They always kept a safe distance from RTA's in case of fire. The police car was parked on the other side of the crash site and an officer with a hi-vis jacket on was talking to someone in the car.

They both jumped out of the ambulance and grabbed the equipment.

As soon as they walked up to the car, the police officer stepped back.

'It's her,' whispered Jay, 'It's Caitlin. Shit.'

Paul kneeled down and spoke to Caitlin as Jay turned to the police officer.

'What happened?'

'We think she lost control of the car. No other vehicles involved which is a miracle on a busy Saturday in the town centre. We're checking the CCTV then we'll know more. She's wearing shoes suitable for a wedding but hopeless for driving.'

'Is she trapped?'

'No, but I didn't want her moved until you lot arrived.'

'Quite right. I'll get on.'

Caitlin was conscious but tearful and neither of them could get any sensible information out of her, so they put a collar on her in case she'd injured her neck and Paul checked for any obvious injuries before they carefully lifted her out of the car and onto the stretcher.

Jay knelt down and whispered, 'Hey, sweetheart, what happened?'

Caitlin turned a tear-stained face to him and whimpered. Jay stroked her cheek.

'Right,' Paul said, 'You drive, I'll stay in the back with her.'

Jay was just about to argue as he wanted to be the one to talk to Caitlin, but he recognised the sense in what Paul said. He was incapable of being impartial, so he got in the ambulance and waited for Paul to tell him he could drive off.

Jay was in agony as he watched the A&E staff wheel Caitlin into Resus. He looked for his other brother, Casey, who worked as a consultant in the department, but there was no sign of him. He would have been able to keep him up to date. There was nothing else for it. They needed to get back in the ambulance and wait for the next call-out. Once paramedics handed over the patient to the doctors and nurses, their role in the proceedings was over.

For Jay, however, it was only just beginning. Why was Caitlin driving a Mercedes? Didn't she get married? What the hell was going on?

'She's safe there, mate. There was no neck injury and no other major trauma that we could see. Her pupils were equal and dilating, she might have a mild concussion but that's all.'

'I know,' said Jay, 'but why was she driving a car? In her wedding dress?'

'Your guess is as good as mine. But overthinking it isn't going to help you and we've got another three hours before our shift ends, so cool your jets, okay?'

'Yeah, you're right.' Jay fell silent and pondered the problem. 'Just not sure whether to go to the party tonight, that's all.'

Paul gave a belly laugh which put a smile on Jay's face. 'Ha ha, you're a funny man, you know that? Good joke. Glad you've not lost your sense of humour.'

Jay was so glad he was in the ambulance with Paul today. He was one of his regular partners and he loved him like a brother. Even though Paul was a six-foot-two tall, good-looking Jamaican guy with dreadlocks and Jay had two brothers of his own. Always room for another one. A brother from another mother.

A good relationship with your crewmate was one of the most important things, in Jay's opinion. And he worked with the best. Which brought his thoughts back to Caitlin.

The phone rang and they were soon on their way to their next call-out; an elderly gentleman who had fallen in the bathroom. He had dementia and was confused.

'Here we go again, said Paul as he switched the sirens and lights on.

Chapter Six

At the end of his shift, Jay went back to visit Caitlin. She had been moved to a ward and people crowded around her bed. Jay hadn't a clue who they all were as he had never met her family.

'Jay!' Caitlin cried as she caught sight of him hovering on the outskirts of the visitors.

'Hi, how are you?' Jay moved towards the bed, ignoring the dark looks he was getting from rent-a-crowd.

He took her hand and studied her face. She had a black eye and the bruise on her cheek was darker than it had been when they brought her into the hospital. The airbag had saved her life but caused injuries to her face.

He wanted to take her in his arms and hold her, tell her everything was going to be alright, that he would protect her and keep her safe. Instead, he stood at the side of the bed, holding her hand and longing to kiss her.

'I'm so glad you're here. I want to thank you and Paul for rescuing me today.'

'Oh, don't be so dramatic, darling, your life was never in any danger with that little bump.'

Caitlin sighed and seemed to withdraw into the pillows.

'Jay, meet my mother,' she said quietly.

'Pleased to meet you, Mrs Hewitt,' Jay said politely.

'Likewise, I'm sure.' She waved her hand in front of her face and moved closer to Caitlin. 'Now, tell me who I need to see about getting you into the private ward. Or better still, discharging you. I'm sure you don't need to be here, and we can look after you perfectly well at home.'

It was obvious that no one was going to introduce him to the other people, so Jay addressed his comments to Caitlin's mother.

'Caitlin needs to stay here overnight, Mrs Hewitt. We need to make sure she hasn't suffered concussion or other injuries.'

'Oh piffle,' said Mrs Hewitt. 'She's fine apart from a few bruises, I really think she should come back with us. Could you go and find the people in charge and tell them that we're leaving now. With our daughter? There's a good fellow.'

Jay could feel the anger churning in his stomach but smiled as if he were dealing with a rebellious patient and tried to keep calm for Caitlin's sake.

'What tests have you had, Caitlin?' he asked.

'I had a CT scan, but I haven't had the results back yet.'

'Was that really necessary?' said a man who Jay presumed was Caitlin's father.

'Mr Hewitt? Pleased to meet you. I'm Jay O'Connor, a friend of Caitlin's.' Jay put his hand out to shake, and Mr Hewitt shook it briefly. 'The scan would detect any internal injury, especially to Caitlin's head.'

'Might knock some sense into her,' said a young man who Jay assumed was Brandon, the groom. He guffawed at his own joke and Jay glared at him. He looked a typical Hooray Henry, a type that Jay despised.

A young woman fought her way to the bedside and said, 'Hi Jay, remember me?'

'Hi Sophie, yes of course I do. How's Lorenzo?'

'Oh, he's long gone. A bit like my car.'

'It was Sophie's Mercedes I customised.'

'Bloody thing's a write-off,' said Brandon. 'It was still there on the roundabout when we came here. Can't be driven now I don't suppose. Will need towing.'

'Oh don't worry, the insurance will pay for it,' said Sophie. 'I'm due a new model anyway.'

'Do you want me to come back later?' Jay whispered to Caitlin.

'No. Please don't leave me.' Caitlin grabbed hold of his hand again and held on tight.

A staff nurse came over and smiled at Jay. He smiled back, remembering a particularly raucous Christmas party he'd gone to a couple of years back and a few stolen kisses with her under the mistletoe.

'Right, I'm sorry but I'm going to have to ask you all to leave as Caitlin needs to rest. You can come back tomorrow.'

Caitlin tightened her grip on Jay's hand, and he sat down on a chair at the side of the bed.

'I say,' said Mrs Hewitt, 'are you the person to ask about transferring my daughter to a private ward?'

'No, I'm not,' said the staff nurse, 'and you'd be wasting your time as she'll be discharged tomorrow. Now, please could you all leave.'

'Yes, Mother, just go,' said Caitlin, adding quickly, 'thank you all for coming.'

'Come on, Nina, we're not wanted,' said Mr Hewitt, taking his wife's arm.

'Fine, but I'm taking the wedding dress with me. I'll get it cleaned,' said Mrs Hewitt.

Sophie kissed Caitlin who hugged her and thanked her for the loan of the car.

'Text me and let me know when you're coming home. I'll be there to provide moral support,' Sophie whispered.

'Thanks, Sophie.'

Brandon approached the bed and Jay felt the tension in Caitlin's hand as she squeezed his hand even tighter.

'When you're better, we'll talk.' He kissed her on the cheek and Jay resisted the urge to thump him in the face. He instinctively didn't like the man.

Jay watched Caitlin as her family walked away. She sighed as if she had been holding her breath and could now relax. Her eyes were shut, and one tear slowly leaked out and rolled down her cheek. Jay couldn't resist leaning over and wiping it gently away.

'What happened, Caitlin?' Jay asked softly as he got up to pull the curtains around the bed.

She burst into tears and sobbed as if her heart would break. Jay sat on the edge of the bed, holding her tightly. She put her arms around his neck and cried all over his uniform.

'I'm sorry,' she said.

'Don't be. There's no need. You can tell me, or not, it's entirely up to you. We can just sit here quietly if you prefer.'

'It's Brandon. Sophie said she saw him and Fenella Barton-Brookes in a hotel and she thinks they were having an affair. Then, at the altar, I asked him outright and he stared at Fenella as if he didn't know what to say and then…'

It all came out in a garbled rush and Jay sensed Caitlin was getting worked up, so he stroked her back and made shushing sounds. What a piece of work that Hooray Henry must be, thought Jay. He wished now he had thumped him in the face.

'It's okay, we'll talk another time. Why don't you just lie down and try to rest. We'll wait for the scan results and then tomorrow you can go home.'

Caitlin lay down again and Jay returned to the chair next to the bed.

'I wish I could stay here. Do you think, if there's something on the scan, that they'll let me stay longer?'

'Depends on what the something is. I doubt there will be, though, Cait. Why don't you want to go home?'

'You've met my parents.'

Jay laughed. 'Are they always like that? Your mother doesn't think much of the NHS I take it?'

'My parents think money can buy them anything they want.'

'But they are your parents and must have your best interests at heart?'

'I suppose.' Caitlin sighed and turned her face away from him.

Jay knew he should go and let her rest, but she seemed so despondent that he didn't want to leave until he'd seen her smile. Then he had an idea.

'You know I'm on my own at the moment?' He had shared his house with another paramedic who'd left the service to travel the world. Jay had been tempted to go with him when he offered. Especially after Caitlin had told him about her engagement to Brandon. But something had kept him here. He had spent several months travelling America a couple of years back and wanted to stay at home for a while. All his family were in Leytonsfield and his brothers both had new babies. And then there was Caitlin. Maybe the reason he needed to be here was to help her.

Caitlin had turned on her side and was watching him. 'Yes?'

'I'm looking for a lodger to replace Steve. I haven't advertised yet, so the spare room is yours for as long as you want it.'

'Come and live with you?'

'Only for as long as you need a place to stay. No commitment or anything.'

'Oh Jay, that's a lovely idea. Thank you. Yes, I will accept your kind offer.' She smiled and Jay felt like punching the air in triumph. If he could make Caitlin smile, then he was a happy man.

'Great. I'll go home and get your bedroom ready.'

Caitlin sat up and looked happier than she had since the crash.

'Are you sure, Jay? I mean, well, I'm not the tidiest person but I'll try to be better.'

She looked vulnerable in the hospital gown with her hair loose and her face covered in bruises. He loved her. But he also wanted to help her. No doubt she and Brandon would patch things up. He knew this wasn't forever. For him, though, it was a chance to be close to her for a few precious days, or weeks. Or for whatever time she wanted. This was for Caitlin and he had to remember that.

'Yes, I'm sure. It makes sense. I'll pick you up early tomorrow as I'm on a late. See you then.'

'Bye, Jay, and thank you.'

He grinned at her and walked away. His heart was

singing at the joy of having Caitlin in his home. He'd look after her. She'd be his for a short time. He was borrowing her, that was all. There was another part of him, the sensible, logical side of his brain, that asked him what the heck he thought he was doing. He ignored it and, dancing on air, he left the hospital.

Chapter Seven

'Oh, it's nice to be back here,' said Caitlin, looking around at the open-plan living room.

'Good. *Mi casa tu casa*,' said Jay, as he put her meagre belongings on the coffee table. 'Although it's nothing special. Not like your parents' house.'

'Yes, it is special, Jay. It's cosy and warm.'

'It's far from what you're used to though, isn't it?'

'Exactly. That's what I need at the moment, somewhere far from home where I can lick my wounds and think about my next move.'

'Right. Cup of tea?'

'Love one. What can I do?'

'You can sit down, and then, when I'm at work, you can go to bed and sleep. I've made up your bed. There's more pillows in the airing cupboard. I didn't know what you're used to.'

'It'll be fine, Jay. Thanks. For everything.'

'It's a pleasure.'

Caitlin followed him into the kitchen and watched as he

took mugs out of a cupboard, and milk from the fridge. Jay O'Connor was the first paramedic she met. As a first-year student, she had to partner a qualified paramedic, and she had been terrified. Jay had made her laugh and put her at ease. She'd always be grateful to him.

When she qualified and started to work as an equal, Jay became one of her closest friends.

Caitlin watched him as he moved confidently around the kitchen. Just as he did when he was treating a patient. He was the kind of person that put others at ease, with his gentle manner and calm approach.

'There we go. You sit down, I'll carry the mugs.'

Caitlin did as she was told.

'I need to wash these clothes and return them to you.'

Jay had turned up that morning with the same sweat pants, T-shirt, and trainers she'd worn before, but with the addition of a cardigan.

'There's no hurry, Josie told me. She's got a wardrobe full of stuff like that.'

'Well, it's very kind of her.'

'What did your parents say when you told them you were staying with me?' Jay asked.

'I sent them a text as I didn't think they'd be up as early as seven.' That was stretching the truth a little bit as her father was in his office for seven every day, but her mother never surfaced before ten. And it was her mother who would be the one to tell her to come home.

'Have they replied?' Jay sipped his tea and watched her. She couldn't lie to him, he had been too good to her.

'Yes. I know I'm being a coward, but I just can't face their anger at the moment. They're furious with me after all the money they spent on the wedding and Brandon's family being friends with ours.'

'I don't think you're a coward. It looks to me as if you've had a lucky escape. If your parents don't see it that way, well, it's not your problem. You're a grown woman and can make your own decisions.'

If only that were true, thought Caitlin. Yes, she was a grown woman, but her parents still thought they could order her life.

'What did they say?'

She looked at Jay with his kind hazel eyes and his sweet smile. He was a handsome man and Caitlin wondered again why he didn't have women chasing him. She had never seen him with any woman for longer than a few dates.

'My mother said, "Come home and stop all this silly nonsense." Then her second text said she'd sent the wedding dress to a specialist dry cleaners who thought there was no damage done. They'd be able to get the bloodstains out, for a price. No damage done to the dress, maybe, but what about me?'

Jay drained his tea, then walked over to where she sat on the couch and sat next to her.

'Listen, sweetheart, you can stay here for as long as you need to. Get better first before you make any decisions.'

Jay had taken her hand and she studied his fingers with the short, well-manicured nails. Strong, capable hands.

'Sophie's coming around later and we're going to get my things. I'll have to see my mother and I know she'll try to convince me to stay, but I'm going to be strong. I'll be here tonight when you get home. Thanks for all your help, Jay.'

She squeezed his hand. His closeness made her feel safe. And something else. When he smiled at her, she felt her body tingle. She smiled back. Then he sighed and got up off the couch. She felt a twinge of loss as he let go of her hand.

'Better go and get ready for work.'

'Hi,' said Sophie as Caitlin opened the door and stepped back to let her in. 'Oh, wow! Isn't it charming, so *bijou* and cute.'

'Come in and look around. Jay won't mind.'

'Don't mind if I do.' Sophie entered the cottage and looked at everything from the furniture and rugs on the laminate flooring, to the prints on the wall.

'Can I go upstairs?' asked Sophie.

'Sure, I'll come with you and put my trainers on.'

It didn't take long for Sophie to see the upstairs of the cottage. 'I bet this whole house could fit into your parents' living room. And mine come to that.'

'Probably,' answered Caitlin.

'Doesn't it make you feel slightly claustrophobic?'

'No. I tell you what does though, the thought of going back to my parents' house. I'm so glad you're coming with me, Sophie.'

Sophie threw her arms around Caitlin and gave her a bear hug. 'I'll always be by your side, you know that, for as long as you want me to be.'

'Thanks, hon, you're one in a million.'

'Right, come on then, let's go and stick our heads in the lion's den.'

Sophie had borrowed her mother's car; an electric blue Aston Martin. It was a racy, exhibitionist's car which described Mrs Amelia Simons perfectly. Ever since her divorce five years previously, she had lived the high life with toyboys, cruises, and all-night parties.

Sophie visited her mother often but lived on her own in a smaller version of her mother's house. She got an allowance from her father and had received a generous divorce settlement. She appeared to be living the life of Riley, but Caitlin suspected, however, that the novelty had begun to wear a bit thin and her bestie was bored. Sophie was on the hunt for husband number two.

As they sped down the road, away from Leytonsfield town centre and towards the outskirts of the town, where the six-bedroomed detached houses in acres of land were, Caitlin rehearsed what she wanted to say to her mother.

Mother dearest was bound to try to convince Caitlin to move back home, so she could continue to work on her, convincing her to marry Brandon. Not because Brandon was a great catch, perfect husband material, or such an honest hard-working man that he could never have hurt her in such a way. No, it was because the Hewitts and the Dodds were merging their companies, to make a bigger, stronger, unbeatable one that would soon be the top dog of the property development world.

The marriage of their offspring was the jewel in the crown.

Caitlin sighed and turned to Sophie who drove in a headscarf and sunglasses like a sixties Hollywood film star.

'Sophie?'

'Yes?'

'Am I doing the right thing?'

'Do you love him?'

'Yes. Well, I thought I did, but ever since I found out about Fenella, I don't know what I feel. I'm not sure I could trust him.'

'What would it take to convince you to trust him again?' Sophie spoke without taking her eyes off the road.

It was a good question and one Caitlin didn't know how to answer.

'I don't know. People lie so easily. How can you ever tell if someone's telling the truth?'

'My mother says everyone's doing it. Screwing around.' Sophie laughed.

'Not everyone? There must be some honest people around.' Caitlin thought of Jay.

'She probably meant everyone in her set. But then they are all swingers, so that tells you a lot.'

'I don't know how anyone can do that. Urgh, the very idea makes me go cold.' Caitlin shivered.

'I think if someone threw their car keys into the bowl and it was a vehicle I liked, I'd grab the keys and run off with the car.'

Caitlin laughed. 'What is it with you and cars?'

'I love them. They're better than men. Reliable, comfortable, and the feeling of speeding down an open road... well, there's nothing like it. Better than having an orgasm.'

Sophie was grinning but still drove steadily with both hands on the wheel at two and ten. Caitlin had to hand it to her, she was a good driver.

They pulled into the gravelled turning circle at the front of the Hewitts house and Sophie switched off the engine. Neither of them moved.

'What does my face look like?' asked Caitlin.

'Your eye looks better with the concealer, and the foundation hides the bruise on your cheek.'

'Good.'

'How are you feeling?'

'Sick.'

'Cait, you're only here to collect your things. They're your parents, they're not going to kidnap you.'

'I know, I'm being silly.'

Sophie opened the car door. 'Come on, let's go and get it over with.'

Caitlin got out too, and they marched up to the front door.

'Hello?' called Caitlin once they were in the hallway. 'Is anyone home?'

'Ah, there you are,' said her mother from the top of the stairs. 'I'm so glad you've come to your senses and have come home where you belong. Is that your doing, Sophie? Well done, you.'

Her mother floated down the stairs enveloped in a cloud of Chanel. Her wrap-around dress clung to her figure and had a slit up the side that showed her long model's legs to perfection.

'Are you going out?' Caitlin asked hopefully.

'No. Whatever makes you think that?'

'Oh, nothing. We're here to collect some clothes and make-up.'

'Why?' Her mother had descended the stairs and now stood in the hall in front of them both. 'Please don't tell me you're going to stay with that young man at the hospital. Why, Caitlin, when you've got a perfectly good home here? We have things to discuss and poor Brandon doesn't know if he's coming or going.'

Caitlin looked down at the floor, uncomfortable under her mother's intense gaze.

'I need some time to get my head straight. Jay has a spare bedroom and I'm staying with him for a few days, that's all.'

'And what about Brandon? Whatever are we to tell him?'

'You don't need to tell him anything, Mother. I'll talk to him.'

Caitlin started walking towards the stairs and her mother followed her.

'Well, I'm not at all in favour of it. Not one bit. And your father won't be either. After all we've done to make your wedding day the best day of your life, and you repay us by going to live with an ambulance driver.'

Caitlin stopped walking and turned to her mother in exasperation. 'Paramedic. We're paramedics, Mother.'

'Oh, whatever you call yourselves, it amounts to the same thing. You could have such a comfortable life married to Brandon. An up and coming entrepreneur like him needs a wife by his side to encourage and comfort him. We really hoped that wife would be you.'

Caitlin had heard enough and started to climb the stairs. 'I'm going to get my things. Come on, Sophie.'

They made their way upstairs to Caitlin's bedroom. Caitlin closed the door and leaned against it with her eyes shut.

Sophie was looking in the wardrobe for suitcases.

Without opening her eyes, Caitlin said, 'They're in the walk-in.'

'Right.' Sophie went to the walk-in wardrobe and came out pulling two large suitcases on wheels. 'Will these do?'

Caitlin opened her eyes. 'Fine.'

'Come on, cheer up, it could have been worse. And the quicker we can fill these, the sooner we can get back to the cottage.' Sophie started collecting toiletries and make-up, stowing them in the cases which she had opened on the bed.

'You're right. I'm not going to let her get to me. I just

wish she would listen sometimes. It's all about what they want. I'm twenty-eight for flip's sake.'

Sophie laughed. 'You're the only twenty eight year old I know who says "flip".'

'Okay. Well, fuck then!'

'That's better.'

They both sat on the bed and laughed. Caitlin was getting a headache and realised that Jay had been right. She should be in bed for a couple of days at least.

They set to and stuffed as much as they could into the cases. When they went back downstairs, her mother was waiting for her.

'Please stay here with us, darling. I'm your mother, it's my job to look after you no matter how old you are.'

'I need to be on my own to think. It isn't going to be for long.'

'What's there to think about? You made a fool of yourself in front of hundreds of people and upset Brandon, but he's forgiven you hasn't he? He told me he would forgive and forget, and you should be jolly grateful you've got such a man still willing to marry you after that performance.'

'Goodbye, Mother,' said Caitlin.

'Bye Mrs Hewitt,' called Sophie as she negotiated the steps with one of the suitcases.

Nina Hewitt stood on the top step and called out, 'If you leave now, you might find there's no way back.'

'She doesn't mean it,' said Sophie, slipping her arm around Caitlin and giving her a hug.

'Let's just go,' said Caitlin. Every nerve in her body was twanging with tension and she felt like crying. But she wasn't going to break down in front of her mother. She had done that for the last time.

Chapter Eight

Jay had just finished a twelve-hour shift and was eager to get home. He had partnered Ali, a paramedic who had been in the service for thirty years, and someone Jay looked up to. The man was quiet and serious in the ambulance but had a wonderful bedside manner with the patients. He was the perfect partner for Jay, being the kind of man who didn't feel the need to make small talk and respected a person's right to be quiet.

'Never speak unless it improves on the silence,' he had told Jay once. Wise words from the Buddha that Jay had never forgotten.

Jay had spoken only when necessary and spent the time between call-outs thinking about Caitlin.

When he arrived home, he had expected Caitlin to be in bed and getting some well-needed rest. After all, it was nearly midnight. But she was in the kitchen cooking beans on toast for him.

'It's the least I can do after you've been kind enough to let me stay here. Sit down, it's ready.'

'Thanks.' Jay sat at the table and surveyed the state of the kitchen with amusement. It looked as if a bomb had hit it. There was a used saucepan next to the draining board, toast crumbs everywhere and two empty baked bean tins.

'There we go,' said Caitlin putting a plate of burnt toast and congealed beans in front of him. 'I didn't know how long you'd be, and I think I misjudged the timing. Sorry. I've been trying to keep it warm for about an hour.'

'Well, thanks anyway,' Jay said as he cautiously put a forkful of toast and beans into his mouth and chewed. The toast was black, and the beans were cold. But he ate some of it anyway, whilst Caitlin watched every mouthful.

Eventually, Jay couldn't eat another bite and he pushed the plate away. 'Sorry,' he said.

'No, I'm the one who should be sorry. I can't cook you see as I've never had to learn how. We've always had a cook at home and Mother thought it was beneath her to do it herself.'

'Don't worry, you tried and I'm grateful for that.' Jay smiled and said, 'You got your stuff I see.'

Caitlin's stuff was all over the floor in the living room. The cases were open, and clothes had spilt out and made their way to the couch and armchairs. A lot of it was on the floor. Some even on the stairs.

'Yes, Sophie went with me. My mother wasn't happy.'

'What did she say?'

'She said that Brandon was willing to forgive and forget.'

'Big of him. Have you spoken to him yet?'

'No, not yet. I know I have to talk to him but I'm not ready.'

'No hurry,' said Jay. He wanted Caitlin to stay for a long time. Even though he'd only be putting off the inevitable.

Jay got up and started tidying the kitchen. He put the leftovers in a bag and then put that in the bin. Then he started loading the dishwasher.

Caitlin was still sitting at the table. She looked exhausted.

'Caitlin, you should go to bed you know. You need plenty of rest to get over this. I'll sort out the kitchen.'

'Thanks. I think I will. Well, goodnight then.'

He turned and smiled. 'Goodnight, sleep well.'

'You too.'

After Jay had finished washing up and cleaning the kitchen, he tidied up the living room, putting all Caitlin's belongings into the cases and carrying them up the stairs. He left them just outside the door of the spare bedroom.

It was after one o'clock by the time he got to bed. He was tired out but couldn't sleep. Caitlin's upbringing was obviously the opposite of his. All four of them had been encouraged to clean up after themselves, tidy their rooms and leave communal areas spotless from a young age. Caitlin had been waited on hand and foot by maids and a cook. The next few days would be interesting.

But for all the mess, Jay was glad she was in his house, sleeping under his roof. He'd have preferred it if she were in his bed, but he knew that would never happen. They were destined to be just friends and Jay was going to make the most of every minute he had with her.

The following day, Caitlin had a long lie-in, not getting up until midday. Jay was on an early shift.

She had just made herself a cup of coffee and was wondering how to spend the day, when the doorbell rang. Her first instinct was to ignore it. It was probably someone selling something or wanting the owner of the house to change their fuel provider. Then she thought it might be her parents or Brandon. She froze, hoping whoever it was would go away. Then she heard a key in the lock and she nearly dropped her coffee.

'Oh, there is someone in. I'm so sorry, but I did ring the bell. I'm Eloise, Jay's mum. You must be Caitlin. He told me you'd be staying for a while. Pleased to meet you.'

Eloise advanced across the living room with her hand out to shake.

'Yes, hello, sorry… I thought I heard the bell. I've just got up, you see…'

Caitlin shook hands with Eloise, feeling stupid now at not answering the door.

'Quite right, too,' said Eloise. 'Jay told me all about your accident. You poor thing. Yes, you should be in bed and getting as much rest as you can. I won't disturb you for long. I've bought some food for Jay. An apple pie and a chicken casserole. I'll just put them in the fridge, shall I?'

'Fine. Would you like a drink? The kettle's just boiled.'

'Oh, that would be lovely. Tea, please. No sugar but a drop of milk.'

Caitlin busied herself with making the tea and trying to think of things to say.

'Jay will be grateful for proper food. I tried to make him beans on toast yesterday and it was a spectacular fail. Poor Jay tried manfully to eat it, but he had to give in eventually.'

Eloise had put the food away and was now sitting on the couch smiling and listening to Caitlin wittering on.

'There you go,' she said giving Eloise her tea. Caitlin sat next to her.

'Don't worry, we can't all be domesticated. I only

learned when I got married and started having babies. My poor Dan lived on takeaway food for years when we were both working.'

'Really?'

'Oh yes. I took evening classes and bought hundreds of cookery books. I love cooking now and, I'm not afraid to admit, I still cook for the twins. Josie's like you, can't boil an egg. The two eldest—Riordan and Casey—are married with families of their own, so I resist popping round to their homes with apple pies, but I must confess, Jay and Josie get food on a regular basis.'

'Well, I'm sure it's delicious and I'm glad you've brought something so Jay can have a proper meal tonight. I am going to learn to cook, though, it's on my to-do list.' Caitlin sipped her coffee, aware of the mess in the living room. 'Another thing on my to-do list is being tidier. Starting with this room.' She didn't want Jay's mum to think she was not pulling her weight in her son's house.

'Don't worry, dear. We'll finish our drinks and then I'll help you tidy up.'

'Thanks, that's kind.'

'I'm sorry about your wedding day. It must have been awful for you. We won't talk about it if you don't want to.'

'No, it's okay. What did Jay tell you?'

'He said your fiancé was caught with another woman who was there on the front row. No wonder you were angry. I would have been blazing mad.'

Caitlin suddenly felt the need to offload to this lovely lady. It would be good to get an outsider's opinion.

'The thing is… Brandon's family and mine have businesses dealing in property. Conversions and developments, that type of thing. Their companies are merging, and my parents have always seen my marriage to Brandon as part of the deal. I've known him all my life.'

'But do you love him?'

Caitlin looked into Eloise's eyes and wondered how to answer.

'Honestly? I don't know. I thought I loved him, but that was when I trusted him and saw him in my future. Now, I can barely see past tomorrow.'

Eloise put her hand on Caitlin's. Her touch was cool and gentle.

'If you want my advice, you need time. Time away from your parents and your fiancée. Time to think and heal. I think you're doing the right thing, staying here. And Jay will appreciate your company, I'm sure. Right. Now, let's get this place tidied up shall we?'

Chapter Nine

It was Friday night—beer and Chinese night—and Jay was taking orders and writing them on the back of an envelope.

Josie had brought wine, and, with Jay's permission, Caitlin had invited Sophie. Paul and Matt were also there.

'Are we doing our usual sharing thing?' asked Josie.

'Oh, that sounds good,' said Sophie. 'How does it work? Do you order everything on the menu and have a bit of each?'

Paul laughed, 'Darlin', it's a big menu and there's only six of us.'

'We order a selection,' said Jay. 'Usually sweet and sour chicken, spare ribs in Peking sauce, beef in black bean sauce, egg fried rice—that kind of thing.'

'And starters, Jay, don't forget the crispy seaweed and sesame prawn toast,' said Josie.

'Crispy wontons, mate,' said Paul.

'Oh and get some of those... what are they? It's on the tip of my tongue...oh, I know, Char Siu Bao.' Matt said.

Sophie was almost jumping up and down with excitement. 'What are they?'

'Chinese pork buns,' said Jay adding them to the order. 'Is that it?'

No one could think of anything else, so he phoned in the order.

'It'll be forty minutes.'

'As long as that,' said Sophie, 'I'm starving. I've never had to wait that long in a restaurant.'

'Have some more wine,' said Paul filling her glass.

'Oh, thanks awfully.'

'So, Sophie,' Paul said as he filled Josie's glass, then Caitlin's. 'What do you do?'

'Me? When?'

Paul laughed. 'No, I mean for work.'

'Oh, I don't work.'

'So…what do you do with yourself all day?'

'Are you one of those ladies who lunch?' asked Josie. She stretched out on the couch and put her head on one of the cushions and her feet in Jay's lap.

'Yes. And I love going on holiday. Cruising especially. River and ocean.'

'I bet that's hard work,' said Matt and Jay frowned at him. 'Just saying.' He shrugged.

Caitlin had been staring at the fire in a melancholy way and didn't seem to be paying attention to the conversation. Although it was June, the air was still quite chilly, so Jay had built a wood fire in the grate that Caitlin sat in front of, warming her hands. Now she rallied to defend her bestie.

'Sophie is still recovering from a particularly bitter, acrimonious divorce. She's still healing. Aren't you?'

'Yes, I am, that's right. It was very painful.' Sophie looked downcast and sipped her wine.

'Sorry to hear that, sweetheart,' said Paul. 'Do you have any children?'

'Oh no, nothing like that. He didn't want kids. He just wanted to have sex with other women. Quite a lot.'

'Quite a lot of which,' asked Matt who seemed hellbent on taking the mickey out of Sophie, 'women or sex?'

'Well, both really. He had a lot of women and had a lot of sex with all of them. He was a complete bastard.' Sophie drained her glass and stared at it solemnly.

'Would you like some more wine, Sophie?' asked Paul, grinning.

'Oh yes, thank you, that would be lovely.'

Jay realised that Sophie was getting drunk very quickly. He glanced at Caitlin, but she was staring at the fire again, lost in thought.

'D'you know, I saw the most beautiful Maserati the other day. I'm debating whether to get it or not. Now that I need another car.'

'Sorry,' said Caitlin in a small voice.

'Oh, don't worry about it. I've got an excuse now to get the Mas.'

'Alright for some,' muttered Matt.

The front doorbell rang and Sophie cheered. 'The food, at last!'

Josie got up and went to get the takeout and Jay went into the kitchen and collected the plates, knives, forks, and chopsticks for those who wanted to show off.

They devoured the food as if they hadn't eaten for days; only Caitlin picked at hers.

Sophie wolfed down everything she put on her plate. She even finished off the free prawn crackers that the others didn't want. Paul seemed amused by Sophie and tried to engage her in conversation, but she was too busy eating, so he gave up after a while.

Afterwards, Paul and Josie cleared away whilst the others kept on drinking and talking.

Jay sat back and listened to the conversation. Caitlin had left the fire and sat next to him on the couch. His body tingled at her closeness and he longed to put his arm around her.

'How you feeling now?' he asked.

'I'm fine. The meal was nice. I keep thinking I need to go and talk to Brandon as, until I hear what he has to say, I won't be able to make a decision.'

'Do you want me to come with you?'

'That's sweet but…no, I need to do this.'

'Are you taking Sophie?'

'No, she'll be away for two weeks. Another cruise. I'll be all alone.'

'Fancy coming to my parents the Sunday after next for a family roast?'

'I don't want to intrude. You've done enough for me already.'

'I want you to come.' Jay hadn't meant to say that and hoped Caitlin knew he meant as just friends.

'You're so sweet, Jay. I wish Brandon were like you. Okay, if you think it'll be alright.'

'Of course it will. I wouldn't have asked otherwise.'

The evening proceeded in the usual fashion. More drink and music but no one got up to dance as they were too full of food.

Sophie was quite drunk but still made sense when she spoke. She sat on a bean bag on the floor which was quite a feat considering she was wearing a scarlet swing dress with a tight bodice and full, flared skirt. She had matched the dress with scarlet stilettoes and a red handbag. Everyone else was casually dressed.

'The question is... if a man is unfaithful, should you forgive him?'

'No,' said Josie.

'No,' said Matt, 'I wouldn't forgive my Ben if he was unfaithful to me.'

'Depends on the circumstances,' said Paul.

Jay said nothing but waited to hear what Caitlin said.

'That's my problem isn't it? Do I forgive Brandon even if I *can* get him to admit the truth?'

'I think it comes down to this,' said Sophie, 'Even if he admits his guilt and apologises, there's nothing to say he won't do it again. With the same woman or another. Once a cheating bastard, always one, I say. Any more wine?'

Paul filled up Sophie's glass with the last of the wine.

'Coffee?'

'Oh, not for me, unless it's a liqueur coffee,' Sophie said.

'No, sorry.'

'Then I'll decline your kind offer.'

'I'll ring you a taxi,' said Jay.

'Oh thank you. You're a nice man. Why can I never find anyone as nice as you?'

Chapter Ten

It had been two weeks since the accident. Caitlin's bruises had almost disappeared, and she was feeling stronger and well rested. She couldn't put it off any longer so had texted Brandon to ask him to meet her at Mellow, the wine bar on High Street. He had texted back to say he'd be there at seven.

Jay was on a late so Caitlin had the house to herself. She showered, washed her hair, and spent ages staring at her wardrobe wondering what to wear. She hadn't spoken to Brandon since their wedding day and had no idea what mood he would be in. Not good would be her guess.

Playing to her strengths, she put on her favourite dress, a Calvin Klein sleeveless midi dress with a floral print, and liberally sprayed her favourite perfume—Miracle by Lancôme. She dried her hair and carefully applied her make-up. Having achieved the look she wanted, she rang for a taxi and waited nervously for it to arrive. It wasn't that far to Mellow, and Caitlin could have walked, but she intended to arrive in style.

The wine bar was full as it was a Friday night and Brandon wasn't there. Caitlin had deliberately waited until seven twenty so he would be waiting for her and she could stage her entrance. She'd pictured herself strolling in, ignoring the admiring looks from the men and the envious looks from the women and sashaying her way towards him, so that he recognised he was in danger of losing the best thing that had ever happened to him.

Instead, she had to squeeze past men who were all taller than her to get to the bar and wait there for ages for a bartender to notice her. She'd shouted her order, twice, as she couldn't be heard above the din of inebriated laughter and raucous jollity.

Then she stood around like a spare part, hoping that a table would become vacant and she could sit down as her high heels were killing her.

By the time she had done all that, it was nearly seven forty and Caitlin wondered if she should just go home. Nobody noticed her, she was the wallflower in the corner waiting in vain for her date to turn up. At least she was near the toilets and could dive into there for refuge if she were chatted up by an unsavoury character who leered at her and breathed beer fumes all over her. But even they ignored her.

Then, at last, just when she'd finished her drink and had decided to leave, Brandon came in. He smiled and held the door open for a group of young women who were obviously at the start of a night on the town. They all giggled and flirted with him, chattering brightly, and holding up other people who were trying to get through the door.

Caitlin watched him with mixed feelings. He was handsome, with a warm smile and come-to-bed brown eyes. Caitlin had once thought that look was reserved only for her. Now she knew better.

Brandon gazed around briefly but he didn't see her hidden in the corner. He went to the bar and was served straight away. When he turned around, a table in the centre of the wine bar had magically become vacant and he sat down and started scrolling on his phone.

Caitlin moved away from her corner and sat at the table. Brandon looked up and smiled.

'Ah, there you are. I've got you a drink.' He gestured at a glass of white wine.

'I'm drinking red.' Brandon ignored her.

'You look nice. And smell nice, too.'

'Thanks.'

At one time she would have been warmed by the compliment but now she wondered if it was one of his stock phrases. Did he use that line on all women? Fenella? Caitlin felt a surge of anger that she tried to suppress. She must hear him out, it would be a waste of time otherwise.

Brandon put his phone on the table and drank some of his wine. Neither of them spoke until, eventually, Brandon broke the silence.

'So… are you going to tell me what that little scene was all about? Your mother was very apologetic on your behalf, but I must say, I'd like to hear it from you.'

'You know what it was about, Brandon. You're having an affair with Fenella Barton-Brookes.'

'I'm disappointed in you, poppet, listening to ugly rumours.'

'Are you denying it?'

'Of course. Vehemently.'

'So, you haven't had sex with her?'

'Well, of course I've had sex with her, she used to be my girlfriend.' Brandon drained his glass and put it down.

'I mean recently.' He was looking down at the table and

playing with the empty glass, running his finger around the top to get a sound.

'That only works if there's liquid in it,' said Caitlin.

Brandon took the glass and stood up. 'Another?'

'I'm drinking red wine, Brandon,' she said clearly.

'Fine. Then I'll get you a red wine.'

Caitlin watched him as he gave his order. He was served straight away.

'There you go—*red* wine.'

'Thank you.'

Brandon sat down and took a sip of his wine. Caitlin watched him.

'You haven't answered my question,' she said.

'Which question was that, poppet?'

'Please don't call me that, you know I hate it.'

'My my, we are touchy. Your mother warned me you were having some kind of a breakdown.'

'What! She said I was having a breakdown? When was this?'

'At the wedding of course, when you ran out of the church for no earthly reason, leaving me with egg on my face to try to explain to all my family and friends why my wife-to-be was acting like a complete fruit loop.' Brandon drained his glass and then started drinking the white wine that Caitlin didn't want.

'I'm sorry—'

'No explanation, Caitlin, no apology, nothing for two weeks. You ignored all my calls, texts, even emails. What the hell was I supposed to think?'

'I'm sorry, but I was upset—'

'Upset! How the hell did you think I felt? I had to spend two weeks explaining your behaviour to all and sundry when I didn't even understand it myself. You made me a laughing stock and I'm not sure I can ever forgive you for that.'

Brandon was on the point of losing it. Caitlin had only seen him lose his temper once, and it hadn't been pleasant.

Caitlin had come here tonight hoping to get an apology from him, and an explanation. Instead, she was feeling wretched, seeing things from his point of view for the first time and desperately wanting his forgiveness.

'Brandon, I do hope you can forgive me. I am so sorry I ran out like that, it was stupid and childish, and…'

Caitlin waited for him to say something, but he was checking his phone again.

'Brandon?'

'That's not all you need to apologise for though, is it?' Brandon put his phone on the table and sat back, glaring at her.

'What do you mean?'

'Your hen night. I've been reliably informed that you were dancing with someone who had his tongue down your throat, and you seemed to be encouraging it. So, what have you got to say about that?'

Caitlin went cold. Fenella must have seen her kissing Jay and had told Brandon.

'I…' What could she say?

'What's the matter? Cat got your tongue?'

'It didn't mean anything, we'd both been drinking and I—'

'I don't want to hear your excuses, but please don't take the moral high ground with me when you're guilty as charged.'

'It's different.' Caitlin was floundering. She had kissed Jay, she couldn't deny it.

'Not at all. Fenella's been a good friend from way back, what's your excuse?'

Caitlin didn't have an excuse. She'd kissed Jay and enjoyed it. But a kiss compared to an affair. It was different.

'Brandon? I don't want to fight with you. I came here tonight so we could sort this out—'

'I need to be somewhere in five minutes, so I'm going to have to cut this short. Are you ready to come to your senses and go home to your parents where you belong? You've caused them no end of grief with your hysterics you know.'

'I know and I'm sorry for that, but I need to be away from them to think. I can't do that at home.'

'Stuff and nonsense.'

'No, Brandon, it isn't—'

'Fine.' Brandon stood up and put his phone in his pocket. 'Let me know when you're thinking straight again. Goodnight, Caitlin.'

He strode out of the wine bar and several women watched him leave.

Caitlin wanted to cry. The evening hadn't gone as she'd expected or planned. She was still being painted as the bad guy. They were right, she'd wasted everyone's time and money. She should have spoken to Brandon the night before the wedding and got a straight answer from him. She still didn't know if he was seeing Fenella. Although how else would he know that she'd kissed Jay? Fortunately, he didn't seem to know that the man whose spare room she was staying in was the same one that she'd kissed. Caitlin wasn't going to enlighten him.

People were beginning to stare at her. Then she realised that she was sitting alone at a table with enough seats for a group, and several people were waiting to grab it when she made a move. She got up and left them to fight it out.

Caitlin had lain awake, going over everything in her mind and coming to no sensible conclusion.

She was still awake when she heard Jay come in from his late shift. She got out of bed and put on her dressing gown, before wandering downstairs.

'Hi. What's up, can't you sleep?'

'Oh Jay, it's so awful.' She felt tearful and longed for him to give her a hug.

'Didn't go well, then?'

'No.'

'Right. Hot chocolate or Horlicks?'

'Either. Whatever you're having.'

Caitlin curled up on the couch and waited for Jay to join her with the drinks.

'There you go. Horlicks will help you sleep.'

'Thanks.'

'So, do you want to talk about it?'

'Yes, please.'

Caitlin gave Jay a rundown of the evening. How confident she had felt at the start and sure that Brandon was the one in the wrong. How he had turned it all on its head and made her the villain and how she thought he was probably right as she hadn't seen it from his point of view until now. She didn't mention that Brandon knew they'd kissed on her hen night.

'There's always two sides to every argument,' said Jay. 'If he denied the affair, perhaps he's telling the truth.'

'Maybe. But Sophie saw them together in a hotel. I never even got the chance to ask him about that. I didn't handle things very well.'

'Perhaps you need more time to think. Talk to him again

when you feel stronger. You're obviously better physically, but you need to heal emotionally too.'

'My mother told Brandon that she thinks I'm having a breakdown.'

'You've had a lot to put up with lately. You need to get over it before you can move on.'

'Yes, you're right. Can you do me a favour?'

'Of course.'

'I need a hug.'

Jay put his arms around her and held her tightly. Caitlin snuggled into him. He smelt of the ambulance, handwash, soap and clean male. She didn't want to let go. Ever. Apparently, neither did he as they sat like that for ages. Eventually, reluctantly she pulled away.

Jay was watching her face and the look in his eyes was hard to read. He was being a good friend to her, that was all. He didn't fancy her or want anything from her. Even so, she had a vision of them falling asleep, wrapped in each other's arms. How comforting that would be.

'Right. Why don't you try to sleep now?'

She sighed. 'Yes, thanks, Jay. Goodnight.'

'Goodnight, Caitlin. Sweet dreams.'

Caitlin went to the bathroom before she jumped into bed and noticed Jay's T-shirt in the laundry basket. She picked it up and held it to her face, inhaling deeply. It smelt of him, with an extra note of musky aftershave. She took it with her into the bedroom and pulled her nightie off, exchanging it for Jay's T-shirt.

Surprisingly, when she woke the next morning, Caitlin realised that her dreams had been sweet, and she had dreamed of Jay.

Chapter Eleven

'Okay, let's get this old bus rolling.'

It was Saturday and Paul was in a chirpy mood as he'd got a date from the online dating site he'd recently joined. Jay was also in a good mood as he was taking Caitlin home the following day for Sunday lunch. It wasn't exactly taking his girlfriend home to meet the family, which is what he wished it were, but he was looking forward to it, nonetheless.

'Let's hope we have a good shift,' said Jay.

'So, how's everything going at Chez Jay? Has Caitlin made it up with her fiancé yet?'

Jay popped a mint into his mouth and offered one to Paul.

'No, not yet. They have talked but nothing was resolved.'

'Only a matter of time though, right?'

'I suppose so.'

Paul chewed the mint thoughtfully and then said, 'You're my mate, okay? Just be careful.'

'Careful of what? That I don't fall in love with her? Oops, too late.'

'You know what you need?' Paul glanced at Jay briefly before looking back at the road.

An ambulance passed them in the opposite direction and they both waved.

'What do I need?'

'You need to start dating again. There's nothing like a new relationship to help you get over an old one, or an unrequited love.'

'The timing's all wrong.'

'Why? Because Caitlin's staying with you? I'd say it's the perfect time. Otherwise, when she leaves, you'll be on your own again. You're my friend, man, I'd hate to see you get hurt.'

'Thanks, I appreciate that.'

Fortunately, they got a call-out and there was no more time to talk. A three-year-old child had put something up her nose and the mother was concerned. She had seen it go in but hadn't been able to get there in time. By the time they'd asked all the questions and taken the little girl into the ambulance in preparation to take her to hospital, she gave an almighty sneeze and the offending object—a pea— came flying out of her nose.

'It was frozen when it went in, but then it thawed,' Paul said.

The mother was relieved, Paul thought it was hilarious and Jay was thankful they hadn't needed to take the child to A&E. He hated wasted journeys.

The rest of the morning passed quickly with minor cases. And then it was time for lunch.

They stopped at McDonald's and had a cheeseburger,

fries, and a milkshake each. Paul returned to his earlier train of thought.

'Why don't you try online dating? I know people who've met their spouses that way, and I've already got a hot date lined up.'

'Not looking to get married right now,' said Jay stuffing fries into his mouth.

'You're thirty, my friend, you're not getting any younger.'

Jay wiped his hands on a paper napkin and turned his attention to the milkshake.

'When's the hot date?' he asked Paul.

'Tomorrow. We're meeting at lunchtime for the first date and then taking it from there.'

'Well, I wish you the best. Hope it works out for you, man.'

'Thanks, but I'd be a lot happier if you could move on from Caitlin. She's a lovely girl but...not for you. I want to see you happy is all.'

Jay tipped the carton up to get the last bit of the milkshake. 'What makes you think I'm not happy?'

'Because I know you. You love women and they love you. You aren't the type of guy to spend the rest of your life alone. Your brothers have now got families. Once Josie meets the right man and gets married, well...'

'I'll be an uncle several times over and still be able to up and travel the world if the fancy takes me.'

'Which it won't.'

'How do you know?'

'Like I say, man, I know you.'

'Come on, back to work.'

Paul was silent until they were back in the ambulance.

This time, Jay drove, and Paul waited for the call-outs to come rolling in.

'You're wrong, you know,' said Jay.

'How am I wrong?'

'Women don't love me for the reason you think. It was the same when I was in school. Girls liked me as a friend, but I was never boyfriend material. Riordan and Casey had admirers, especially Casey, but me... no. I was the funny little O'Connor brother. I made people laugh.'

'You just haven't met the right one yet.'

'I have, but she's probably going to marry someone else. A man who doesn't deserve her.'

'Sophie seemed to like you. She said she wanted to meet a man like you.'

'She was drunk and anyway, she called me nice. No one wants to be described as nice...or sweet, or funny.'

'Better than being called a cheating bastard.'

'Ah, well, that's where you're wrong. It's the arrogant ones that women like.'

A call-out came through which stopped the conversation.

Paul read it out. 'Eighty-five-year-old woman, lives alone, fell, badly cut leg. May have hit her head.'

'Right. We're on it.' Jay switched the siren on, loving how the cars parted for them as they raced to the scene.

When they arrived at the patient's house, her elderly neighbour greeted them.

'I heard the dog barking, you see, and I thought it was funny as she doesn't bark much when Betty's home, so I thought I'd better go round. I looked through the window and saw her. Well, I couldn't see all of her you understand as she was lying behind the sofa, but I saw her legs sticking out.'

'You did the right thing to call us,' said Jay.

'Hello, Betty,' said Paul, kneeling down and examining her.

The dog, a tiny Yorkie wearing a pink collar with a bell attached to it, barked, and ran up and down, obviously distressed by what had happened to its owner.

'You'll have to go to hospital, Betty. Can I call you Betty?' asked Jay. He had learned from experience not to take anything for granted with patients.

'Oh yes, that's my name, but I can't go to hospital unless SpongeBob comes with me.'

'Can't he stay with your neighbour? You need stitches in that leg.' Jay looked at the neighbour hopefully.

'Oh no, I have to look after my husband, you see. He's got Alzheimer's. I would do otherwise, she's a lovely little dog.'

'The dog's a she?' asked Jay.

'Yes, we thought she was a male at first and then she got used to her name. She belonged to my son who died recently and she's the only thing I've got left now. I lost my husband twenty years ago and I'm all alone.' Betty was on the verge of tears and Jay wished he could do something to help her.

'We can't take you and the dog to hospital, sorry, love,' said Paul.

'Well, I'm not going then. I'll stay here and see my GP. Or the district nurse.'

'I don't like the look of that wound and you've got a bump on your head too. You'll have a headache soon if you haven't got one already.' Paul frowned but the lady was not for moving.

'If I get a headache I'll take an aspirin.'

Jay couldn't help smiling at Betty's attitude. He loved the

elderly, especially those like Betty, fiercely independent and not wanting to be a bother to anyone. But, like Paul, he wanted her to go to hospital as elderly skin didn't heal well and could easily become infected.

Paul took Betty's temperature, pulse, and blood pressure. 'Your temperature's fine, but your blood pressure is a bit high and so is your pulse rate. I'm not happy about leaving you, to be honest, Betty, you need to be looked at.'

'Can't you just put a plaster on it?'

'No, darlin', I can't.'

Betty looked defeated suddenly. SpongeBob was trying to climb onto her knee, still distressed as her beloved owner was sitting on the floor. The bump on her head could make her dizzy, so they had to move her slowly.

'There is a solution.' They all looked at Jay expectantly. 'I'll take her. Look after her while you're being treated, then bring her back to you.'

'Have you had a lot of experience with dogs?' asked Betty as if she were interviewing him for a job.

Jay grinned. 'I have. We had dogs as a kid and both my brothers have dogs.'

'And what would happen to her when you're working?'

'I have a friend staying with me and she isn't working at present. She'll look after her. Take her for walks. It'll be fine and only for a day or so.'

Betty still looked worried. 'I don't know.'

'It's the best offer you're going to get, Betty. I'd accept if I were you,' Paul said.

'Oh, alright then. Thank you. Most kind. I'll tell you where her lead and food is.'

Paul was looking at Jay as if he had gone stark staring mad. Jay was thinking how nice it would be to have a dog around the place.

They got Betty and SpongeBob into the ambulance and Jay sat with them while Paul drove them to hospital. The dog was sitting on Betty's knee and staring at Jay as if warning him not to mess with her mistress.

They were so quiet in the ambulance with no one speaking, that Paul asked if everyone was okay.

'We're fine, aren't we, Betty?'

'Yes, dear, we are.'

Betty was a love and Jay wished he could get to know her better, but she didn't seem to want to talk. Perhaps she was in pain, or maybe that bang on the head had given her a slight concussion. She wasn't at all confused but the sooner they got her to hospital the better.

It had been the right call. They couldn't have left her at home on her own. Anything could have happened. And where would SpongeBob have been then?

As they pulled up outside A&E, Jay said, 'We're here.'

Betty took Jay's hand and gave it a squeeze. 'Thank you for doing this. You have no idea what it means to me.'

'You're very welcome, Betty. She'll be looked after, I promise.'

———

'What have you got there?' Caitlin was sitting in the living room, surrounded by a mess as usual. Somehow she didn't seem to be aware of it. Jay sighed and shut the front door. He picked his way gingerly across the debris-strewn floor cuddling the little dog to his chest.

'Her name's SpongeBob and she's staying with us for a few days.'

'Why? Anyway, I thought SpongeBob was male.'

'The one on the telly is—this one isn't.' Jay sat on the couch next to Caitlin so they could get acquainted.

'Hello, sweetheart, you're cute, aren't you?' Caitlin let SpongeBob sniff her face as she stroked the little dog.

'She likes you.'

'Does she? How can you tell?'

Jay was tempted to be facetious and say it was because the dog hadn't sunk her teeth into her. But he didn't know how Caitlin felt about dogs. She could be allergic to them for all he knew. He should have phoned Caitlin to find out before bringing SpongeBob home.

'She's just checking you out but her tail's wagging.'

'Oh, right.'

'Didn't you have dogs as a kid?'

'Oh no, my mother would never let me have any pets because she didn't want their fur to get onto the furniture.'

'Not even guinea pigs or rabbits? You could have kept them outside.' Jay stroked SpongeBob who had moved over to his knee but was keeping her gaze fixed on Caitlin.

'No, because their fur would have clung to my clothes and I would have brought it inside. My mother hated a mess.'

Jay was beginning to understand why Caitlin was so untidy. She was rebelling silently against her mother's tyranny. Children should be allowed to make a mess so long as they cleared it up afterwards. And pets were an essential part of family life.

'Well, I'm sure that you two are going to get on well. In fact, you're going to have to as she's staying here whilst I'm at work. You'll have to feed her and take her for walks.'

'Me? I don't know how to do any of that.'

'Well then, it's about time you learned. Get your shoes

on and we'll take her for a walk together. I'll show you how easy it is.'

Jay changed into jeans and a sweatshirt, SpongeBob watching him from his bed. He sat next to her and put his trainers on, talking to the little dog all the time. He carried her downstairs where Caitlin was waiting.

Jay pulled SpongeBob's lead from the plastic bag that contained her food and bowls. He also pocketed some poo bags. Immediately she started barking and her stumpy little tail wagged as hard as it could.

'See, she knows she's going for a walk. Clever girl!'

'Who? Me or the dog?'

'The dog, of course. Nothing clever about you.' Caitlin broke into indignant laughter and thumped him on the arm. 'Ouch! That hurt.'

'Serves you right.'

They locked the door and started walking towards Manor Park. Jay breathed deeply of the early summer air and the warm sun felt good. Caitlin walked by his side, watching SpongeBob who was trotting along by Jay's side, perfectly happily.

'See,' said Jay, 'It's easy to take a dog like this for a walk as she's used to the lead. It'll be a doddle looking after her. You don't really mind, do you, Caitlin?'

Caitlin glanced at the dog, then back to Jay. Then she smiled. 'You're a bit of a softie, aren't you, Jay? And no, of course I don't mind. She'll be company whilst you're at work. I'm starting to get bored.'

It was on the tip of Jay's tongue to suggest that she could do a bit of housework, but he didn't want to spoil the mood, so kept quiet.

They passed children who wanted to fuss SpongeBob and other dog walkers who smiled and wished them a good afternoon. It would have been nice to have taken Caitlin's hand and pretended that they were a happy couple enjoying a late afternoon stroll.

Then SpongeBob adopted the pose that told Jay she was about to relieve herself. When she'd finished, Jay took a poo bag out of his pocket.

'Do I have to do that?' asked Caitlin.

'Yep. It's not that bad. Watch and learn, Caitlin.'

Caitlin dutifully watched as Jay deftly turned the bag inside out to use as a glove and quickly grabbed the offending, but small, mound, and tied it in a few seconds.

Caitlin was looking sceptical and Jay burst out laughing.

'She's a tiny dog, with tiny poos. Think of the things you have to do as a paramedic and people's mess you've had to clear up. It's nothing compared to that. It's a transferrable skill.'

'If you say so,' said Caitlin and started to walk away.

'Never mind, SpongeBob, we'll win her round,' he said, thinking that Caitlin had a greater shock to her system in store the following day when she met all the O'Connors; grown-ups, kids, and dogs. If she survived that, she could cope with anything.

Chapter Twelve

Caitlin was assaulted by a wall of sound as soon as Jay opened the back door of his parents' house. There was laughter, loud voices, dogs barking and a delicious smell of lamb cooking.

'You've got a dog!' shouted Jade.

'Cool,' said Tom, 'the family's got four dogs now.'

'Come in, you two,' said Eloise.

Jay put SpongeBob down while he hugged his mother and Jade and Tom were soon sitting cross-legged on the floor while the little terrier plus their own dogs scampered from one to the other to be stroked and petted.

Caitlin stood to the side watching but was soon pulled into the family circle. She was introduced to people she didn't know and greeted those she had already met.

'Why the dog?' asked Riordan.

'Why not?' answered Jay.

'Jay is doing a patient a favour. We're fostering the dog while the old lady's in hospital,' said Caitlin.

'She was hurt and tachycardic but wouldn't go to

hospital because of SpongeBob who used to belong to her son who'd recently died.'

'Is it a boy?' asked Jade.

'No, sweetie,' said Jay, 'They thought she was a boy so called her SpongeBob, but then found out she was a girl, but she was used to the name by then.'

'Sounds a very dubious story that,' said Casey lounging against the doorframe. 'I suspect they just liked the name.'

'It's a good name,' said Eloise, putting the carrots and peas on to cook.

'Why did you have to take the dog?' Riordan said, obviously unsatisfied with the explanation. 'There are charities who look after the pets of people living alone. Why did you have to put your hand up.'

'Because he's kind like that,' said Eloise, turning to pat Jay on the cheek.

'He's a soft touch,' said Josie, 'but that's why we love him.'

'Is he going red yet?' asked Casey with a grin.

'Water off a duck's back, Bro, water off a duck's back.'

The meal was like a banquet. There were ten adults, counting Tom. The toddlers, Abigail and Lucy sat in high chairs and Jade had her "Special Chair" that she used when she came to visit her grandparents, which was every day, piled high with cushions so she was just the right height.

Dan O'Connor sat at the head of the table and Eloise was at the other end. The siblings and their other halves spread out in the middle.

Caitlin wasn't sure where to sit and didn't want to tread on anyone's toes by sitting in their place, so she waited until everyone else was seated, then sat next to Jay. Tom, Josie, and Zoe helped carry the dishes to the table and Dan and Riordan poured the wine and juice for the kids.

Once everyone was seated with steaming plates of food in front of them, Dan proposed a toast. 'To family and friends,' he said.

'To family and friends,' they all replied.

Then several conversations started at once and Caitlin thought, again, how different this family was to hers. In her family home, mealtimes were spent in silence, with occasional comments from her father. The atmosphere was oppressive, and Caitlin avoided meals with her parents as much as possible.

The O'Connors, however, were chatting away as if they hadn't seen each other for years. Dan, Zoe, and Riordan were talking about the GP Practice and some of the improvements that were planned.

Casey and Tom were talking about the school swimming competition that Tom was taking part in. From what Caitlin could hear, Casey was coaching him. Lexi and Josie were talking about the latest series of *Love Island*, and which of the men were the best looking. The toddlers were having fun throwing their food on the floor, while their mothers calmly wiped it up, before the dogs could eat it.

No one worried about having elbows on the table or eating with the wrong knife and fork. The meal was delicious, the atmosphere relaxed, and Caitlin felt it was okay to join in a conversation, but equally okay to sit back and just listen. Nobody seemed to mind what she did.

Caitlin was conscious that Jay was quieter than usual, and she asked him if he was okay.

'Never been better. How about you?'

'Fine. The same. I love your family.'

Jay looked around the table. 'Yeah, they're not a bad lot really.'

'It was kind of you to ask me today. I'm the only one who isn't part of the O'Connor family.'

Jay said nothing but his eyes were full of pain.

'Jay? What is it? What's wrong?'

He shook his head as if to clear it. 'Nothing. Why not, just for today, pretend that you're an O'Connor? If you want to that is.'

Caitlin thought for a moment, realising what an honour Jay was bestowing on her. To be a part of this family would be a dream come true.

'There's nothing I'd like better,' she said quietly.

After lunch, the family played games with Jade and Tom. Mainly snap and draughts; games that Jade could take part in. Caitlin had never played some of the games and Tom took great delight in teaching her.

'You're a fast learner,' said Tom.

'Well, thank you, Tom. It's because you're such a good teacher.'

Later, Casey, Lexi, Tom, Jade, Jay, and Caitlin took the dogs out for a short run and even let SpongeBob off the lead. Caitlin knew they were taking a risk as she could take fright and run off but Jay was confident that she'd stay with the other dogs as they seemed to have bonded.

Jay was proved right.

When they got near to the canal, however, they put all four dogs on leads.

It was a beautiful spring day and Caitlin was feeling relaxed and happy. Being in such a peaceful spot with people she felt completely comfortable with, made her realise everything that was missing from her own life. She needed to talk to Brandon again. Her mother hadn't contacted her since she had gone home to get her things and it wouldn't be long before she went back to work. Physically her scars had healed, even though nothing was sorted in her personal life. She didn't feel ready.

'This is where that boy fell in and Dad and Uncle Casey saved his life,' said Tom.

'Yes, I was there too,' said Jade who hated to be left out of anything.

'I heard about that,' said Caitlin, 'some childhood prank, wasn't it?'

'A dare that went wrong,' said Casey.

'It could have ended badly if it weren't for Casey and Riordan,' said Lexi.

'And me, I was there,' said Jade.

'Yes, darling, and you, too.' Lexi hugged Jade.

How loving they all are, thought Caitlin. Would she be as patient as Lexi and Zoe if she had a child? They've got strong men at their side. Supportive and hands-on men. Caitlin tried to picture Brandon as a new father and couldn't.

'You're quiet,' said Jay.

'Just thinking. I've had a lovely time today, Jay, thanks for everything.'

'You're welcome any time you want.'

Caitlin longed to slip her hand into his but didn't want to send him the wrong signals. It wouldn't be fair after all he'd done for her.

Jay watched as Caitlin was dragged off by Jade and Tom to show her something they'd spotted. Casey took her place and looked as if he had something to say.

'So, how's things, Little Bro?'

'Couldn't be better, Big Bro. How are things with you?'

'Peachy.'

'Great. You want to say something?'

Casey was looking at the ground as he walked, as if the answers were on the canal path. 'Josie mentioned something about you being in love with Caitlin, even though she is engaged to someone else.'

'Ah… the O'Connor grapevine. Nothing gets past my twin.'

'Is it true?' Casey was talking quietly, and Jay kept his voice low as well.

'Yes,' he whispered.

'If you want to talk about it…' Casey trailed off. Neither Casey nor Jay talked much about their feelings. But in this case, there was nothing to say anyway.

'No, it's okay. I've got a handle on the situation. I love her, she loves someone else. End of.'

'Nothing's ever that straightforward, Jay. I heard her fiancé was playing away.'

'Her fiancé's a knob with nothing between his ears and please don't ask me why she's marrying someone like that because I've no idea.'

'Okay, well… don't forget though. We're all here for you whatever happens.'

'Thanks Casey, I'll remember.'

At the end of the day, surrounded by choruses of good-byes, the dogs running around in circles as their owners tried to get them in the cars, the kids jumping up and down and throwing themselves at people for one last hug, Jay realised what a treasure his family was.

When Caitlin married her Hooray Henry, and whatever other heartache he had to face further down the line, he would always have his family. A warm, safe haven to return to when he needed their unconditional love and support. He didn't care about money, property, or position. As long as he was part of this clan, he had everything he could possibly want. Except Caitlin.

Chapter Thirteen

'Let me look at you! You look fabulous! Did you have a good time?' Caitlin stepped back to let Sophie enter the cottage. She was tanned, her blonde hair was two shades lighter and she wore designer sunglasses perched on top of her head.

'Hi darling, did you miss me?'

'Missed you like crazy,' said Caitlin. They air-kissed and then Sophie caught sight of SpongeBob.

'OMG she's gorgeous! Where did you get her?'

'I didn't know you liked dogs.' Caitlin watched as Sophie scooped SpongeBob up into her arms. 'A patient asked Jay to look after her while she's in hospital and, of course, he said yes. Sadly, the patient has to stay in longer than anticipated and I think SpongeBob will be with us for a while yet. Jay told her it wouldn't be a problem. The man can't resist a damsel in distress.'

'Like you?' Sophie put SpongeBob on the floor.

'Well, yes, I was in need at that time. Don't know what I would have done without him.'

'Have you got him into bed yet?'

'Sophie! He's a friend, it's not like that.'

Sophie sat on the couch after throwing a pile of clothes and magazines onto the floor. SpongeBob jumped up and straight onto her knee. Sophie hugged the little dog and kissed her on the top of her head.

'That's even better. You're living here rent free, he does all the cooking and cleaning and you don't even have to sleep with him.'

'You're impossible. Do you want a drink? Tea or coffee?'

'I'd love a drink, but haven't you got anything stronger?'

Caitlin opened the fridge and found half a bottle of white wine. She poured Sophie a glass and half a glass for herself. She wasn't a daytime drinker but didn't want to leave her friend to drink alone.

'Just bring the bottle, hon,' shouted Sophie.

'There you go.' Caitlin sat beside her and Sophie started pulling things wrapped in sparkly paper out of a designer shop carrier bag. SpongeBob tried to put her head in the bag.

'Now.' Sophie turned to her and looked serious. 'I haven't got you as much as normal, as this cruise was highly lacking in shopping opportunities. But I think you'll like this.'

'You didn't have to get me anything,' said Caitlin unwrapping a present. 'Oh, it's gorgeous, Sophie, thank you so much.' She held up a clutch bag covered in gold beads.

'Well I always get you something, don't I?'

'Yes, you do. You're a good friend. Did you meet anyone?' They both knew she meant a man.

'There was one, but he wasn't husband material.'

'That's a shame. When's the next cruise?'

'Oh, not for ages yet. I'll have to find something or

someone else to amuse myself with until then. Maybe I'll make a play for Jay... Oh, that rhymes... if you're not interested that is.'

'No, I don't think that's a good idea.' Caitlin felt panicked at the thought of Sophie and Jay together, but when she analysed the feeling, she couldn't come up with a logical reason why. After all, they were both free and single.

'Why ever not? If you don't want him. Maybe you do want him, is that it?'

'He's just a friend, Sophie, that's all.'

Have you ditched the ghastly Brandon yet?'

Sophie drank her wine in one and filled up the glass again.

'We met once, and he told me to contact him when I'd come to my senses. I tried to apologise to him, but—'

'What the hell have *you* got to apologise for? He's the one who's been screwing around.' Sophie drank some wine, then looked penetratingly at Caitlin and asked, 'You haven't been screwing around, have you?'

'No, of course not.' Caitlin decided not to mention the kiss with Jay.

'Good. That's alright then. So tell me why you felt the need to apologise to that louse.'

'Because I didn't take his feelings into consideration. When I ran out, I left him to try to explain why he was suddenly minus a bride when he didn't even know why.'

'If the man had half a brain cell, or even a microscopic piece of one, he would have guessed. Especially with Fenella the witch sitting on the front row.'

'He denies that they're having an affair.'

'Do you believe him?'

'I don't know.'

Sophie took a selfie of herself and SpongeBob and uploaded it to Instagram.

'Let's have one of the three of us, come on, Caitlin.'

Caitlin moved up to be close to Sophie holding the dog in front of them.

'D'you know, I've just had the most brilliant idea!'

'Really?' Caitlin was used to Sophie's brilliant ideas which quite often turned out to be disasters for someone else.

'Why don't we put Princess SpongeBob on Instagram with her own page? I bet she'd get thousands of likes.'

'Oh, I don't know. We'd need to get Jay's permission first. And probably Betty's.'

'Betty who?'

'She's the patient and rightful owner of SpongeBob.'

'We don't need to go to all that trouble. I bet neither of them use Instagram.'

'I think Jay does.'

'Oh, go on, let's do it, it'll be fun. I'll order some ribbons and little dresses for her. And we can go travelling in my new car and take pictures of her at each place. Like a travelogue. It'll be great! Please. Say yes.'

Caitlin could never say no to Sophie. It had been the same when they were in school together. Sophie thought up adventures for them and she got dragged in. Her parents had warned her to stay away from Sophie Simons as she was bad news; one of the reasons Caitlin stuck to her friend like glue. That, and the fact that she loved her. And owed her big time. She was constantly aware of the debt that she would never be able to repay.

'Oh, alright then. What car did you get?'

'The Mas.'

'Thought so. Is it outside?'

Sophie nodded and then squealed like a little girl. 'Come and see.'

Sophie, still carrying SpongeBob, dragged Caitlin up off the couch, and to the front door.

'Let's go for a ride and I'll show you what she can do.'

'We'd better leave the dog.'

'No, bring her too. She can make the first journey in "The Life and Times of Princess Spongelicious". That's her stage name. I can't wait to set up her profile on Instagram. She could have her own blog, become a social media star. Oh, it's so exciting!'

Caitlin knew which car was Sophie's even before they reached it. It stood out amongst the Fords, Minis and SUVs parked outside the houses. For one thing, it was a mustard yellow colour—the only car in the street that was. The other thing was that the top was down.

'Two thousand and eleven, Maserati Gran Turismo soft-top convertible. Isn't it gorgeous?'

Caitlin studied the car and had to agree that, yes, if you were a lover of cars, then this one was pretty special.

'It's beautiful, Sophie. Really lovely.'

'Right. Hop in and let's go.' She pushed SpongeBob into Caitlin's arms and ran around to the driver's side. 'Come on, let's go.'

They sped off in the direction of the motorway.

'Where are we going?' asked Caitlin.

'To start Princess Spongelicious's new career. Hold on tight.'

Several hours later, Sophie dropped Caitlin and SpongeBob off outside the cottage.

It was late and Jay would be in bed, so Caitlin tiptoed up the stairs, still carrying the dog. As she passed his bedroom door she could hear the sound of soft snoring. She smiled and carried on to her bedroom.

'Shush,' she said to SpongeBob as she moved as quietly as she could to the bathroom and cleaned her teeth and removed her make-up. When she returned to her room, SpongeBob had already made herself comfortable in the centre of the bed.

Caitlin pulled Jay's T-shirt on and got into bed. Her phone pinged with a text message. It was from Sophie and simply read, 'Check it out,' with a link to Princess Spongelicious's new Instagram page. There were dozens of pictures of the places they'd been, all centred around Manchester city centre. Spinningfields, The Northern Quarter, pubs, wine bars and coffee shops.

Caitlin had to hand it to Sophie, she took good pictures and they were already attracting some positive comments and post likes. It was harmless fun. Sophie had found a new interest and Caitlin was getting out of the house. Sophie had already planned an itinerary for Princess Spongelicious, and the next few days were going to be busy. She would have to go back to work soon and talk to Brandon and her parents. But not yet. She'd think about all that later. At the moment, she was having too much fun.

Chapter Fourteen

Jay hadn't seen Caitlin for several days. She had been spending her time with Sophie, driving around in the new car, getting in late when Jay was asleep. He didn't feel jealous of the fact that Caitlin's best friend could afford a car that cost more than the cottage he lived in. He didn't care about things like that. It did, however, remind him, as if he needed reminding, that Caitlin and Sophie came from a completely different world to the one he occupied.

They came from money. Their parents were rich. Even if Caitlin didn't marry Hooray Henry, she would expect to be able to live in that world. If not Brandon, there'd be someone else from the circles she moved in, ready to take his place. Jay couldn't hope to compete. That thought made him sad.

It had been a slow day so far and Jay felt out of sorts for some reason. He needed to get his act together as they could have a difficult call-out at any time and he had to be ready.

He was working with Sally who, as an experienced paramedic, had seen it all as far as the extent of human tragedy goes. He loved listening to her talk about some of the funnier call-outs she'd attended. Today, however, Sally was quiet, so Jay respected that and didn't speak.

They had attended a woman who was an alcoholic and diabetic. Two conditions that didn't mix. She had collapsed with a hypoglycaemic attack and they had stabilised her before taking her to hospital.

Their next call-out was a man who'd fallen through a French window and had cuts and bruises. They patched him up and took him to A&E.

After lunch they got a call-out that struck fear into both of them. A twelve-month-old boy had been found by his mother face down in the bath. She had left him to answer the phone. He wasn't breathing.

'Right, lad,' said Sally, 'pedal to the metal for this one. We need to get there ten minutes ago.'

Jay could hear the unease in Sally's Scottish tones. She was a plain-speaking woman and she was afraid. His blood ran cold.

When they got to the house, five minutes later, Jay having driven like the proverbial bat out of hell, they found the young mother in hysterics, a neighbour trying to calm her down and the baby, lying on the sofa, wrapped in a towel.

The baby wasn't breathing and had no heartbeat. His lips were quite blue.

As he started CPR and Sally got the defibrillator ready Jay felt a rush of anger that he fought to control. Nobody had tried to resuscitate the child. They'd lost precious minutes that could have saved his life. Simple CPR wasn't hard to do—it wasn't rocket science.

He felt Sally's hand on his shoulder and looked up. The

expression on her face mirrored the way he was feeling. The mother was pleading with them to save her baby, so Jay continued CPR even though he knew it was not going to bring the child back.

He had to try. It was the only thing he could do.

———————

Jay got back to the cottage to be greeted with the usual mess. Caitlin was sitting on the couch, painting her toenails and SpongeBob was curled up next to her. The dog was wearing a big pink bow on the top of her head. The house smelt stale and he could see by the amount of dust on the television and the mantlepiece that no cleaning had been done for several days.

Jay was exhausted, heartsore, and angry. He always felt this way when they lost a patient, especially a baby. Fortunately, it didn't happen often. Sally had tried to talk to him about it afterwards, but he'd just wanted to get home.

If he'd been thinking straight he would have gone home to his parents and poured his heart out to them. Instead, he had to keep his temper and be pleasant to Caitlin. He had invited her to stay in his home, so had no one to blame but himself.

'Hi, Jay. You okay?'

'Not really. Bad day.'

'Oh, I'm sorry. Do you want to talk about it?'

'Not really.' He didn't know what he wanted. All he knew was that a whirlwind was rotating inside him, making him feel emotions he didn't want and had no idea what to do with. Other paramedics would go to the gym and thrash it out on the treadmill. Or go running and keep going until they dropped with exhaustion. Or get drunk.

'Did you have a good day?' Perhaps Caitlin could take his mind off his pain.

'Yeah, it was great. Sophie took us to Chester. We went to the zoo, went shopping. Oh, we found a lovely antique shop there.'

Jay couldn't speak. The whirlwind inside him was getting faster and he shook his head to try to clear it. He coughed but it came out as a harsh sound.

Caitlin looked up quickly and nudged the nail polish that she had balanced on the arm of the couch, so it fell onto the rug, spilling its contents.

'Oh, shit,' said Caitlin. She bent to pick it up and carried on painting her toenails.

'Look what you've done. Caitlin—aren't you going to clean it up?'

'Yeah, in a minute.' She didn't even look up at him.

Jay felt a red mist descend and he clenched his hands into fists so hard that he could feel pain. But even the pain didn't prevent him from losing control.

'Don't bother, the rug's ruined.'

Even then Caitlin didn't realise the state he was in. 'Oh, chill out, will you, I'll buy you another one.'

'My mother bought me that rug when I moved in. It has —had—sentimental value.'

Caitlin looked up then. 'I'm sorry, Jay. I'll clear it up now. Sorry, okay?'

'No, it's not okay. I have had the worst day I've had for years and I come home to a complete mess. I can't cope with this any longer. You are treating my home like a dumping ground for all your crap. Can't you at least tidy once in a while?'

Caitlin stared at him and her eyes were huge in her face. He had never spoken to her like this before, but something had been released inside him and he couldn't seem to stop. All his anger and pain was directed at Caitlin.

'I'm sorry, I'll buy you a new rug.'

'That's your answer for everything, isn't it? Just buy a new one. Well, there's some things that money can't buy, Caitlin. But you, spoilt little rich girl, wouldn't know about that, would you?'

Caitlin stood up and put her hands on her hips. 'Don't call me that, okay? Don't you dare call me that!'

Caitlin turned and ran up the stairs.

Jay called after her, 'That's right—run away like you always do.'

When he heard Caitlin's bedroom door slam, he sat down heavily on the couch and put his head in his hands.

———

Caitlin was in shock. Jay had never spoken to her like that before. He'd always been a perfect gentleman, thinking of her feelings and looking after her. But he was right. She was untidy and messy. All she had thought about recently was going out with Sophie and having fun. She'd used Jay's home like a hotel, expecting someone else to keep it clean and tidy. And that someone was Jay.

An apology was needed. She wanted to get things back on the right track. Jay was a close friend. A very dear, lovely friend who had done so much to help her. Jay's good opinion was important to her and she needed to get it back.

Caitlin left her bedroom and listened at Jay's door. At first she couldn't hear anything, then detected the sound of muffled crying. She was taken aback. She'd never heard a man cry before. Except maybe the patients and their relatives. It was a distressing sound and Caitlin couldn't bear the thought that she might have caused it.

Caitlin opened the door slowly and peered in. Jay was sitting on the edge of his bed, his face in his hands, sobbing.

'Jay, I'm so sorry. Please don't cry.' She knelt down in front of him and put her arms around him, but he couldn't seem to stop crying. 'Lie down, Jay.'

He did as she asked, and she climbed onto the bed and they held each other tightly. Eventually, when Jay's tears had been all cried out, Caitlin felt the time was right for a heart to heart.

Chapter Fifteen

'It was the last call-out of the day. I spent my time doing CPR on a dead baby.' Jay felt calm but empty. He didn't want to go over it all again but knew talking about it would help. And then he needed to apologise to Caitlin.

She was holding him tightly and he breathed in her aroma. A light floral scent that she always wore and the faint tang of the nail polish.

'Oh, Jay, that's awful! My worst nightmare.'

'Yeah, mine too. The mother was begging us to save him, but we knew he'd gone before we even got there.'

'Who were you on with?'

'Sally. She was the strength I needed. I knew I had to call it, but I couldn't. She intervened eventually. The mother had to be sedated.'

'Oh God, that is awful. I'm so sorry, Jay. If I'd known, I'd…'

Jay hugged her to him. 'You didn't know. It was all my fault, I should never have taken it out on you. I'm sorry, Caitlin. Will you forgive me?'

'Only if you'll forgive me first.'

'There's nothing to forgive you for.'

'Yes, there is—for being a dirty, lazy, spoilt, rich bitch.'

Jay wished he hadn't said that to her. He could hear the hurt in her voice.

'Hey, don't say things like that. I was distraught, I didn't mean what I said. You're lovely. Untidy, I'll give you that, but still lovely.' Jay sat up a bit so he could see Caitlin's face. She'd been crying, her eyes were red, and her make-up smudged. 'Have I really upset you that much?' The last thing Jay wanted to do was upset Caitlin. He wanted to look after her, care for her and instead, he'd made her cry.

'It isn't you. It's being called a spoilt little rich girl that upset me. It reminded me of being bullied at the private school I went to because I wasn't like the other girls. They all came from aristocratic families who could trace their ancestors back for generations. The landed gentry. Some of them lived in castles. They had no money, but they had a name. My family had no name, but they had enough money to send me to boarding school.'

'But why were you bullied? Surely you weren't the only girl in that situation?'

'There weren't many of us and we were ostracised. My only friend at that school was Sophie. She protected me from the bullies and I'll never be able to repay her.'

'There's more to Sophie than meets the eye.' He would never have put her in the role of protector, but people never ceased to surprise him.

'And you're right about me always running away. That's been my default position with a situation I can't handle or one that makes me uncomfortable, but I'm going to stop doing that and face up to things. I'll go and see my parents and Brandon. I promise. I can change, Jay.'

Jay hugged Caitlin to his chest, wanting to feel the touch of her skin next to his. He wanted to kiss her so much but was afraid of what that could lead to. She wasn't his and he had to keep his distance.

He thought of the kiss they'd had on her hen night. They'd been on a packed dance floor, under hot lights, surrounded by couples, but they could have been the only two people in the club as the background had faded away and all that he saw was Caitlin's face and her rosy mouth as she asked him to kiss her.

She was quiet now and Jay wondered what she was thinking.

'I think I'm going to take my uniform off,' he said quietly.

'Okay,' said Caitlin. 'Do you want to get into bed? We'd be more comfy.'

'Good idea.' Jay was glad that Caitlin wanted to stay with him. Maybe just for a while longer. He couldn't believe that she wanted more than just to be a friend to him. But whatever she was offering, he'd take it.

Jay quickly stripped down to his boxers and slipped under the duvet. Caitlin had taken off her outer clothes and kept her bra and panties on.

He lay on his back and Caitlin lay on her side next to him, her head on his shoulder and one leg over his legs. It was such a comfortable position, he could easily fall asleep if it weren't for the way his body was reacting to the situation. His heart thudded in his chest, pumping his blood around his body.

He had thought that this would be enough. To lie in the darkness with her by his side was something he dreamed about regularly. But now he was there, he wanted more. He wanted her, all of her, completely.

He couldn't lie still any longer and caressed the soft skin on Caitlin's back. He buried his face in her hair and breathed in the scent of her shampoo. He sighed deeply as he felt Caitlin's hand stroking his chest and her fingers tangling in his chest hair. She played with one of his nipples and he groaned.

'Cait?'

'Umm?'

'I want you.'

'I want you.'

The words had been whispered in the darkness and Jay turned towards Caitlin and kissed her. Gently at first, slowly, an exploration, discovering her secrets, as if kissing were enough, the feelings and sensations of her tongue, her lips would sustain him.

Jay moved her gently onto her back and kissed her chin, her neck, the top of her breasts as they pushed out of the bra. He unclipped the bra and pulled it off her, then kissed her breasts all over until she was writhing slightly under his touch. He took one nipple in his mouth and played with the other one, rolling it gently between his fingers.

Her breasts were small but beautiful. Petite, like the rest of her. He swapped over and took the other nipple in his mouth.

He continued his exploration of her body, licking her stomach until she cried out then lower still until he reached her panties. He pulled them off and spread her legs so he could kiss her. She was wet and ready for him, but he wanted to make it good for the first time. And maybe the only time, but he refused to think about that.

He licked and nuzzled her, and she grabbed his hair and encouraged him. She wriggled on the bed and thrust upwards, so he took pity on her and brought her to orgasm. Caitlin cried out and called his name as she climaxed.

Jay moved back up the bed until he could kiss Caitlin again. She lay panting and he watched until finally she turned to him and said, 'Your turn.'

After removing his boxers, he let her do what she wanted with him. He lay on his back and gave himself up to her.

Caitlin mirrored his actions as she moved down his body, kissing his nipples, his belly, then taking hold of his balls and gently massaging them while she took him in her mouth. He was close to his climax and wanted to make it last, but Caitlin's administrations were too good, and he ejaculated into her mouth. He cried out and waited until his heart rate returned to normal and his breathing steadied.

'That was amazing,' he croaked.

'It was. It was lovely. The best.'

Caitlin lay next to him again and this time, Jay felt he could sleep. But he didn't want to. This night was special. He had no idea what was going to happen the following day and he didn't care. There was only this night and the chance to spend the rest of it with Caitlin. He didn't want it to end yet.

They lay together without speaking. Jay was wondering how long it would take for him to recover as he wanted to make love to Caitlin. Usually, it didn't take him long.

'Jay?'

'Yes.'

'Thank you for listening to me tonight. I didn't mean to start moaning on about school, not when you were the one hurting and needing the shoulder to cry on.'

'It's fine. I'm glad you told me. And I should thank you for listening to me. I can usually control my emotions, but losing a baby is something I've never been able to get used to.'

'I know. God, that poor woman.'

Jay didn't want the ambience to be brought low by thinking of sad things, so he kissed Caitlin and thankfully felt his body respond.

'I want to feel you inside me,' she whispered in between kisses.

Jay sat up and opened the drawer in the bedside cabinet, to find a packet of condoms. He took them out and then looked at Caitlin again, but she was smiling.

'I'm on the pill, Jay.'

'I still think we should use protection.' He opened the packet and took one out.

'Let me,' Caitlin said taking it from him. So he lay back and let her put it on him.

Caitlin wasted no time with preliminaries. She straddled him and he held her hips as she rode him. He took longer to climax this time and was able to hold back until Caitlin had orgasmed.

Caitlin had a smile on her face that warmed Jay's heart.

'Okay?' he asked.

'Amazing,' she said and carefully moved off him so he could dispose of the condom.

When he returned, she was lying with one arm over her head, her dark hair covering her breasts and a sweet smile on her lips. Jay loved her in that moment with an intense longing. He didn't know what would happen in the future, but he would always cherish the memory of the first time he made love to Caitlin.

Perhaps there could be a future for them. He desperately hoped so. But if not, at least he had this.

The following day, as Jay had a day off, he slept in.

Caitlin had spent the night in his bed but must have got up when he'd still been asleep. He woke in a good mood and followed the aroma of breakfast down to the kitchen. He looked around in amazement. The living room was clean and tidy, with no clothes, make-up, magazines, or any other of Caitlin's possessions in sight.

'Wow, I can actually see the carpet,' he said. 'You have been working hard.'

'I've turned over a new leaf,' said Caitlin who was wearing an apron, possibly for the first time ever. 'I've bought croissants for breakfast and have made fresh coffee. I've cleaned and tidied and taken SpongeBob for a walk.'

'Good for you.' Jay sat at the table and poured some of the coffee for them both. He took a croissant and was pleased to see it was still warm.

'I've made an appointment with my doctor to be signed off sick leave and I've told work to put me back on the rota.'

'Are you sure about this, Caitlin? Are you ready?'

'I am, more than ready. You see a new Caitlin Hewitt before you.'

'Well, much as I liked the old one, I'm pretty impressed with the new one.'

'Thank you. It's about time I faced up to the realities in my life. I need to talk to my parents and Brandon before I decide on my next move.'

Jay nodded, sincerely hoping the new Caitlin Hewitt would find room for Jay O'Connor in her new life.

Chapter Sixteen

Caitlin felt as if she had never been away. Welcomed back with open arms, she felt proud to put her uniform on and climb up into the ambulance with whoever she was partnering that shift.

Today, it was Sally and they were working a night shift. It was Caitlin's turn to drive.

Despite telling Jay that she had turned over a new leaf, she still hadn't spoken to her parents or Brandon and knew that, until she did, she couldn't move on with her life. One thing she did know, however, was that her feelings for Jay had changed the night they made love. Caitlin couldn't stop thinking about him and how different he was to Brandon. Jay was kind, sensitive, gentle but also strong, reliable, and fantastic in bed. Brandon was none of those things.

The evening started in the usual way for a Saturday night in Leytonsfield, which was probably being repeated in every town and city up and down the country. People out for a good time—stag and hen nights, teenagers too young to drink but finding a way to do it anyway, rowdy, and boisterous at the beginning of the night but with the potential for alcohol poisoning, drug overdoses, fights, knifings, and goodness knows what else as the bewitching hour came closer. Once the bars and clubs closed, people took it onto the streets and the paramedics were in the thick of it.

They treated a young girl who had slipped off the kerb in heels too high for her and twisted her ankle. She had been drinking but wasn't totally inebriated. Her night out was cut short by a long stay in A&E waiting for her ankle to be X-rayed.

The next casualty was a man who had been in a fight in a club where his assailant attacked him with a broken bottle. He got off lightly but needed stitches in his face.

'How're you bearing up?' asked Sally as they returned to the ambulance after they had taken their break.

'I'm fine. Really. But thanks for asking.'

'Right. You still living with Jay?' Caitlin knew that Sally wasn't being nosy, she was just making conversation.

'I'm still in his spare bedroom yes, but I need to make a decision soon about my future.'

'Serious stuff, eh?'

'Yes. You know about my disastrous wedding day, don't you?' Caitlin was aware that everyone would know about it by now.

'Aye, I was sorry to hear about that. You're not going to marry the bastard, are you?'

Caitlin chuckled. 'Not if he's guilty as charged, no, I'm not going to marry the bastard. But I need to hear him deny it. We haven't really talked.'

'Best do that sooner rather than later. Until then your future's uncertain.'

Before they could talk further, a job came through.

'Right, here we go. We have a job to go to,' said Sally.

'It's at the Leytonsfield Hotel. Man in his late fifties, query heart attack.'

'Right, sirens going on,' said Caitlin.

They sped through the busy streets to reach the hotel. Even at the late hour people were out and about celebrating Saturday night.

When they got to the hotel, the concierge escorted them to the third floor. The door was open, and an extremely anxious woman stood at the side of a double bed, wringing her hands, and crying. A man was lying on the bed with a blanket over him. He looked unconscious and as she stepped closer, Caitlin stopped and stared at him, then looked at the woman and back to the man on the bed in utter bewilderment.

'Don't just stand there gawping at him—do something!' The woman was shouting at her, but Caitlin was in a daze. Then Sally's voice penetrated the fog in her brain.

'Caitlin? What the hell's the matter?'

Caitlin turned and whispered to Sally, 'The man on the bed is my father.'

'Right, then I'll take charge, you do exactly as I say. Forget the fact he's your dad, treat him like any other patient. I take it the woman isn't your mother?'

Caitlin shook her head.

Sally bent over Caitlin's father to examine him, but spoke to the woman, asking her to describe the symptoms exactly as they occurred.

'He just clutched his chest and then… he sat on the bed and said he felt sick. He was sweating.'

'Did he just sit on the bed or was it more of a collapse, do you think?'

'More of a collapse. He was in agony.'

'Okay. What's your name, love?' asked Sally.

'Heather,' said the woman. 'Is he going to be alright?'

'We're doing everything we can for him. I'm doing an ECG which should tell us if he's had a heart attack. We'll get him in the ambulance as soon as and take him to the General. Has he had chest pains before?'

Sally was working on her father but talking to the woman called Heather. Why was she asking that woman? She could have told her that he hadn't. But then Caitlin realised that she didn't know. She had been away from home for a while and before that, she hadn't seen her father very much. He was always working. Or so she'd thought. Now she wondered if he had been working at all. Had he been with this Heather woman?

Ask her what her relationship is to my father, thought Caitlin, even though she was frantic for his safety. Who is this woman? She was fully clothed, but her father had his trousers on with the belt undone, no shirt and bare feet. She gave the room a cursory glance. There was an overnight bag on the floor that belonged to her father.

'Caitlin,' said Sally loudly.

'Yes?'

'Help me get him on the stretcher.'

Caitlin could feel her own heart beating fast as she did what Sally said. She needed to stop thinking and just do her job. Pushing her anxiety and all the questions buzzing around her head to one side, she concentrated on getting her father into the ambulance while causing him as little distress as possible.

The caring professions were often told to treat every patient as if they were a relative. Caitlin had always tried to follow that advice. Now, however, she realised how impossible it was to be impartial when the patient was known to you.

'You can drive,' Sally commanded once her father was in the ambulance and in the most comfortable position they could get him in.

Heather climbed into the ambulance and took her father's hand. She was crying again but ignored Caitlin completely.

'We're ready,' said Sally, glaring at her. Caitlin didn't take offence, she knew she wasn't acting professionally but she was stunned at seeing her father on the bed and couldn't get her head together.

'Okay,' said Caitlin putting as much strength into her voice as she could.

'Good girl,' said Sally gently.

Sally drove this time, while Caitlin sat in a daze still, staring out of the window. She'd hated leaving her father in Resus but knew it was the best place for him. She wanted to be with him, holding his hand, not that woman.

'We've only got an hour or two of the shift left. Let's hope there's nothing major. In the meantime,' Sally glanced at Caitlin, 'if you want to talk about what just happened I'm willing to listen.'

Caitlin sighed. 'I know I screwed up and was no earthly use to you back there. You had to do all the heavy lifting and I'm sorry—'

'No, you dunce, I don't mean that. You were fine. My God, if I'd gone to a hotel room and found my father with another woman I'd be screaming blue murder. The fact that he's no longer on this earth would make me scream even louder, of course.'

Caitlin laughed, tears squeezing out of her closed eyes.

It felt good to let go but her laughter wasn't really appropriate.

'Sorry...'

'Don't be sorry, laughter is a good thing. Puts things into perspective.'

'Oh Sally, I don't know what to think. Who was that woman?'

'Well, I'll take that as a rhetorical question shall I? She was obviously with him for a bit of hanky-panky I imagine. She was upset though. Must care about him a lot.'

'I don't know what to do. I need to tell my mother, but I don't want to betray my father. I'm stuck in the middle.'

'Aye,' said Sally, 'You are that.'

A call-out came through. Caitlin answered and then waited for the details to come through.

'A man has been beaten up outside The Late Club.'

'Right. Let's get on with the job.'

Caitlin asked for a change of shift the following day so she could go to see her father. Fortunately, there was someone who wanted to swap their shift, so Caitlin got the day off.

When she got to the Intensive Care Unit, her mother was already there, sitting upright and perfectly poised on the plastic chair next to Alan's bed.

Caitlin was familiar with the ICU but seeing her father lying in bed, attached to tubes, wires and cables, surrounded by the machinery keeping him alive, was distressing. He was lying in a semi-upright position supported by pillows, wearing an oxygen mask. A computer screen just to the right of his bed showed his vital signs; heart rate, blood pressure and the amount of oxygen in his blood.

'Dad?' she said softly. He fluttered his eyelids but didn't open his eyes. She took his hand and squeezed it.

'Long time since you called your father that,' said Nina.

'I've never seen my father in this state,' Caitlin retorted, 'it's a shock. And he is still my dad.'

'Well, I'm glad to hear you say that. I just hope it hasn't come too late.'

Caitlin sat on a chair on the other side of the bed to her mother, holding her father's hand. She tried not to disturb all the equipment around the bed.

'Too late? Have they said something? What have you been told?'

Her mother glared at her and shook her head impatiently. 'Nobody's said anything. They never do, do they in places like these?'

'They're busy. They will tell us if there's been any change. He probably just needs to be monitored for a day or so.'

Caitlin stroked her father's hand, noticing how wrinkled his skin was becoming. He was nearly sixty and the liver spots were starting to appear on the backs of his hands. Strange how she'd never noticed before. She'd been too obsessed with her own problems to worry about her parents. Things would change from now on.

She'd start by improving relations with her mother. Judging by the look on Nina's face, however, that was going to be easier said than done.

'I'm sorry, Mother,' Caitlin said.

'You should be. This is all your fault, you know. Your poor father's been frantic with worry about you after that stunt on your wedding day. If he dies, it'll be down to you.'

Caitlin's head shot up. 'He's not going to die. And I'm really sorry if I've caused either of you stress. I never meant to.'

'Have you told that so-called friend of yours that you no longer want anything to do with her?'

Caitlin thought of Sophie, her warm and bouncy bestie

who was always looking for the next adventure. She was more supportive than her mother had ever been.

'No, I haven't and I'm not going to either. Sophie's a good friend.'

'Then you're not all that *sorry*, are you? If you don't want to make amends and undo all the trouble you've caused, then you can't really care about us.'

Caitlin felt shrivelled inside. She had no idea that her father was feeling stressed because of her. She needed to talk to him, ask him about Heather. Maybe things weren't as they seemed, and they weren't having an affair. Perhaps there was a perfectly simple explanation and she was wrong to assume the worst.

Then, she saw the hotel room in her mind's eye. Her father with no shirt on, Heather in a dishevelled state. Sally's caustic remark about hanky-panky made her realise that it was exactly as it seemed.

Caitlin looked at her mother. She always dressed immaculately and even her husband's heart attack hadn't changed that. She wore a coral shift dress, with shoes and handbag to match. A cream jacket was neatly folded on her lap. Her hair was in a neat bun and her make-up was subtle but perfect.

'You look nice,' Caitlin said.

'Well, you don't,' Nina answered. 'Why don't you do something with your hair? It's long enough to put up. It's always round your face. It looks untidy, Caitlin.'

'I didn't have time.'

'No, you never have time for the important things, do you? You need to grow up and start acting more responsibly.'

'Yes, Mother.' The answer that she always gave. But this time it was different. She could easily blurt out that her father was having an affair just to get back at her mother, but she wouldn't. She would act responsibly and ask her father when he was better. Find out the facts before she went charging in all guns blazing.

'Have you spoken to Brandon yet?'

'No, not yet.'

'Well, you should. It's wicked to keep the poor man dangling like that. Put his mind at rest and tell him you're sorry for your childish behaviour then we can set another date for the wedding.'

Caitlin, who would have liked to see Brandon dangling over a precipice, said, 'I don't know what I'm doing yet, Mother.'

Her mother stood up. 'Oh for goodness sake. You're marrying Brandon Dodds, that's what you're doing. I'm going to the ladies.'

Caitlin breathed a sigh of relief, then turned her attention to her father who must have been heavily sedated as he hadn't moved since she'd arrived.

'Dad? I'm sorry for everything. I want to talk to you when you're better. I love you, Dad.' She kissed his cheek then decided now would be the perfect time to escape. 'I'm going now, but I'll come back tomorrow after work. See you then.'

As Caitlin left the hospital, a tear rolled down her cheek. It was true what people said. You don't know what you've got until you're in danger of losing it.

The following day, Caitlin was on an early, so she called in to see her father after her shift.

Her mother had visited that morning, and Caitlin had

hoped to be alone with her father, but when she got there Heather was sitting at his bedside.

She looked a lot better than she had at the hotel. She was dressed in a white blouse, maroon skirt and jacke,t and her hair was tidy and fell to her shoulders in a reddish-gold wave. Caitlin had to admit that she was an attractive woman.

Heather watched as Caitlin approached and looked around for a chair.

'Have this one,' said Heather starting to rise.

'No, I've got one.'

Caitlin sat down and examined her father. He looked better than he had yesterday. She glanced at the screen, pleased to see that his observations looked normal. His heart rate and blood pressure had come down.

'He's better, isn't he?' Heather asked eagerly.

'It certainly looks that way,' said Caitlin. 'Have you spoken to anyone yet?'

'No.'

Caitlin wasn't going to make conversation. She hadn't thought that she might have to speak to Heather before her father, but maybe this was the golden opportunity to find out what the woman meant to him.

'I'm sorry you've had to find out about us like this. It must have been a terrible shock.'

'Yes,' said Caitlin, 'it was.'

'You'll be wanting to know who I am and how long it's been going on?'

'Yes, I do.'

'I love him, Caitlin. This isn't any old slap and tickle in a hotel. He loves me too, we want to be together.'

It had gone from hanky-panky to slap and tickle and now this woman was trying to tell her they were in love. She didn't know what to think and knew that she needed to talk to her father.

'How long *has* it been going on?' At least she could get the facts from Heather.

'Five years.'

'Five years!'

'Yes. We're in the same line of business. He had a heart scare three years ago—you knew about that, of course.'

How to admit to his father's mistress that she didn't even know he'd had heart problems. What kind of a daughter did that make her? Caitlin felt angry at herself for not knowing her father had been ill. Five years ago she was just starting her paramedic training and was so wrapped up in it, she couldn't see what was under her nose.

'No, I didn't know.'

Heather smiled. 'He was probably protecting you. He loves you very much, you know.'

'Really?'

'I realise how hard this must be for you, and I'm sorry about that, I really am. For the way you found out, I mean. I love your father and he loves me. This has been a wake-up call to stop sneaking around and get everything out in the open. Life is precious and Alan and I want to spend ours together.'

'My father will never leave my mother. He loves her and they've been together for too long to throw it all away. He'll end it with you, and everything will go back to normal.' Caitlin spoke with as much confidence as she could. Heather, however, looked at her as if she were a child who had told her she still believed in Santa Claus.

'Oh, Caitlin, I do hope that we can be friends. I think we'd get on. I'm sorry for any pain we've caused you.'

'I need to talk to my father. This has all been a bit of a shock. I need to hear it from him.'

'Yes, of course, I understand perfectly. I'll be waiting for the right time.'

Caitlin got up and marched away. She expected Heather to call her back, but she didn't. When Caitlin got to the door, she looked back once to see what Heather was doing. It appeared she had forgotten her already for she was bent over her father's bed, tenderly wiping his face, and whispering to him.

Chapter Eighteen

Jay was on duty with Paul, who kept throwing him suspicious looks. As Jay drove, he couldn't keep the smile off his face.

'Are you going to tell me, or do I have to beat it out of you?'

Jay laughed. 'I have no idea what you mean.'

'You've been grinning like a Cheshire cat which can mean only one of two things; you got laid, or you've won the lottery.'

'I don't do the lottery,' said Jay grinning.

'Okay… so that only leaves one option. Who's the lucky girl?'

'I don't know whether I should talk about it. It was only once, and we haven't spoken about it since.' Jay didn't want to think about the cold, hard facts; that Caitlin hadn't mentioned the night they had spent together and had seemed to be avoiding him. He knew all about her father's heart attack and had tried to be supportive, but Caitlin seemed preoccupied and unwilling to talk about her feelings for him. His feelings, however, had ramped up to the point where he was looking in jeweller's shops at engagement rings.

'You got it together with Caitlin, right?'

'Correct.'

'Oh man, you're playing with fire.'

'You don't approve of Caitlin, do you?'

Jay kept his eyes on the road, so he couldn't see the look on Paul's face. But he knew, from his tone of voice, that he was in for one of his bro lectures. They always began, "I love you, Bro which is why I have to be honest." Paul was a good friend and the kind of guy you wanted on your side. Jay would listen—he always listened when Paul spoke—but he would do whatever he felt right.

'Go on then,' Jay said, 'I'm listening. Be quick though, before we get a call-out.'

'Okay, if you insist. I love Caitlin as a friend, she's a great colleague and I love working with her. But she ran out of the church on her wedding day, man. She's flaky. Unreliable. She's not the woman for you.'

'Right, I've heard enough. I appreciate your advice but... I love her.'

'I understand that, and if she felt the same way, I'd be over the moon for you. I want you to be happy, man, you know that.'

Just then a call came in and Jay switched the sirens on.

'What've we got?'

'Hit and run. Man in his nineties trying to cross at a zebra crossing was hit. Car didn't stop.'

'Bastard,' said Jay.

When they got to the scene the patient was conscious and sitting on the kerb. He had blood streaming from a head wound. The police were in attendance and they'd need the man to make a statement. But stopping the blood flow was the first priority.

Paul and Jay assessed him and got him in the ambulance.

Jay drove, while Paul stayed with the patient. Jay could hear laughter in the back and smiled. If anyone could cheer a patient up it was Paul. He had a way with people that Jay envied. He exuded confidence and likeability and patients felt safe in his presence.

Once they'd dropped their patient off, it was time for their break. Paul headed off to find a fast food outlet and Jay took advantage of being at Leytonsfield General to check on Betty and give her an update on SpongeBob.

When he arrived at the ward, he discovered that Betty had suffered a major stroke that morning and had been moved to the Stroke Unit and wasn't receiving visitors.

Betty wasn't having any luck as far as her health was concerned. At least she could rely on him and Caitlin to look after her precious dog.

The rest of the day was relatively quiet. Paul didn't mention Caitlin again, so Jay didn't either. But he was determined to speak to her that evening if she was in. He wanted to tell her how he felt about her. After all, he had nothing to lose and everything to gain.

When Jay arrived home, Caitlin was already in. She'd showered and changed into jog pants and T-shirt, and she was setting the table in preparation for the takeaway that Jay had picked up on the way home. He'd sent her a quick text checking that she'd be in and telling her he would bring food.

'Hi,' he called as SpongeBob ran to greet him. He fussed the little dog, petting her and telling her what a good dog she was.

'Hi, Jay,' Caitlin replied. 'What have you bought? It smells good, whatever it is.'

'Indian. Korma for you and rogan josh for me.'

'Great. What would you like to drink?'

'Beer would be good. Can you keep the food warm? Just nipping up for a quick shower.'

'Sure.'

As Jay showered, he went over in his mind how he would explain his feelings to Caitlin. He pulled on jeans and a clean T-shirt and ran down the stairs to the kitchen.

As they ate, Caitlin kept her gaze on her plate as if she didn't want to talk, but Jay was determined to find out where he stood.

'This is good,' Caitlin said. 'I can't believe how hungry I was. Did you have a good day?'

'I did have a good day but… I need to talk to you about something.'

Caitlin looked up then and searched his face. 'Have I done something wrong?'

'No, of course not. Why would you think that?'

'You sound serious,' Caitlin said.

'The other night?'

'When we slept together? Do you regret it? I understand if you do. After all, you invited me into your home and I appreciate your friendship, but that doesn't mean I want to take advantage of you, or…' Caitlin trailed off and Jay reached out and put his hand over hers.

'I don't regret it. Not at all. In fact…'

'What? Do you want to do it again? I don't know if that's a good idea. I mean, it's just sex, I know, there's no love involved or anything, but it might complicate things and right now, I'm so mixed up with my father and Heather. My head's in a mess.'

Jay withdrew his hand and continued to eat his curry. She thought that love wasn't involved, and it was just sex. That told him everything he needed to know. She didn't have feelings for him except for those of a friend.

'Have you decided what you're going to do about Brandon yet? Are you going to marry him?'

'I haven't decided yet. I need to see him face-to-face to talk to him. I need to be convinced that he isn't having an affair. At the moment I've got more important things to think about with my parents.'

'How is your dad?' Jay kept his voice light and his thoughts to himself.

'He's better. I phoned the ICU earlier and he's being moved to a cardiac ward. He's out of danger.'

'That's good. I'm pleased for you, Caitlin.'

'Thanks.'

After the meal, Jay grabbed SpongeBob's lead and headed for the door.

'Do you want me to come too?' asked Caitlin.

'No, it's okay. I won't be long.'

Once Jay was outside the cottage and striding down the road, he breathed deeply a few times, slowing down when he realised that SpongeBob's little legs were struggling to keep up.

'Sorry, girl.'

He headed for the park where he could let SpongeBob off her lead to run free for a while and sat on a bench and watched her. Some kids were playing football on the field and couples were walking by, hand in hand. It was a pleasant August evening. The second half of summer when the days were shortening and, in a few weeks, the kids would be back in school. The seasons changing and turning constantly in the background of Jay's life, counting down the years.

He hadn't told Caitlin how he felt. But what was the point? She obviously didn't feel the same way. They'd had one night of sex and he'd been ready to declare undying love. He was an idiot. Paul was right. Caitlin wasn't the one for him.

Why did that thought cause such a raw ache inside of him? Because, if he couldn't have Caitlin, he didn't want anyone else.

He looked up but couldn't see SpongeBob. The kids had gone, and the field was empty. He jumped up and ran to where he had last seen her. Nothing. He turned in a full circle looking in every direction. There was no sign of her.

He started running towards the copse of trees to the side of the field.

'Excuse me, mate! If you've lost a little dog, she's in there.'

He turned and a young boy on a bike pointed to the trees.

'Great! Thank you.' Jay ran towards the trees and the boy cycled off.

His heart was racing, and he nearly collapsed as he spotted her moeching around at the base of a tree. She was completely oblivious to everything else, sniffing the ground, her little tail wagging in the joy of being a dog.

Jay was so relieved to see her that he picked her up and cuddled her.

'Right, missy, you're staying on your lead. We have to keep you safe for when your mum gets out of hospital. No more running off.'

When Jay's heartbeat returned to normal, he put SpongeBob on her lead and headed home. This time, there'd be no heart to hearts, Caitlin was a friend, that was all.

Perhaps Paul was right, he should join a dating site. But the thought gave him no pleasure at all. In fact, he would rather have stuck pins in his eyes.

Chapter Nineteen

Caitlin's next day off was a full week later. Her father was doing well and was due to be discharged, but Caitlin knew she needed to speak to her mother before that happened. She hadn't seen Heather again, but the brief talk she'd had with her father had confirmed what Heather had said; that they were in love and intended to be together.

Even though she had a key, Caitlin rang the bell and her mother answered.

'Hi, can I come in?'

'Of course, this is your home.'

Her mother stepped back to let Caitlin in, and she moved into the hallway to the smell of pine furniture polish and the Chanel that was her mother's signature scent. Everything looked as it usually did, but the house felt empty as if waiting for people to come home and bring it back to life.

Caitlin wondered how her mother had coped alone in a big house, but she didn't want to upset her by asking. At least her standards hadn't slipped. Her mother wore a deep mauve silk pantsuit that looked stunning on her tall, lithe figure. Caitlin was glad she'd made an effort with her clothes by wearing a dress and heels, but she still felt shabby in comparison to her mother.

'Would you like something to eat or drink?'

'Tea would be nice.'

'Okay, come into the kitchen and I'll make you a pot.'

'Where's Daisy?' Her mother had never made tea, or anything else, before. She'd always left it to the maid cum cleaner. Daisy had been with them for years and Caitlin was very fond of her.

'Daisy has retired, and I haven't got around to finding her replacement.'

'I didn't know. I would have liked to have said goodbye.'

'Well, you've left it too late, she's gone to Cyprus to live with her sister.'

'Right.'

Caitlin sat down at the kitchen table while her mother made her a pot of tea. Surprisingly, she was quite adept at it. She poured two cups and handed one to Caitlin.

'Don't sit there, Caitlin, let's go into the drawing room.'

Her mother left the kitchen and Caitlin trailed after her. She sat in an armchair and her mother sat on the sofa opposite her.

'It's good news about Father, isn't it? I bet it'll be great having him home again.'

Her mother smiled. 'Yes, it will.'

Caitlin sipped her tea and wondered how to broach the subject. She'd better just come out with it. Her mother was starting to look bored.

'Mother? I need to ask you something but it's a bit delicate.'

Her mother sighed and waved her hand as if giving Caitlin permission to speak. 'Ask away.'

'You know that I was one of the paramedics who found Father. In the hotel.'

'Yes.'

'Well… there was a woman with him. They had been… well, together, if you know what I mean.'

'Oh, for goodness sake, Caitlin, if you mean Heather just say so. Of course, they'd been *together* as you coyly put it, she's his mistress.'

'You know about her?' Caitlin stared at her mother in amazement.

'Of course I do, I'm not stupid. Pity I can't say the same about you though.'

Caitlin was gobsmacked. She drank the rest of her tea and then asked, 'Is there more tea in the pot.'

'Help yourself,' said her mother.

When Caitlin got to the kitchen she poured milk into her cup and then tea. She added one teaspoon of sugar and drank it down. Then she poured more milk, sugar, and tea. She was used to a mug that could hold three times the amount of tea than this delicate little teacup. Then she returned to the drawing room, where her mother was flicking through *Vogue*.

'I don't understand.'

Her mother sighed deeply. 'What don't you understand?'

'How you can stay with a man who's cheating. I know he's my father but… for goodness sake, have you no pride?'

Caitlin thought she'd gone too far, and her mother would throw her out telling her never to darken her door again. Instead, she laughed.

'Oh, you poor deluded girl. You still think marriage is all about love, roses and champagne, don't you?'

'No, I don't. I know you have to work at a marriage, and it can be hard work. I know that it's a partnership and is about compromise and give and take, and…' Caitlin trailed off as she couldn't think of anything else and her mother was staring at her as if she had gone mad.

'I can see I've been lax in my duties. I've never instructed you on the truth about marriage, have I?'

Caitlin shook her head, wondering what was coming next. Her mother had never instructed her about anything. She barely spoke to her.

Her mother sat up straight and Caitlin mirrored her.

'Marriage is a business contract. Both parties get something out of it, and it is rarely equal. Alan never loved me, but he needed me. I know how to organise dinner parties, how to run a household and give him children—although that didn't go to plan.'

'What do you mean?'

'You were supposed to have been a boy, someone to carry on the business. I couldn't face going through another pregnancy, so we had to work with what we had. Sending you to that expensive boarding school was meant to teach you how to behave in society. We hoped that you'd make a good marriage and that would make up for it.'

'I must have been a terrible disappointment to you.' Caitlin understood now why her parents were so ashamed of her when she told them her dream of becoming a paramedic.

Her mother leant forward and stared Caitlin in the eyes. 'You have a chance of making up for all that. After all we've done for you, it's time for you to return the compliment. You're old enough now to help shoulder the burden.'

Caitlin felt a shiver down her spine at the intense way her mother was staring at her.

'I d-don't know what you mean,' she stuttered.

'The business is in financial trouble. Has been for a while. The Dodds are willing to help us out, but part of the agreement is that you and Brandon get married. If this merger doesn't go ahead then we will have lost everything and it will all have been for nothing, and we could go bust. We'd lose the business and our home.'

'I don't understand—are you saying that my marriage to Brandon is the only way to keep the business and the house?'

'Yes, Caitlin, that's exactly what I'm saying.'

'And if I don't marry him?'

'Then we lose everything.'

'But…where does Heather fit into all this?'

'It's nothing to do with Heather. She's just the mistress. I'm his wife.'

Caitlin could see the door to her future slamming shut. For what choice did she have? To save the family home and the business—everything her father had worked so hard for —she would have to marry Brandon, a man she now knew she didn't love. She was pretty sure he didn't love her. It would be a replica of her parents' marriage. She would be the trophy wife.

'I need to talk to my father.'

'He'll only tell you what I have.'

'I need to go now.' Caitlin got up and started towards the door. She felt numb and wanted to be on her own to think about what her mother had told her.

When she reached the front door her mother, who had followed her, spoke.

'I'm sorry it's come to this. Really I am. If there was any

other way, we would never put this burden on you, but, sadly, there isn't.'

Caitlin couldn't think straight so she simply said, 'I'll be in touch,' before running down the gravel pathway and away from the house as quickly as possible.

Chapter Twenty

When Caitlin reached the cottage, she slammed the door and stood with her back against it, listening to the silence.

Sophie, who was now SpongeBob's official minder, had kept her charge as Caitlin didn't know how long she would have to stay with her mother. She had anticipated tears, and anger, and had been prepared to be there for her mother in whatever capacity she needed. Turned out the only thing her parents needed was for their daughter to throw her life away on a marriage that was sure to fail, to a man she was growing to despise. While the man she was starting to have feelings for—real feelings, ones that lasted—was living in the same house as her.

Caitlin walked to the couch and sat down, staring into space. It had taken her a while to realise it, but she now knew, without reservation, that she loved Jay O'Connor. It wasn't just the sex, good as it had been, it was the man himself. She had never known anyone who could be so gentle and so strong at the same time. He cared about her. He had put up with a lot since she moved into his home.

Sophie had been right, Jay had done all the housework while she was "healing" which was another way of saying she'd been a lazy bitch.

Now, it was too late. She couldn't tell him how she felt. Marriage to Brandon, that was her future. She'd lose everything so her parents could keep what they held dear. Was that fair? She'd have to stop working as a paramedic as Brandon would expect her to keep house and accompany him to social events. Shift work for the ambulance service wouldn't fit into that kind of lifestyle.

When she'd spoken to Brandon about it, in the days when she still thought she loved him, he had agreed to her working until the babies started coming. He had just been telling her what she wanted to hear. How could she have been so naïve?

But it wouldn't be just her job she'd leave behind, it would be her friends. And Jay.

Caitlin felt a scream building up inside her and she let it fly, thumping the cushions as hard as she could. 'No! No! No, I can't do it,' she screamed. She stopped screaming when she began to feel sick. Ten deep, calming breaths later she felt better. Strangely enough she didn't cry. Perhaps she was too angry.

Caitlin sat with her eyes closed and tried to empty her mind. Don't panic, she told herself, there must be a way. Yes... her father wouldn't let her marry a man she didn't love. Would he?

Her mobile rang and she looked at the screen, wondering if she should answer it or not. It was Sophie. Maybe her bestie could cheer her up.

'Hi, Sophie? How's it going? How's the princess?'

Sophie was almost incoherent, and Caitlin struggled to understand what she was saying.

'What? I can't hear you, slow down.'

'I said the Mas has been stolen!'

'Oh no! That's awful... have you told the police?'

'Yes, they're putting an APB out.'

'A what?'

'All-points bulletin. So everyone can be on the lookout.'

'Well, that's good then. I'm sure a distinctive car like yours will be spotted in Leytonsfield easily.'

'It may not be in Leytonsfield. Once they hit the motorway they could be anywhere. That car can do nought to flying in mere seconds. There's something else. I'm really sorry, Caitlin.'

'You're sorry... why?' Then she realised. 'Please don't tell me SpongeBob was in the car. She wasn't, was she?'

'I am so, so sorry. I put that new security car seat belt on her lead, and she looked happy curled up in the back with her toys. I only nipped out for a few minutes, I promise. Oh God, I'm so sorry.'

'Where are you?'

'Starbucks. Waiting for the police to phone with news.'

'You can do that here. Come to the cottage. Jay will be home soon, I want you here when we tell him.'

Caitlin heard Sophie groan and she understood how she felt. Jay was going to go apeshit.

Could this day get any worse?

Jay let himself into the cottage and missed SpongeBob running to greet him. She always jumped up and danced on her hind legs until he picked her up. He smiled at the thought.

The smile drooped when he caught sight of Caitlin and

Sophie, standing in the middle of the living room looking at him in horror.

'What?' he asked, prepared to be amused by another tall tale of misadventure and mayhem by Sophie and Caitlin. They were a right pair for getting themselves into strife.

'You better sit down,' said Caitlin. She looked pale and shaken and Jay began to sense that something was very wrong.

'Tell me. What's happened?'

'Someone's stolen the Maserati,' said Sophie.

'I'm sorry, that's rotten luck. Where?'

'In the town centre. But that's not all,' said Sophie, looking more serious than he'd ever seen her.

There had to be more. It was a shame that her car had been stolen, but... Then he realised what was wrong.

'Where's SpongeBob?' Jay looked at Caitlin.

'I...'

'She was in the back of the car. It was my fault entirely and I take full responsibility. I'm so sorry, Jay—' Sophie was wringing her hands and tears were streaming down her face.

'You left her in the fucking car!'

'Jay,' Caitlin stood close to Sophie as if she were showing support for her bestie. 'It wasn't Sophie's fault, it could have happened to anybody.'

Jay sat on the couch and put his head in his hands. That little dog was the only thing that Betty had to remember her son by. The poor woman was recovering from a stroke and relying on him to look after SpongeBob. He'd failed spectacularly. How was he going to tell her?

Caitlin came and sat beside him, but he didn't feel like talking to her at the moment. He looked at Sophie.

'Okay, so tell me what you are doing to get my dog back.'

'I've phoned the police and—'

'Apart from that.'

'Jay, we'll find her, don't worry…' Caitlin put her hand on his arm. He stood up abruptly and moved away from her.

'Actually, I've had a thought,' said Sophie. Jay glared at her. 'I wonder if this is, like, a hostage situation?'

'A what?' Jay didn't know whether to laugh or cry.

'You mean like a ransom?' asked Caitlin.

'Yes, exactly. Someone who had seen her on Insta and had decided to steal her, and demand money for her safe return.'

'Please don't tell me you've put her on Instagram?'

'Oh yes, she's quite the celebrity. Look.' Sophie offered Jay her phone and he scrolled through the posts. They all followed the same pattern. SpongeBob wore different outfits; dresses, ribbons and bows, jackets, and frilly stuff. The background was different each time, but it looked as if she was in bars, coffee shops, arcades and near tourist attractions.

'Princess Spongelicious.' He read the name with as much disgust as he could muster.

'I thought it sounded classier than SpongeBob.' He handed Sophie's phone back to her.

'I'm going to get changed, then I'm going out,' Jay said. He was starting to feel very angry indeed.

'You're going out?'

'Yes, Caitlin, I'm going to round up my family, or all of those who are free, and we're going to search the whole of Leytonsfield to find SpongeBob. Is that alright with you?'

'Jay, I know you're angry, but—'

'No, you have no idea how angry I am at the moment. I think it would be better if we didn't speak. Unless, by some miracle, you find her before I do.'

Jay ran up the stairs. He changed as quickly as he could, leaving his uniform on the bed. Then he left his cottage without a backward glance.

He got in his car and drove to his parent's house while trying to calm down. Losing his temper wasn't going to help matters. He was furious with Sophie for caring more about her stupid car than the dog she was supposed to be looking after. He was angry with Caitlin for not loving him and putting him through hell. But, more than anything, he was angry at himself for not doing a better job of looking after SpongeBob. He had made a promise to Betty and, if they didn't get the little girl back, he would have to break the poor woman's heart.

He let himself in through the back door that led straight into the kitchen. His parents hardly ever locked that door despite all their children warning them that one day they would be burgled. They justified it by saying that they wanted the whole family to have access to the house whenever they needed it.

'Darling, hello, what's wrong?'

'Mum, I need help. SpongeBob's gone missing and I have to find her. Is there anyone around who can help me look?'

'Of course. We all will. I'll ring Riordan and you ring Casey and Josie. Don't worry, we'll round up the troops. Your father can drive, and the younger ones can walk. Oh dear, what a terrible thing to happen, but don't worry, she'll turn up.'

Jay stepped into his mother's arms and gave in to a hug

that made him feel five years old again. Then they got busy ringing the rest of the family.

Soon, the kitchen was full of O'Connors all ready and willing to do whatever it took to help bring SpongeBob home.

'Right, Tom,' said Riordan. You look after Jade. Josie, can you go with the kids?'

'Sure.' Josie hugged Jay and kissed him on the cheek. 'We'll find her,' she whispered.

Jay knew he had to start searching before he got too emotional and started blubbing.

'Come on then, let's go.'

Chapter Twenty-One

When Jay had left, the house was quiet, except for the sound of Sophie crying.

'He hates me. Doesn't he? I know he does.'

'He doesn't hate you, Sophie, he's just concerned about SpongeBob. Jay hates to let people down and if she doesn't turn up and he has to tell Betty…' Caitlin trailed off as the enormity of the situation started to sink in.

'I wish I hadn't put her on Instagram. I never dreamed it would end up like this.'

Caitlin went into the kitchen and returned with a bottle of white wine and two glasses. She poured one and gave it to Sophie. Then poured one for herself.

'Do you really think it's down to the Instagram profile?'

'Well, why else would someone steal a dog?'

'To be honest, Sophie, it appears they stole your car, but they might not have known she was in the back.'

'Maybe,' Sophie wiped her face and drank her wine, thinking deeply. Caitlin could always tell she was thinking as she got a deep frown line between her eyebrows.

'Should we ring the police again?' Caitlin suggested.

'No. I've got a better idea. Why don't we put a post on Insta, telling everyone that she's disappeared? Then people in the area can look out for her.'

'I suppose it's worth a try. Better than doing nothing,' Caitlin said. She wished Jay had let her go with the O'Connors to look for the dog. She had loved the day she spent with them, feeling a part of things, welcomed. Perhaps she wouldn't be as welcome now. She blamed herself. She should never have put all the responsibility for SpongeBob on Sophie. She had her own life to live.

Caitlin glanced at Sophie who was busy on her phone. No doubt updating all Princess Spongelicious's followers.

Caitlin was sick of wine, so she made herself a cup of tea and settled down to wait. She wanted to text Jay but was sure he'd tell her if there was any news. He probably didn't want to speak to her at the moment anyway.

Two hours later, Sophie was drunk, and Caitlin had bitten her nails down to the quick.

Sophie's phone rang but she was in no state to answer it, so Caitlin picked it up. It was the police.

'Hello?'

Then followed the best phone call Caitlin had ever had. They had found SpongeBob. Or rather, someone had taken her to the police station having found her tied up to a post outside a supermarket in Stockport and shivering with cold. They thought she must have been there for a while. Could somebody come and pick her up?

'Yes, of course, straight away. Oh, thank you so much.' Caitlin ended the call and danced around the room.

'Wha's happening?' asked Sophie with one eye open.

'I'm going to get SpongeBob from the police. Someone

found her. We should reward them for being good citizens. I'll ring Jay.'

'Good. I'm sorry about… all of it.' Sophie burst into tears and Caitlin hugged her friend.

'It wasn't your fault, okay? I'll be back soon. Just stay here.'

Caitlin got in her car and texted Jay to meet her at the police station where SpongeBob was safe and well. Any serious conversations could wait until later.

The O'Connors had been everywhere. Josie and the kids went to the park, Casey drove round the estate. Riordan and Eloise travelled further afield and even went onto the motorway in case the callous bastards who'd stolen the car had jettisoned the poor little dog when she was discovered. Jay went with his dad and looked in the centre of Leytons-field where the shops, pubs, restaurants, and wine bars were.

There was no sign of her anywhere and Jay was growing more and more frantic with every minute that went by. He felt sick to his stomach and could swear he was having palpitations.

'What if we don't find her, Dad? I'll never be able to live with myself.'

'We'll find her son, just keep your eyes out.' Dan O'Connor's calm voice and reassuring manner made him feel a bit better.

When Jay got the text from Caitlin he nearly collapsed with relief. He called off the troops and thanked them for their help by sending a heartfelt text to all of them saying how much he loved them and was grateful for them in his life.

Then he turned his attention to Caitlin who would be waiting at the police station for him. He'd been a bit harsh with her and regretted it now. It wasn't her fault. Nobody was to blame except the person who'd stolen Sophie's car.

When he arrived at the police station, Caitlin was in the waiting area with SpongeBob on her knee. She was cuddling the little dog and talking to her.

'Hi,' he said sitting down next to her.

'Jay, I'm so sorry for this, I really am. Sophie is too.'

'Let's not talk about it now. I just want to get this girl home and in the warm.'

'Right. Yeah. Good point. Where's your car?'

'Back at my parents. Dad dropped me off. We'll go in your car and I'll keep SpongeBob on my knee.'

When they got back to the cottage, Sophie was crashed out on the couch, so Caitlin put a blanket over her and left her to sleep it off.

Jay and Caitlin went into the kitchen, after checking that the little dog was unharmed. She was so pleased to see them that she wouldn't leave their sides and wanted to be carried everywhere by Jay.

'So… what's the story? Who did they say found her?'

'Two women recognised her from her Instagram account. She was wearing her signature plaid bow in her hair. She's got them in all colours, not just the standard red. Sophie said she needed something to distinguish her from all the other dogs on Instagram. She's got blue ones, purple, brown, even tweed… sorry, I'm talking too much.'

Caitlin blushed and Jay longed to hug her. He'd given her such a hard time but would make it up to her somehow.

'So, where is it now, this… bow?'

'Well, that's the thing, isn't it? *Where* is it?'

'Yes…that's what I just asked.'

'Well I think the women took it for a souvenir. They recognised her because of her Instagram page. The policeman I spoke to said they kept calling her Princess, not SpongeBob which made him suspicious at first, but then they showed him her Instagram profile.'

'Right. So, if it hadn't been for Sophie, we might not have got her back. But then, if it hadn't been for Sophie we wouldn't have lost her in the first place.'

'Maybe we should just call it quits,' said Caitlin hopefully.

'Good idea.'

'Tea?' asked Caitlin and Jay couldn't help smiling. The British answer to every problem. Put the kettle on.

'Love one,' he said.

———

Caitlin was aware of Jay sitting at the kitchen table, singing quietly to himself. He must be so relieved that SpongeBob was back, unharmed. He'd been so angry before, Caitlin had never seen him like that. She'd thought he was going to turn green and split his trousers.

'Did you go and see your mum?' he asked.

'Yes, but she already knew about Heather. She called me naïve.'

'Why? Because you believe in fidelity in a marriage? Most people do, don't they?'

Caitlin sighed. How could she explain it to him when she didn't understand it herself? How could you spend the rest of your life with a man you didn't trust? A man who was having sex with other women? She didn't know which was worse, a series of women who meant nothing, or one woman who meant everything.

'Cait?'

'Yes?'

'Are you okay?'

'Yes, now we've got her back. Losing her put everything into perspective.'

'I absolutely agree. Nothing against Sophie, but I'm going to ask my parents to look after SpongeBob while we're working. Then I'll pick her up on my days off. I think it's for the best.'

'Yes, you're probably right.'

Caitlin was relieved that the crisis had been averted, but she still had her original problem to think about. Should she marry Brandon and save her parents from penury, or should she tell Jay she loved him?

'More tea?' Caitlin got up to refill their mugs.

'Go on then, one more then I think I'll hit the sack.'

'Me too. It's been quite a day.'

'It has indeed.'

Caitlin sat down again after putting a mug of tea in front of Jay. She was finding it difficult to look him in the eye as the temptation to unburden herself and tell him everything was pressing down on her. But she couldn't. The poor man had suffered enough for one day.

They sat in silence while they drank their tea, then both stood up and Jay rinsed the mugs and put them away in the cupboard.

'Well… goodnight then Cait.'

Please kiss me. Or just give me a hug. Something. Anything.

'Goodnight, Jay, and I am really sorry.'

'Let's not mention it again, shall we? All's well that ends well.'

'Right. Goodnight then.'

Neither of them mentioned the fact that the Maserati was still missing.

Chapter Twenty-Two

By the beginning of September, Caitlin had made her decision. She was going to move back home.

When Jay arrived back from work, she was carrying her cases down the stairs.

'Hi. Did you have a good day?'

'Where are you going?' Jay was watching her with a bewildered expression on his face.

'Well…as my father is going to be discharged tomorrow, I thought I should go home and help look after him. My mother won't be able to cope on her own.'

'Can't she hire a nurse?'

'Oh no, she'll want to look after him herself. With my help.'

'I don't understand your family,' Jay said, making his way to the kitchen and pouring a glass of water. 'Your father's been having an affair for five years, but your mother is still playing the loving wife. It's crazy.'

'I know, I agree but they've been together a long time and it's just how they are.'

And it was how she'd have to be if she married Brandon. Everything for show.

'Jay. I need to thank you for all your help. I don't know what I would have done without you. You've been a great friend and I don't deserve—'

'That night we made love, Caitlin, did it mean anything to you?'

She stared at him, her heart racing. She should tell him. Admit that it meant everything, and she was madly in love with him. Tell him the truth.

'Jay…'

'Okay, I can see that it didn't. It was just sex. Same for me. Just in case you're interested. I just needed to make sure. So I guess we can go our separate ways without looking back. You'll marry your groom finally and I'll…' Jay stopped, and Caitlin saw the pain in his eyes.

'Jay, please don't think it meant nothing. That's not true.'

'Do you want any help carrying your bags?'

'No, I can manage.'

'Right then. I'm going to have a shower, so…'

'Right, I'll go then.'

'Bye, Caitlin.'

Jay ran up the stairs and she heard his bedroom door slam.

Jay stood under the shower, letting the warm water wash over him. He'd lost her. It was over. He stayed there a long time, trying to get clean. But he knew it wasn't his body that needed cleansing. It was his heart. He'd lost the only woman he'd ever loved. Ever would love.

When he was dry and dressed again he wandered back downstairs and sat on the couch listening to the quiet. Some people loved silence. His brother Riordan, for instance. He could sit and say nothing for hours, happy with his thoughts.

Jay was more like his brother, Casey, who could never keep still. He wanted to be active, talking, laughing, joking, and interacting with the people he cared about.

Jay didn't want to be alone with his thoughts for they were blacker than they'd ever been. Caitlin had walked out the door and he didn't know how to cope with it. He didn't even have SpongeBob to cuddle.

Perhaps he should make a list. The pros and cons of his life. His mother had taught him that. When he had a decision to make the best thing to do was to write it all down. Pros: he had a lovely home although he needed to get another housemate to help pay the bills. His family were still there and would supply shoulders to cry on should he need them. Work: he had his job which he loved and all his mates and people he partnered. Of course, Caitlin was one of them and he couldn't avoid seeing her and working with her sometimes. How did he feel about that? Mixed. It would be better if he never saw her again but that wasn't going to happen so long as they were both paramedics. Once Caitlin married her Hooray Henry she would probably give it up anyway.

Jay lay full length on the couch and stared at the ceiling. So where had all that got him? Not very far. All he wanted to do was think about Caitlin. How soft her hair was as it fell around her shoulders. She coloured it and it shone with a reddish sheen in certain lights. Her beautiful eyes were hazel but a softer colour than his own. His were deep hazel, almost chestnut. Caitlin had great tits. And a great arse. And…

Jay sat up and then stood.

He started pacing up and down. He should have fought for her. But fight who? He couldn't give her the life she was used to. It was her decision who she married, and it looked as if she had made her mind up. The excuse of going back home to look after her father hadn't rung true. People with that kind of money would just pay a nurse to look after him. She was trying to let him down gently. He would have preferred it if she'd been honest with him.

His phone rang and he answered it when he saw that it was Paul.

'Hi, Paul.'

'Hi, my man. How are you doing tonight? Or should I say *what* are you doing tonight?'

'Nothing.' Not this night or any other night in the future.

'What's up? You sound a bit down.'

'Caitlin's gone back home to look after her dad. She hasn't said anything to me, but I think she's made her mind up to marry Hooray Henry.'

'I'm sorry to hear that for your sake, but I might just have something that'll take your mind off her and give you the chance to meet someone else.'

'I'm not doing online dating, Paul, I told you. Even for you, I can't. Getting dressed up to meet a complete stranger who'll bore the pants off you…' Jay trailed off as Paul was laughing down the phone and Jay couldn't help but smile. Paul always had the ability to cheer him up.

'Chill, man, I'm not talking about that. This is some-thing totally different.'

'What?'

'Speed dating. I was going to go tonight with a friend, you know, for moral support, but he's let me down and has pulled out. So, I asked myself who is the closest friend I have who would never let me down and would come with me tonight and, of course, I thought of my good buddy Jay, who just happens to be on the lookout for a woman too.'

'Speed dating? Are you kidding me? Have you ever done it?'

'Never, but I'm willing to try anything once. You don't know 'til you try, man, and the woman of your dreams could be there tonight just waiting for you.'

The woman of his dreams had just walked out, without a backward glance. And it was this thought that made him say yes.

'Seeing as it's you, I'll go. Only once mind, and I'm only going to keep you company. Agreed?'

'Agreed. I knew you wouldn't let me down.'

Paul drew up outside the cottage and Jay peered through the window to see what his friend was wearing.

Jay had deliberated for ages before he decided on smart black jeans with a denim shirt, not tucked in, and with the sleeves rolled up. What did guys wear for speed dating? It was only after he realised that he was only there for Paul's sake that he relaxed and decided it didn't matter.

Paul stepped out of the car and Jay was pleased to see that he was wearing a suit jacket with a white T-shirt and black jeans with boots. He wore his dreadlocks loose and, as always, he looked stylish and smart.

Jay left the cottage and locked the door. In a strange kind of way, he was looking forward to tonight. If nothing else, it proved he was trying to move on, and it would be educational.

The event was being held in an upstairs room at the Leytonsfield Hotel. When Jay and Paul walked in and gave their names, they were handed a scorecard and a name tag with their nicknames. The woman on the desk had to write Jay's quickly when Paul explained that the golden fox wouldn't be coming and in his place was…Jay had to think of a nickname quickly. He wished Paul had warned him about this.

'Want a drink?' Paul asked.

'Badly,' Jay answered.

Paul threw back his head and laughed which drew some approving looks from the ladies standing around looking nervous.

They had just got their beers when a bell rang for the event to start. The women sat at a table and stayed where they were for the evening. The men, who took the seat on the other side of the table, were the ones who moved around when the bell rang after four minutes of sparkling conversation and witty repartee.

Jay had no idea of the etiquette, so he smiled and said hi to the first woman he sat in front of. She looked nervous and so he said, 'I'm a paramedic. What do you do?'

The change was instant and scary. She shrank back from him as far as she could and said, 'Oh, no, not hospitals, I can't be doing with them. Hate the places. My parents both died in hospital and the last thing I want to do is be reminded of those awful places.'

Jay sat for the full four minutes and listened to a tirade from Ms Nervous on her feelings about hospitals. He didn't speak, mainly because he couldn't get a word in edgeways and also because there wouldn't have been any point. He was relieved when the bell rang, and he could move on.

The next lady looked more hopeful, so he smiled and

decided to try a different approach. But before he could say a word she leaned over and asked, 'Do you like dogs?'

Jay thought, great, a normal woman and he answered, 'Yes, I love dogs.'

'Oh no, I hate dogs. Got bitten when I was a kid. No sorry, I can't be with someone who owns a dog.'

So that was another cross on the scoreboard. Jay looked across to Paul who was deep in conversation with an attractive lady looking at him as if he held the secret of eternal life. Glad someone's having fun.

Fortunately, the four minutes passed quickly, and Jay had moved on to number three. This time he would be enigmatic and only speak when he thought it was safe to do so.

'Hi,' number three said.

'Hi,' answered Jay.

'I've never done this before, have you?'

'Uh…no I haven't. Why are you here tonight then?'

The woman was a redhead with lots of freckles. She was attractive in a girl-next-door kind of way. Her nickname was "Rhinestone Cowgirl" which intrigued Jay.

'Well, I've recently broken up with my boyfriend and I'm trying to move on. My name's Emma by the way.'

'Pleased to meet you, Emma, I'm Jay.'

'What's your story? Are you trying to move on too?'

'Yes, you could say that.' Jay didn't want to discuss Caitlin with Emma, or anyone else for that matter, the feelings were too raw.

'Are you a professional?' Emma obviously had a list of questions that she worked her way through.

'I'm a paramedic.'

'Oh, how wonderful! I want to be a nurse, but I don't have enough qualifications, so I'm studying for my A levels at the moment. Then I intend to go to university and do a nursing course.'

'What subjects are you studying?'

'Psychology and sociology. I love psychology—you know, finding out what makes people tick, it's fascinating. Sociology is harder, but still quite interesting.'

'Do you mind me asking how old you are?' Jay was conscious that the four minutes was nearly up, and he was enjoying talking to Emma.

'Not at all. I'm twenty-four. How old are you?'

'Thirty.'

'Oh, cool, I like older men.'

'Why Rhinestone Cowgirl? If you don't mind me asking.'

'Oh, not at all. It's because I like country and western music. I love folk music too. Have you ever been to the ceilidhs in Leytonsfield?'

'No… can't say that I have.'

'Oh, you should, they're great fun. I go regularly.'

'Right.' Jay couldn't think of a thing to say to that, so he continued to be enigmatic as it seemed to be working well so far and said nothing. But he needn't have worried for Emma had another question.

'Your nickname, Biker Jay, I'm guessing you're into motorbikes?'

'Correct.'

'I've never ridden on the back of a bike, but I've always wanted to have a go.'

'You should, they're great fun,' said Jay mirroring Emma's comment.

Emma burst into girlish laughter and Jay realised he was enjoying himself.

Then the bell rang, and he had to move on. The rest of the women were nice, but not his type, but at least he had one tick. Not bad for a first attempt at speed dating.

Chapter Twenty-Three

'Caitlin, why haven't you spoken to Brandon yet? I can't avoid the Dodds forever and you need to put the poor man out of his misery. He's been distraught since that day you broke his heart. If you don't, then I will.'

Nina swept into the kitchen as Caitlin was taking the dishes out of the dishwasher. Daisy's replacement hadn't been appointed yet and Caitlin suspected she was acting as the maid until she married Brandon. Another of her mother's subtle punishments for disobeying her.

'Mother, please don't say anything. I want to speak to Father first before I make any decisions.'

'Your father needs rest. He doesn't want you bothering him with your concerns. He's just had a heart attack and isn't strong enough yet. You should know that as a so-called medical worker.'

Caitlin didn't reply. There wasn't any point. Her mother would do as she wished regardless of what she said. And her dearest wish at the moment was saving her home, the business and being able to live the lifestyle she was used to. And she was prepared to throw her daughter under a bus to achieve that.

Later that morning, when her mother had left to attend a luncheon with some friends, Caitlin slipped quietly into her father's room. He was asleep so she left just as quietly. She'd try again later.

As she came down the stairs, the doorbell rang. She would have loved to ignore it, but they could keep ringing and wake her father up. Her mother was right, he needed rest. She opened the door.

'Caitlin. Thought no one was home. Where's the maid?'

'Brandon. What a surprise. Come in.'

He strode into the hall, looking tanned and fit. Brandon had a gym in the basement of his home, and he made good use of it. He didn't look the slightest bit distraught or broken-hearted.

'Wouldn't mind a drink if there's one going.'

'Tea or coffee? Or would you like a cold drink?'

'I'd love a drink that came out of a whisky bottle but no ice.'

Caitlin sighed. She wandered into the kitchen feeling despondent. How had she ever thought she was in love with this man? He was an arrogant...

'Good to see you home where you belong. I knew you'd see sense eventually. Took a bit longer than I'd liked, but I'm prepared to put all that behind me. As far as dates are concerned,' Brandon took the glass Caitlin offered without looking up from his phone or thanking her, 'I'd say we're probably looking at the end of October at the earliest.'

'For what?'

'Ha ha, good joke. Glad to see you've not lost your sense of humour. Your mother's managed to salvage the dress, thank goodness. Didn't fancy having to fork out for another one. Bloody expensive.'

Caitlin sat at the kitchen table while Brandon stood, leaning against the island, and scrolling through his phone.

'Brandon? Why did you pay for the wedding dress? I thought my father paid for everything.'

'You are a little innocent you know. Nina told me she'd put you straight about the state of the Hewitts finances. Can't believe you didn't know about it beforehand. They've been losing money hand over fist for years. That damned school they sent you to must have made a tidy hole in the old money pot.'

'I never wanted to go to that damned school. I hated it there.'

'Now, now, poppet, no need to be ungrateful. Everything your parents did was for you.'

'Brandon… I don't think—'

'Something else I need to talk to you about. Clear the air before the big day. I don't want you working as an ambulance driver once we're wed.'

'Paramedic,' Caitlin said automatically.

'It's not the image I want my wife to present to the world.'

Caitlin got up and went to the window, marvelling at how beautiful the garden was. SpongeBob would love it. Maybe she'd bring her back when she went to visit Betty in the nursing home. She'd moved in a few days ago. The hospital had done everything they could for her, and she now needed rest and rehabilitation to get her to a state of fitness enabling her to go home.

'Caitlin! You haven't listened to a word I've said. You are a dolly-daydream. Could you concentrate please.'

Caitlin turned so her back was to the window and gave Brandon her full attention.

'I'm listening, Brandon. So, tell me, what kind of image do you expect your wife to present to the world?'

'Well,' Brandon strode around the kitchen importantly, still scrolling on his phone, 'I would expect her to be conversant with the upper echelons of society and be able to hold her own in a conversation with the wife of an important business contact or customer—'

'Just the wife? Not the business contact or customer themselves?'

'No, Caitlin, you don't need to worry yourself about them. They are my department. Yours is to look good when we go to social events, organise dinner parties at our home, and generally support me in every aspect of our lives.'

'What about the other way round?'

'Explain.'

'What about you supporting me in my life?'

'Don't be ridiculous.'

'Why is it ridiculous to want my husband to support me?'

Caitlin knew she was wasting her time trying to reason with Brandon, but she was so angry, albeit the anger was bubbling away below the surface where only people who knew her well could tell she was ready to blow and couldn't resist poking the bear.

Brandon looked at her then, possibly for the first time since he'd arrived.

'Have you spoken to Nina about this? She assured me she'd told you what to expect from marriage. She said you understood.'

'Marriage is about love, compromise and respect. It's an

equal partnership, not a business contract, or an employment contract, or any other kind of bloody contract!'

Brandon looked at her and frowned. 'I don't understand you. I'll put it down to the worry of your father being ill. I know when my father was ill it put everyone on edge. Thankfully, he's okay now and I'm sure Alan will be too. Just keep calm, poppet, and listen to your mother.'

'My mother?'

'She knows best. Mothers do. Right, I'm going to go now but will be in touch about venues and dates. It'll be a smaller affair, of course, but I'm afraid that's down to you.'

Brandon left the kitchen without a backward glance. Caitlin heard the front door slam and sank onto a chair.

'Has he gone? Pompous git.'

'Dad? Were you listening to all that?'

Her father came into the kitchen and sat on an adjacent chair.

'Not from choice, but I heard most of it. I suppose he's been drinking my whisky again?'

'Sorry.' Caitlin smiled and shrugged.

'Not your fault, darling. How about you make us some tea and take it into the drawing room. I need to talk to you about something.'

'Fine.' At last, thought Caitlin, she'd be able to ask him about Heather.

Chapter Twenty-Four

'How's the great romance going?' asked Paul.

'It's not a romance,' answered Jay as he drove the ambulance through the crowded streets thronged with Saturday afternoon shoppers. 'We're good friends.'

'But you like her, right?'

'Why are you in such a great hurry to pair me off with someone? Yes, I like her.'

'How much? On a scale of one to ten, how much do you like her?'

Jay thought about the question. He liked Emma a lot. In fact, if it weren't for the fact that he was still in love with Caitlin, he would give her a high score. But comparing her to Caitlin, which he knew wasn't fair, he couldn't really give her a high number.

'Okay, six.'

'Is that all? She's more than a six, man, come on... Beautiful redhead with those cute freckles, blue eyes...'

'You obviously noticed her too. Was she one of the ticks on your scorecard?'

Paul laughed. 'No, man, I could see you were smitten, so I was doing you a favour. Anyway, I'm happy with Pandora.'

'Ah yes, the lovely Pandora, who hung on your every word. A bit shy, but a nice lady.'

'Just my type. Taking her out tonight. Maybe try the new Mexican place.'

'Good for you. I'm seeing Emma later, but I'm taking SpongeBob to see Betty in the home first.'

'How's Betty doing?' Paul unwrapped a protein bar and passed half to Jay.

'Not good to be honest. She's having physio, occupational therapy, and speech therapy, but the lady's eighty-five and there's only so much use of her left side she can get back.'

'Shame.'

'Yeah, big shame. Seeing SpongeBob will cheer her up though.'

Their conversation was cut short as a call-out came through. Jay listened to the one-sided conversation.

'Okay, hit the road.'

'What've we got?' Jay asked.

'Woman, forty-five years old. Repeat offender. Remember Geraldine?'

'Yep.' Everyone he worked with had come across Geraldine. 'Where is she?'

'Manor Park. Doing a spot of sunbathing apparently.'

She was a diabetic who also happened to be an alcoholic. They regularly collected her from various places around Leytonsfield to take her to the hospital. Geraldine was told by every paramedic who picked her up, and then every A&E doctor who treated her that drinking alcohol caused her blood sugar levels to drop, so she needed to check her glucose levels if she was going to drink. If the level was lower than the safe zone, she should eat a snack to bring it back up.

Problem was, Geraldine was a serious alcoholic who was rarely sober, and she preferred to drink than to eat. She was severely malnourished and in danger of liver failure, as well as dying from hypoglycaemia. And the symptoms from a hypo were the same as being drunk.

It was a vicious circle that poor Geraldine kept on going around. Jay sometimes felt that they were all chasing their tails and getting nowhere, but sometimes all the paramedics could do was pick the patient up and take them to the hospital, hoping that a miracle would happen in between call-outs that meant the patient could get the help they needed or get their life together somehow.

When they got to Manor Park, Geraldine was lying on the grass with several members of the public sitting near her to keep their eye on her. No matter where Geraldine chose to collapse, there were always people around to help her. Whether that was from good luck or clever planning Jay wasn't sure. He just knew that most people were basically good and willing to help a fellow human being when they needed it.

'Geraldine,' said Paul, his deep voice with its slight Jamaican accent commanding everyone's attention. 'What you been doing, woman?'

Geraldine laughed as Paul knew she would. He had an instinct for which patients needed the gentle treatment and those, like Geraldine, who responded to being told off like a naughty child. She loved Paul and flirted outrageously with him. She listened to his advice and then completely ignored it.

'Nice to see you, Paul,' said Geraldine. 'Have you come to rescue me?'

'You know it. I need to check you over. Can I take your glucose levels?'

'Sweetheart, you can take whatever you want. If I've got it, you can have it.'

Paul threw his head back and laughed. 'You kill me, woman, you really do.'

Jay left them to it and sat on the grass looking around at the people enjoying the sun. Geraldine wasn't in any danger and was in safe hands. They would need to take her to hospital once Paul had stabilised her blood glucose and checked her vital signs.

Jay wished he could lie on the grass and watch the clouds float by. He used to do that as a kid with Josie. The two of them would lie for hours, discussing things important to them and looking for clouds that looked like animals or countries. Sometimes Jay would fall asleep and Josie watched over him until he woke up.

'Right, Geraldine, your carriage awaits.'

'Is it a gold carriage pulled by white horses?'

'No it's yellow and green and Jay's going to drive. You and I are going to have a chat, okay?'

'Okay.' Geraldine was compliant when she was in the company of the medics, but as soon as she got home and returned to the loneliness of her bedsit, she returned to her old ways.

Once they had deposited Geraldine in the care of the Accident and Emergency Department, they got on the road again.

There wasn't long to the end of the shift and Jay was looking forward to seeing Betty again and the reunion with SpongeBob. Then he was seeing Emma for a drink in one of the older pubs in the town. She wasn't keen on the wine bars and trendy places, she preferred quieter venues where she could hear herself think, and they could talk.

He refused to let himself think of Caitlin. That part of his life was over. Forever.

The nursing home was on two levels. The bottom floor was for patients like Betty, who needed one-on-one care. The top floor was for patients who were mobile and didn't need as much nursing.

Betty had a pleasant room, with a door that led into the garden. She was sitting in the doorway, in her comfy armchair, her left arm supported by pillows, waiting for SpongeBob.

'Here she is,' said Jay as SpongeBob ran to Betty and jumped up, doing her little dance. Jay picked her up and put her on Betty's knee, making sure the old lady was comfortable and SpongeBob didn't wriggle too much.

The look on Betty's face was heart-warming and Jay stood and watched the reunion, feeling quite emotional himself.

'Have you been okay, Betty?' Jay asked.

Betty nodded. Her speech wasn't too good, but she managed to make herself understood if asked direct questions that she could nod or shake her head to, and if she wanted to say something, she wrote it on a small pad she kept with her at all times.

Jay avoided asking her too much, content with her reaction to having her little dog on her lap again.

Before the visit was over, he asked her if there was anything she wanted. She pointed to SpongeBob and Jay nodded.

'Of course, I'll try to bring her more often. It's lovely to see you again.'

He kissed her cheek and squeezed her hand. Betty gave a lopsided smile and blew them both a kiss.

As Jay drove home, he wondered what else he could do for Betty, to try and make her life easier. Hopefully, with the rehabilitation, she'd regain the use of her left side and go home with carers coming in to help her. For now, he'd just take SpongeBob to visit as often as he could. That was the best thing he could do for her.

Chapter Twenty-Five

Caitlin carried the tray containing the teapot, mugs, sugar, and milk, through to the drawing room. Her father was already settled in an armchair, looking pale and small.

She was used to seeing her father as larger than life, quick-tempered and hard working. But now he sat and stared into space, almost as if he'd withdrawn from life.

'Are you okay, Dad?' Caitlin asked.

'Yes, fine. Just wanting my tea.'

'Right, I'm on it.' Caitlin smiled at her father's attempt to be his old self. It wasn't convincing at all.

She poured the tea into mugs, added milk and sugar, just as he liked it, and put the mug on a small table at the side of his armchair.

'Thank you,' he said, then sighed. 'I expect you want to know about Heather.'

'Yes, I do. She told me you're in love and you've been seeing each other for five years.'

Her father nodded. 'True. We were childhood sweethearts and we wanted to get married. We were both too young of course, but even when we weren't, it was forbidden. My father threatened to cut me out of his will which meant I wouldn't inherit the business. I was a fool. I gave in to his blackmail and married your mother instead.'

As her father took a sip of his tea, Caitlin wondered if he realised that she was in almost exactly the same position. The only difference being that Jay didn't know she loved him, and only thought of her as a friend.

'Did you love my mother?'

'No, Caitlin, I'm sorry to say I never did. I never stopped loving Heather. Five years ago, I finally manned up enough to do something about it.'

'Does my mother know you don't love her?'

'Yes, she knows all about Heather. She doesn't seem to care. Your mother isn't a demonstrative woman. She doesn't care about physical love. All she seems to value is her possessions; her home, car, holidays, clothes. And how she's perceived. Everything about your mother is show.'

Caitlin drank the rest of her tea and refilled her mug and her father's.

When she looked up, he was watching her.

'What?'

'I was just thinking how different you are to your mother. You're passionate and romantic, a dreamer and someone who feels deeply. You don't love Brandon, do you? You're prepared to marry him for our sakes, to ensure this house and the business stay in our hands. Tell me you love him, and I'll say nothing more. I'll let the marriage and the merger go ahead. I'll still see Heather because she's the only one, apart from you, that I live for. I'll provide for your mother and keep up the pretence.'

'What will you do if I tell you I don't love him?' asked Caitlin.

'Then I'll free you from any responsibility whatsoever with regards to the business. You'll be free to love and marry whoever you please.'

'And what will you do?'

'I'll sell the business to the Dodds. I'll sell the house. Your mother will get half, then Heather and I will travel the world.'

'You'll leave Mother?'

'Yes, but I'll leave her well provided for.'

'You'll lose the business you love and have worked so hard to build up.'

'It means nothing without the person you love by your side.'

Caitlin had never heard her father speak about his feelings before and it shook her to think of the life that he must have had married to her mother. He'd kept it hidden for so long until he found Heather again.

'I'm sorry that you've had to go through all that and I'm glad you've got Heather, but I hate the thought that you might have to sell everything to the Dodds. They don't deserve to be the recipients of all your hard work.'

'It doesn't matter, Caitlin. I can't stand by and watch you marry someone you don't love. I know what that's like. I don't want that for you.'

'You're looking tired.' Caitlin stood up and offered him her arm.

'I am. You're right. I need to be in bed. Thank you.'

'For what?'

'For not judging me. For not blaming me for that travesty of a wedding ceremony. And for being a good daughter. One I don't deserve.'

'Come on, Dad, I'll walk you to your bedroom.'

Friday night and Mellow was packed. Sophie wore another of her 1950 numbers, a halter neck, polka dot dress in red. Caitlin wore jeans and a T-shirt. She wanted to drown her sorrows, not draw attention to herself.

They had managed to get a small table in the corner where they were well hidden from practically everyone. Just what Caitlin wanted.

'Have the police had any leads on the Maserati?'

'No,' sighed Sophie, 'I think it's long gone.'

'You are insured?'

'Oh yes, of course.'

'Good. That's something then.'

'And how's SpongeBob? I miss her you know. She was a special little dog. I had to close her Instagram account. I told all her followers it was because of the trauma she'd gone through. She was retiring from the public eye to live a quiet life in the suburbs.'

Caitlin laughed. 'I'm sorry to laugh, but…'

'Oh, don't worry, I can take any amount of ridicule, especially from my bestie. Go on, snigger if it makes you feel better.'

'Sophie…'

'I'm kidding!' Sophie said draining her glass. 'Why don't we buy a bottle?'

'Okay.'

While Sophie was at the bar, probably buying the most expensive red wine that Mellow sold, Caitlin went over the conversation she'd had with her father. He'd let her off the hook. She no longer felt pressure to marry Brandon. But, in its place, was another kind of pressure. If she didn't marry him, her father would sell the business to the Dodds and the house to… who knew who? She hated the thought of that. Her father had worked so hard to build up his business, it seemed so unfair that the Dodds would reap all the rewards.

As she was deep in thought, she sensed that someone had stopped in front of the table. She looked up into the heavily made-up face of Fenella Barton-Brookes.

'Well, well, it's the little not-quite-wifey out on the tiles.' Fenella's gaze travelled from Caitlin's untidy hair that hung down over her face, to the T-shirt she'd had for years, to the scruffy jeans and trainers. Then her gaze travelled back to her face.

'Good evening, Fenella,' said Caitlin, 'on your own tonight?'

'Of course I'm not on my own, don't be so preposterous.' Fenella's snooty look had turned to one of anger.

'Oh, I know… you're working behind the bar. Are times a bit hard for you at the moment? Is Brandon not spending his money on you? Well, that's because he's saving up for the wedding. He was looking at the Seychelles for the honeymoon, or maybe the Maldives. What d'you think?'

Fenella, whose face was turning an angry red, said nothing, but glared at Caitlin, one hand on her hip, a glass of rosé wine clutched in the other. Caitlin studied her. A short blonde bob framed a face that could easily grace any fashion magazine. Her nose was chiselled, her lips full with thick red lipstick in a perfect bow. Her eyes were heavily made up with a smooth winged line at the outer corners— the perfect cat's eye look.

Caitlin had to admit, she was an attractive woman.

'Oh, hello,' said Sophie as she returned with a bottle of

expensive red wine and two glasses. 'Are you staying, Fenella? Shall I fetch another glass?'

Fenella said nothing but gave Sophie the same insolent stare that she'd treated Caitlin to. Sophie was too busy pouring the wine to notice.

'Thanks,' said Caitlin as Sophie put her glass in front of her.

'So, to what do we owe this honour?' Sophie sat down and sipped her wine.

'Still wearing those awful Minnie Mouse dresses I see. You do know you look ridiculous?'

Sophie sipped some more wine and then stood up again.

'It may have escaped your notice, Fenella, but we're not in school any more. You can't bully me or my friends now. So, unless you have something intelligent or informative to say I think you should push off and leave us to enjoy our evening.'

'Says the woman stuck in some kind of weird time warp.' Fenella gave her the once over again and Sophie sat down and spread her skirt out and then poured some more wine. She gazed out of the window and ignored Fenella.

'Actually, I do have something to say.'

'Well please spit it out and then leave us in peace.' Caitlin was getting fed up with the silly woman standing there, thinking she'd got the upper hand. It crossed Caitlin's mind, briefly, to pretend to agree to the marriage on the condition that Brandon stopped seeing Fenella and that, if he did, he would have to pay Caitlin half of all he owned. He'd never agree to it, of course, but it might be fun to see how he wriggled out of it.

'I'm pregnant with Brandon's child.'

'What?!' Caitlin wasn't sure she heard correctly.

Sophie drained her glass and filled it up again. Caitlin was surprised to see the bottle was nearly empty.

'You have my full and most sincere commis'rations.' Sophie was already drunk.

Caitlin felt anger start to burn inside. 'I don't believe you. Brandon swore he wasn't seeing you.'

'He lied. He's lied to you about a lot of things. He has no intention of marrying you, he just wants the business.'

'Can't have one without the other.'

'I think you'll find he can. Brandon always gets his own way—in the end.'

'When's it due?' Not that she really cared but she was curious.

Fenella smiled then, which told Caitlin that the wretched woman did have the upper hand. 'I'm not showing yet, but the baby will arrive next March.'

This comment was met by stony silence from Sophie and Caitlin. Sophie, because she was pouring the last of the wine into their glasses and Caitlin because she had absolutely nothing to say. If she'd found out before the conversation with her father it would have been a different matter. But why should she care now? She wasn't going to marry Brandon. Still, she felt betrayed and humiliated.

March. Nine months before that was June. They had been at it like rabbits when the wedding was about to take place. Brandon had never stopped seeing Fenella, and now she was having his baby, he never would.

'Ciao,' said Fenella. She had done what she came over to do and sashayed away from the table before disappearing into the crowd.

'Another bottle?' asked Sophie, standing up and weaving slightly. If she was getting drunk, then so was Caitlin.

'Bring two.'

'That's my girl!' said Sophie and pushed her way to the bar.

While Sophie was gone, Caitlin mulled over the conversation she had just had with Fenella. There was something wrong—a kind of *What's wrong with this picture?* thing. Then it came to her. Fenella claimed she was pregnant, but she was drinking wine. So, she was either lying or being spectacularly irresponsible. But which one was it?

Chapter Twenty-Six

Jay got the drinks in while Emma looked around for a seat.

The Old Oak was one of Leytonsfield's oldest pubs with a good choice of ale and a pleasant atmosphere. Emma had requested it when Jay invited her out for a drink. She was becoming a good friend. They talked about all kinds of things and she was willing to try anything once, like a ride on his bike. And she drank beer.

'Here we go.' Jay put the drinks down on the table.

'Ah, this is nice. It's so great to get out of that house now and again.'

Jay knew Emma still lived at home and had three younger siblings.

'It must be difficult to study in a noisy house.' Jay opened a packet of chicken flavoured crisps and offered them to Emma.

'Thanks. You're not kidding. I'm sometimes forced to spend the day in the library just to get away. They're not the quietest places in the world, either.'

'You can always use my cottage when I'm working. I can let you know what rota I'm on and give you a spare key.'

'Oh no, I couldn't. That's too kind of you Jay. I wouldn't want to impose.'

'It's no imposition, I promise. And if it helps you…' he trailed off, wondering if he was doing the right thing. He didn't want to send out the wrong message.

'That is so kind of you. Okay, I accept. Thank you so much.'

'Right. I'll get some keys cut and text you my rota for next week.'

'Brilliant. I'll be able to get so much work done on my own.'

A week later and Emma had settled into the routine of spending the day studying when Jay was on duty. At first he had been a bit nervous of the idea of having a stranger in his house, but Emma was such a sweet girl and so desperate to get into nursing, that Jay felt it was the least he could do to help her.

On Friday, after a long, tiring week, Jay organised another beer and Chinese night. Of course, he didn't invite Caitlin or Sophie, but Emma stayed after spending all day at the cottage studying.

'This is Josie, my twin, and Matt, and of course, you know Paul.'

'Hi, Emma,' said Josie.

'Hi,' said Matt.

'Hello, again,' said Paul.

After Jay had ordered the food, they relaxed until it arrived.

'Josie? Did you train as a registered nurse before midwifery, or did you just do the midwifery training?' Emma asked.

'I just did the midwifery. I knew from the start that I only wanted to deliver babies.'

'Wow. I don't know what area of nursing I want to go into yet.'

'Well, there's no hurry. Jay said you're doing A levels?'

'Yes, Jay's kindly offered me his home so I can have a quiet place to study.'

'What a caring boy,' said Paul. 'Although I don't know why you don't just move in permanently. Jay's looking for another housemate, aren't you?'

'Well, I—' Jay couldn't believe Paul would land him in it like that. He wasn't ready to live with anyone again after Caitlin, although the extra money would come in handy.

'Oh no, I couldn't,' said Emma.

'Is it the money?' asked Josie. 'You're a student and I remember what that was like.'

'No, I could afford the rent, it's just that… well, I don't want to impose.'

'You wouldn't be imposing, would she, Jay?' Josie looked at him with raised eyebrows.

'No, of course not.' Jay said with as much enthusiasm as he could muster.

'Great, that's settled then. I'll help you move in if you like,' said Josie looking pleased with herself.

Later, when they'd eaten the food and were consuming vast quantities of beer and wine, Jay got Josie alone.

'What the hell do you think you're doing? I've only just met Emma. She's a friend, nothing else, and now she'll get the wrong idea.'

Josie was loading the dishwasher and turned to whisper, so no one else could hear. 'It's clear she's got the hots for you. This is exactly what you need to get over Caitlin. Another woman. And a beautiful one at that. Emma's stunning. That red hair… I envy her. I always wanted hair like that.'

'Josie, what's her hair got to do with anything? Yes, she's nice, but I don't want to get involved.'

'Nice? That's a word you hate, isn't it? You hate being called that but now Emma is nice.'

'Okay, more than nice.'

'Much more, Jay, she's gorgeous. Too good for you when I think about it.'

'Exactly, she's far too good for me, so why are you trying to push us together?'

'Because, much as I love you, I also know you need a kick up the arse now and again.'

Paul came into the kitchen to get some more beer from the fridge. 'What are you two whispering about?'

'Oh, just twin stuff,' said Josie, 'you wouldn't be interested.'

Josie wandered back into the living room to talk to Emma about nursing. Matt was on his phone to his fiancé, Ben. Paul was looking at Jay enquiringly.

'Okay, I'll come clean. I don't know about Emma moving in permanently. I feel a bit uneasy about it.'

Paul put his arm across Jay's shoulders. 'Go with the flow, Bro—just go with the flow.'

———

Later that night, when they'd all gone home, Jay opened his

emails and found one from Steve, his ex-lodger who had gone off to travel the world.

He read about surfing in Australia, visiting temples in Bali, scuba diving in Fiji and other exotic, exciting adventures. Jay hadn't envied Steve at all when he had told him of his plans to take a year off and work his way around the world, or as much of it as he could get to see in twelve months.

Steve had urged him, on more than one occasion, to take some time out and join him in Indonesia, Thailand, or New Zealand. Just the names of the countries stirred up something in Jay. He had loved his trip to the States, maybe it was time to go travelling again.

He hadn't enjoyed the beer and Chinese evening as much as he usually did. He felt that people, no matter how well-intentioned, were making decisions for him. He should be making his own decisions.

Emma was sweet, but he didn't want to lead her on or give her the wrong impression. He knew they would never be anything but friends.

Maybe he could turn the situation to his advantage. If Emma lodged with him permanently, even if it was for a year or so, he could happily join Steve on his travels, leaving his home in safe hands. He would leave her enough money for bills and his family were nearby if she needed anything. She seemed to have hit it off with Josie.

Jay sent off a quick email, asking for Steve's itinerary. He didn't want to commit himself to anything, but if he should join him—and it was only an if mind—when and where would be a good time and place?

When he had sent the email, he felt a bit better.

He had thought that he would be able to work with

Caitlin even though they meant nothing to each other. But in a moment of brutal honesty, he knew that he couldn't. He couldn't bear the thought of her married to Hooray Henry. Maybe this was the time to get away. Get her out of his system and then he could move on.

Chapter Twenty-Seven

'Mother, can I talk to you?'

'It's "may I talk to you" if you're asking permission, Caitlin, and "can I talk to you" if you are asking me if you are capable of talking, which, of course, you are. Your grasp of the English language is appalling. I suppose it's due to rubbing shoulders with the hoi polloi.'

Nina was in the drawing room draped over her favourite chaise longue, sipping a glass of bubbly. She looked content with her lot, almost happy. Caitlin knew, of course, that her mother was never happy.

'I want to tell you something. Please.'

'Is it important?'

'Yes, very.' Caitlin came into the room and sat on an adjacent armchair. She pulled the sleeves of her cardigan over her hands, then realised her mother was glaring at her, so she folded the cuffs back.

'I can't believe you still do that,' said her mother turning her head to gaze out at the garden.

It was a habit she'd acquired when she was a child and

bit her nails. Her mother had tried everything to stop her; nail varnish that tasted bad, plasters on all her fingers, making her wear gloves, and one time her mother put cayenne pepper on her fingers. Caitlin had taken to hiding her hands as often as she could. She only did it nowadays when she was stressed.

'The last time Sophie and I were in Mellow, Fenella Barton-Brookes was there.'

'Oh, for goodness sake, Caitlin, I do hope you're not going to start all that silly nonsense up again. Brandon is marrying you, not Fenella.'

'Brandon is screwing Fenella! She claims she's pregnant with his baby.'

'Please don't use words like that, and anyway, it's complete nonsense. She was teasing you, that's all. She knows how ridiculous you're being and she's having a little joke. You're far too sensitive and naïve for someone your age. Don't you think it's about time you grew up?'

Caitlin was speechless and close to tears, but her mother was right, it was time she grew up and stood up for herself.

'I suppose the bullying I received from Fenella and her cronies at that horrible school was only teasing to you? Apart from the constant remarks, put-downs, and stalking, they stole my school books, destroyed a project I'd been working on for months, broke anything of mine they could get their hands on and poured water in my bed and told everyone I wet the bed. It was constant for almost a year until Sophie joined the school and protected me.'

Nina stood up and started wandering around the room. She looked agitated but Caitlin knew it wasn't because of the suffering her daughter had gone through at school but because she was irritated. Her mother had never been a good listener, especially when it involved something she didn't want to hear.

'Caitlin, if you hadn't been such a limp lettuce, maybe you could have earned the respect of Fenella and her friends. In fact, if you made the effort to be civil to her, you could be friends now.'

'I don't think so, Mother, I hate the woman's guts. I'm very particular about who I'm friends with.'

'Well, you could have fooled me. You spend your time with a divorcee who is no earthly use to you at all if you want to move in the best circles. And those ambulance drivers are certainly not going to help you get ahead in society.'

'Paramedics.'

Caitlin realised that trying to reason with her mother was like pissing in the wind, as Sophie would have said. The thought of her bestie gave her courage.

'I'm curious, Mother—when you went to school, were you bullied or were you one of the bullies?'

Her mother turned away so Caitlin couldn't see her expression.

'I refuse to speak to you if you continue with this nonsense. Forget the past, Caitlin, it's what happens in the future that counts.'

'Well, there's one thing that won't be in my future—a wedding to Brandon Dodds.'

'Oh, not this again! Good grief, girl, you're giving me a headache. You are going to marry Brandon and that's the end of it.'

'No, I'm not.'

'Yes, you are.'

'No, she isn't.'

They both jumped as her father joined in the conversation. He must have been listening outside the door. Caitlin wondered if he'd taken up eavesdropping as a hobby.

'Alan, I thought you were resting. Why don't you go back to bed, dear, I can handle this.' Nina walked towards him, but her father avoided her and went to sit on the couch, opposite Caitlin.

'I think you've done enough damage, Nina. Caitlin knows her own mind and I'm glad she's not marrying Brandon. The man's not good enough for her.'

'What about… the other thing.'

'I think your mother is referring to the business and the merger, Caitlin, don't you?'

Caitlin was so stunned to be in cahoots with her father that she merely nodded and said nothing.

'She knows all about it, Nina. In fact she knows more than we do. What you don't seem to realise is that your daughter is more grown up than you've ever been. She's seen life, real life, and death, in her job. Caitlin knows what's important. Not being part of an elite, or a group of people with their heads up their arses but having real friendships that last. People who are there for each other at work because they are dealing with a person's life and they have to rely totally on their colleagues.'

'Oh, Dad,' said Caitlin.

'When I had my heart attack—'

'Oh, not this again, Alan, we all sympathise, but—'

'Yes, this again, so do me the honour of shutting up and listening.'

Caitlin glanced out of the corner of her eye at her mother. She was nervously clicking her thumbnail and middle fingernail together. So, she had nervous habits too. Caitlin couldn't help smiling.

'When I had my heart attack I thought I was dying. I

did see my life flashing before me like people say you do, and I didn't like what I was seeing. I've got it all wrong. All the things I've valued all my life, the same things that you want, Nina, are worthless. Money, success, property, membership of the golf club. What use were those things to me when I thought my heart was giving out on me? But then, two angels turned up.'

Alan turned his attention to Caitlin who had tears in her eyes. 'Dad, you don't have to—'

'Yes, Caitlin, I do. It needs to be said. You and…'

'Sally.'

'Sally, yes that's right. Scottish lady. More balls than any man I've ever known. You just got on with it, calmly, no fuss, just saved my life.'

Alan put his hands over his face and Caitlin knelt by his side with her arms around him. Tears leaked through his fingers.

'Dad, I really love you. You know that don't you?'

'And I love you, too, Caitlin, and from now on I'm going to be a better father to you. I don't know how much more time I've got on this earth, but whatever it is, I'm here for you, whenever you need me.'

Caitlin was crying openly now, and her mother was staring at the pair of them as if they'd gone mad. But, surprisingly, she didn't speak, just stood in the middle of the drawing room looking mutinous.

When her father's tears had dried, he wiped his face. 'Right. While we're all in the mood for serious discussion, I may as well tell you that I've made a decision. There'll be no wedding, no merger and I'm keeping my business.'

'What? And what are you going to use for money?' Nina laughed scornfully.

'Well, that brings me neatly to the second thing I want to say. I think you may want to sit down, Nina.'

'Oh, for Pete's sake. What now?'

'I'm leaving you, Nina, that's what. Heather and I are moving in together and we're both going to run the business. You can have the house and I'll keep the business.'

'What about the Dodds?' asked Nina.

'Fuck the Dodds,' said Alan and Caitlin felt like jumping in the air and fist pumping in glee.

'Alan!'

'Dad! That's brilliant, I'm so pleased that you're not going to lose your company.'

'Thank you, Caitlin, and I'm glad you're not marrying that stuck-up oaf.'

'What about me?' asked Nina looking worried for the first time.

Alan said nothing, just yawned, as if the future of his soon to be ex was of no interest to him whatsoever. Caitlin didn't know what to say either. Her mother would be okay, women like her always were.

Chapter Twenty-Eight

'Long time no see. How've you been, Caitlin?' Paul said as they scrambled into the ambulance for an early shift.

'I'm great, Paul, how are things with you?'

'Yeah, really good.'

Caitlin had been pleased when she saw on the new rota that she was partnered with Paul. She got on well with him and he was just brilliant with the patients. And, of course, she could ask him about Jay.

Now she was free to marry whoever she wanted, her thoughts automatically turned to Jay. Since she'd moved back in with her parents, she hadn't seen him, nor spoken to him. She had no idea how he was doing and was desperate for news of him. A couple of times she had picked her phone up with the intention of ringing him but put it back in her pocket when she realised she had no idea what to say. She didn't even know how he felt about her. She was waiting for them to work together but that never seemed to happen either.

'How's Jay?'

'Fine. He's moving on with his life. Got a new girlfriend and is really happy. It's good to see.'

'A new girlfriend?' That was quick. Caitlin's heart dropped to her boots. How can he have moved on so fast? Didn't that prove that he had no feelings for her whatsoever? She thought back to the night they had sex and how wonderful it had been. Well, it had been for her anyway. Perhaps it was nothing more than a satisfying quickie for Jay.

She wanted to ask Paul more questions. Who was this girl? But the radio alerted them to a call-out.

'What have we got?' asked Paul who was driving.

'Male, thirty-six, overdose. Lives alone.'

Paul looked at the address on the screen and switched on the sirens.

When they arrived at the address, the front door was open slightly and they went in, announcing themselves as the ambulance service as they did so. It was dark and dingy, and smelled of dust, mould, and decaying food.

'Hello, anyone home?' Paul called out. There was a faint answer that seemed to be coming from the front room, so Paul pushed the door open slowly and peered around it. Caitlin was right behind him.

'Hello, did you call the ambulance service?'

A young man was sitting in a tatty armchair with a coffee table in front of him. There were bottles of pills and a bottle of vodka on it. He was wearing jeans and a T-shirt and looked quite neat and tidy, not unkempt, or uncared for.

'Yeah. I've taken some pills.'

Paul started to take the man's pulse and Caitlin tried to engage him in conversation as she took his temperature.

'What's your name, love?'

'Mike.'

'I'm Caitlin and this is Paul. We're here to help you. Can you tell us what you've taken?'

'Paracetamol.'

'How much?'

'Ten tablets.' Caitlin noticed that the vodka bottle hadn't been opened.

'Right. We're going to have to take you to hospital, Mike,' Caitlin said. Ten tablets if caught in time, would probably not kill a person, but if left untreated could cause irreversible liver damage.

'When did you take the tablets, Mike?' asked Paul.

'About an hour ago.'

'Okay. Are you on your own? Is there anyone we can call for you?'

Mike shook his head and looked so sad that Caitlin wanted to hug him. The man was obviously struggling with personal issues and Caitlin was thinking a mental health team referral was going to be needed.

When they got him in the ambulance, Paul drove, while Caitlin monitored Mike's vital signs to make sure his heart rate or blood pressure didn't increase suddenly.

'How are you feeling, Mike?' asked Caitlin.

'Tired.'

'Okay. No abdominal pain or feeling sick?'

'No.'

'Have you eaten today?'

'No.'

'When was the last time you had a meal?'

'Few days ago.'

Mike's monosyllabic answers and his lethargic demeanour worried Caitlin and she wanted to get him to the Accident and Emergency Department as quickly as possible to be assessed by the medics there.

'Are you okay, Mike?' Caitlin asked. She was watching him closely in case he fell asleep or became unconscious. He may not have told them the full story about what tablets he'd taken but he seemed quite alert, though depressed.

'Yeah. Sorry for causing you all these problems.'

'You haven't caused us any problems, Mike. We're here to help you. If you want to talk, I'm a good listener.'

'Don't know what to say. Just don't see the point of anything. It'd be better if I weren't here.'

'Better for who, Mike? Have you got family?'

'Not seen them for years.'

Thankfully, they soon arrived at the hospital and Caitlin was glad when they could hand their patient over to the doctors for assessment.

When they got back in the ambulance, Paul drove again, and Caitlin thought about Mike.

'That poor man. He didn't seem to have anyone in his life he could turn to.'

'He was lonely. That was his main problem. Whatever his other issues were, I'd like to bet loneliness was the reason he tried to take his own life.'

'Was it a cry for help, do you think? Rather than a serious suicide attempt?'

'Difficult to say. He hadn't taken that many tablets and hadn't drunk any of the vodka. Perhaps he was going to do it and then got cold feet.'

'Yeah, poor man.' Caitlin sighed and thought about his house, how dark and dingy it was.

'Anyway, he's in the right place now. Hopefully, he can get the care he needs.'

'Yes, I hope so. It's so sad to think of all the lonely people there are in the world.'

'Hey—don't let it get to you, or you'll end up being depressed yourself.' Paul said. 'How's your friend, Sophie?'

'She's fine, thanks. Did you hear she had her new Maserati stolen?'

'Yeah, I heard all about that from Jay. Has she got it back yet?'

'No. The police think it's probably on the continent by now.'

'Shame. And what about your wedding day? Is that getting closer? You're not going to do a runner again, are you?' Paul laughed and Caitlin couldn't help smiling.

'The wedding's off, Paul. Brandon has made his lover pregnant and I've dodged a bullet.'

'No way! What a bastard.' Paul stopped for traffic lights.

'Could you do me a favour?'

'Sure.'

'Would you tell Jay, please? I'd like him to know.'

'Yeah, of course, I'll tell him, but like I said before, he's got Emma now.'

'Where did he meet Emma?'

'Speed dating. We went together. They hit it off straight away. Jay says they've got a lot in common.' The lights turned to green and they continued on.

'Right. What does she look like?'

Caitlin knew she shouldn't be asking these questions. She should just accept that Jay had someone else and move on. But like a scab you can't help picking, she needed to know everything she could about the woman who had won the heart of the man she loved.

'She's beautiful. Red hair, green eyes, and freckles. And she's going to be a nurse. Josie's helping her with her studies.

Wouldn't be surprised if she's met the rest of the O'Connor clan by now. Jay will want to show her off to his family.'

'Yes, of course.' Caitlin brought to mind the Sunday lunch she had with the O'Connors and how she'd felt at home straight away. And now another woman was enjoying the warmth and acceptance of Jay's family.

It seemed she'd lost. If Emma was the woman Jay was destined to be with, then she wished them both well. She'd move on too. Maybe meet someone else one day.

But no matter how Caitlin tried to rationalise it, she felt like crying. She should have said something earlier. She'd left it too late to tell Jay she loved him.

Chapter Twenty-Nine

Jay got home from an early shift to find a spotlessly clean house and the table set for the evening meal complete with a pristine white table cloth and shiny cutlery. There was a vase of flowers on the coffee table in the living room, with gladioli, roses, and sun flowers in autumn colours. Jay loved flowers and had stopped to admire them. They were perfectly arranged as if they had been delivered by an expensive flower shop.

'Hi Jay!' Emma came bounding down the stairs looking gorgeous in a pair of tight jeans and a sleeveless cream blouse. Her hair was loose, and she wore make-up, but not enough to cover her freckles. She'd sprayed herself liberally with perfume.

'Hi Emma...who sent you the flowers?'

'No one, I bought them when I was out shopping. Why? Don't you like them?'

'I love them. The place looks... amazing.'

'Good. I wasn't sure whether you'd appreciate me

adding a few feminine touches, but if you don't like anything, just tell me.'

'Sure.' Jay looked around at all the extras that had appeared. There were cushions on the couch and animal faces looked out at him questioningly. There were a lot of cushions with dogs on them. The rug on the floor was one of those large, thick fluffy ones. He didn't usually bother with rugs as he'd been to too many call-outs where people had tripped on a rug and fallen hitting their head on the furniture. Not just the elderly either. People in their forties and fifties. Especially when they'd had too much to drink.

'Dinner will be ready soon, so you'll have just enough time to nip up for a shower beforehand. I'll have a nice drink waiting for you when you come down.'

'Right. What are we having?'

Emma grinned, 'Well, I've made some chicken noodle soup for starters, then steak and salad, followed by Eton mess. How does that sound?'

Jay wasn't sure what to say. His dad and brothers would say that their wives either wanted something or had done something that their men-folk weren't going to like and were buttering them up before they broke the news. This wasn't a usual mid-week meal. Not for anyone he knew that is.

'It sounds great, Emma, but you don't need to go to all this trouble.'

'It's no trouble. Now, off you go and I'll get you that drink.'

Jay obediently went upstairs.

He put his head around the door of the bathroom to find it in a sparkling clean condition. The tiles shone so that he could see his face in them, and the shower curtain was new. He usually bought the cheapest ones that he could shove in the washing machine now and again. This one, however, was a heavier curtain in a seashell print and there was another, smaller, cream rug replacing the bathmat and pedestal set he'd been using.

The bathroom smelled wonderful and Jay looked around to find the source. A sandalwood and jasmine candle sat on the windowsill which was clear except for a small mirror and a bottle of handwash.

Reluctant to enter his bedroom in case Emma had done a make-over there as well, he opened the door cautiously. No change. Phew. Jay quickly found clean clothes to change into. No more strolling from the bedroom to the bathroom in the nude to save time. Not that he'd done that when Caitlin was living with him.

At the thought of Caitlin, he felt the familiar pang of loss. He hadn't heard from her since she'd moved out. He didn't know whether she was marrying Brandon or not. He had been on the verge of ringing her so many times but then decided that she probably didn't want anything more to do with him. Why else would she have moved back with her parents? If she'd wanted to talk to him, she would have rung or texted.

Emma was serving the meal as Jay wandered downstairs still lost in thoughts of Caitlin.

'Good timing!' she said as she poured a glass of red wine for them both.

Jay sat down and sipped his wine. He would have preferred a beer, but Emma had gone to so much trouble that he was determined to be grateful.

'This is wonderful, Emma, and I really appreciate it, but it must have taken you all day. What about your studies?'

'Oh no, it didn't take long. I love cooking and especially cooking for other people. It's not much fun on your own.'

'That's true.' Jay tucked into his soup, which was delicious. And the bread rolls that went with it were wonderful.

'Well, cheers then,' Emma said holding up her wine glass, 'to us.'

'Cheers,' said Jay. 'You didn't make the bread rolls as well, did you?'

'Of course,' Emma replied.

'You're the real deal,' said Jay, 'maybe you should go into catering instead of nursing.'

'Oh no, I know what I want and it's nursing. Cooking is just for fun.'

By the time the meal was over, Jay was feeling stuffed to the gills and drowsy from the wine. All he wanted to do was sleep, but Emma had other ideas.

'Go and sit down, Jay, while I load the dishwasher and then I'll make you a coffee. I've got a choice of movies for us to watch unless you want to see what's on Netflix?'

'Oh, whatever you want,' Jay answered. It looked as if Emma was expecting them to spend the evening together. He hadn't got anything else planned, so he scrolled through Netflix to see what they could watch. There was nothing that took his fancy.

He wished he still had SpongeBob so he could get out of the house and take her for a walk. Maybe he should ask Emma to look after her and she could live here again. She'd bought cushions with dogs' faces on, so she must like them. He'd broach the subject later.

Emma sat down on the couch next to him and flipped through the choice of movies.

'You watch whatever you like,' said Jay, wondering how long he could wait before making his excuses and going upstairs to check his emails.

'Do you like sci-fi?' Emma asked him.

'Yeah, I do.'

'Okay.' She found an obscure movie that Jay had never heard of and they sat and watched it. Emma's gaze was fixed on the screen, but Jay felt his eyelids drooping and before long he fell asleep.

When he woke, about half an hour later, he felt something pressing on him and the strong smell of perfume. He opened his eyes to find Emma with her head on his shoulder. She was still awake. He sat up and turned to speak to her.

'What... ?'

'Oh, you're awake sleepy head. I had visions of having to put you to bed myself.' Emma sat up and kissed him on the cheek. 'I've paused the film so we can watch it from the point you fell asleep.'

'Listen, Emma. This is nice, but I think I'm going to go to bed now.'

'Really? But it's still early. Do you want to do something else?'

'No. Thank you. I'm tired and I'm on an early again tomorrow.'

'Oh, that's a shame.' Emma sounded disappointed but Jay was feeling uneasy and wanted to be alone to think about things.

'Thanks for everything you've done. The meal was lovely, and the house, too...'

'It's nothing, Jay, really. I love homemaking. I've never had the chance to do it before.'

'Right. Okay. Well, goodnight, Emma.'

'Night Jay.'

Jay felt relieved when he reached his bedroom. What the hell was all that about? She'd acted as if they were a couple, even a married couple. Maybe she'd never shared with anybody before and didn't know how to act. He would have to talk to her and explain that they didn't live in each other's pockets and could do their own thing. Then he felt bad for having those feelings. Emma was just trying to do something nice for him. He wouldn't say anything… for now, anyway.

When he got into bed, he felt too on edge to fall asleep straight away. But the food and the wine had relaxed him more than he realised and he soon slept and dreamed of Caitlin.

Chapter Thirty

Caitlin's father was true to his word and moved in with Heather. To celebrate, they invited Caitlin out for a meal. They chose the Italian restaurant, Rocco's, which was classy and expensive.

Caitlin knew that jeans and a sweatshirt wouldn't do for this venue and rifled through her wardrobe looking for the perfect thing to wear. Maybe the reliable little black dress would do the job. Fortunately, she had a few to choose from.

She looked at her drop-dead sexy ones, that were backless, short, and revealed more than was decent at the front. No, definitely not. What was needed was something stylish, chic, and sophisticated. Caitlin wished she could ask her mother's advice but didn't dare. Apart from anything else, that would be rubbing salt into the wound.

Eventually, she chose one of her favourites. The hem came to an inch above the knee, it was sleeveless and quite plain, but the stretch material accentuated her slim waist and small breasts. She wore a black jacket to match and tasteful gold earrings.

As she came out of her bedroom, her mother was leaning on the balustrade at the top of the stairs waiting for her.

'Going out?' she asked.

'Yes, Mother, I've been invited to dinner by Father and Heather.'

'Anywhere nice?'

'Rocco's.'

'I see.' Her mother said nothing more but fixed her with a steely stare.

Caitlin turned to walk downstairs but her mother's voice stopped her in her tracks.

'How sharper than a serpent's tooth it is to have a thankless child.'

'What?'

'Don't you mean, "I beg your pardon"?'

'I'm sorry, I didn't hear what you said.'

'It's a Bible quote in case you didn't understand it. It refers to how ungrateful some children are.'

Caitlin had never known her mother to read the Bible, attend church, or do anything else that would point to her being a Christian. Religion had never been mentioned in her family.

'Yes, I gathered that. I'm just a bit puzzled as to what I should be grateful for. You sent me to a school I hated, tried to marry me off to a man I despise, and you have never listened to me or asked me what I wanted. Ever.'

'Everything I've done for you has been with your best interests at heart. You have wanted for nothing.'

Except love, affection, warmth and understanding. Caitlin thought about Eloise O'Connor and her all-encompassing unconditional love. How safe she'd felt in Eloise's arms. Her mother was like the ice queen of Narnia. Caitlin couldn't remember a time when her mother hugged her, even when she was tiny.

'Goodbye, Mother, don't wait up.'

'I certainly won't. I may get the locksmith in and change all the locks while you're out gallivanting. Then what would you do?'

'I'd go and stay with Father and Heather. They've already asked me actually.'

'Well go then! Go and leave me here on my own. You ungrateful little bitch—get out!'

'Goodbye, Mother.'

'Traitor!'

Caitlin didn't look back as she walked down the stairs and left by the front door. After she'd reached the road, she stopped to control her shaking. She wanted to cry but didn't want to ruin her make-up. Fortunately, the taxi she'd booked arrived five minutes later and she got in the back and told the driver the destination.

Caitlin closed her eyes and breathed deeply. Her heart was still beating out of her chest and she wanted to appear calm and composed when she faced her father and Heather.

By the time she got to Rocco's Caitlin was feeling a bit better. Her mother was hurting, and she could understand why. Nina Hewitt was a beautiful woman, and as a young model, she had commanded the attention of every man she met. She could have had any of them, but she'd chosen Alan. Now, when Nina was older and no longer in demand, her husband was leaving her for a woman who, while attractive, couldn't compare to Nina's beauty.

Caitlin wondered if her mother had ever loved anyone. She had never known her maternal grandparents as they had died before she was born, and her mother had never talked about them. Any attempts Caitlin had made to ask about her grandparents, what they were like and where they'd lived, for example, was met with a rebuff.

When Caitlin felt composed enough to join her father and Heather, she took a deep breath and opened the door to the restaurant.

Her father had come to the front door to greet her. He'd probably wondered what she was doing hanging about outside.

'Hi darling, you look lovely.'

'Thanks, Dad.' Caitlin kissed him on the cheek and followed him to their table.

'Hi Heather.'

'Hello, Caitlin, nice to see you again and in more pleasant circumstances.'

'Yes. I've been looking forward to this meal.'

'Me too,' said Heather.

Heather looked cool and sophisticated in a pale grey maxi dress with bracelets and ear-rings in silver. She wore a smart pair of sandals with heels. She hadn't stood up as Caitlin approached the table but smiled a welcome.

'We haven't ordered yet, we wanted to wait for you,' said her father.

'Sorry, am I late?'

'No, dear, we were early'.

'Right.' Caitlin picked up a menu and studied it.

'To start, I'm having *funghi gorgonzola*, then *aragosta con linguine*,' said her father.

'I'll have the same starter, but I don't want the lobster, so I'll have the smoked salmon with cream sauce,' said Heather.

'Caitlin? You like lobster, don't you?'

'Yes, I love lobster.'

'Great, that's settled then.'

Caitlin smiled as her father summoned the waiter and gave him their orders. He ordered the wine too. Alan Hewitt was always in charge, in every situation, and Caitlin was pleased to see he was getting his mojo back and taking control, even though she hadn't had much of a say in what she was going to eat. No matter, she loved Italian food and could probably have eaten anything on the menu.

Once that was out of the way, they all sat back and waited for their meal. Nobody spoke and Caitlin hoped this evening wasn't going to be awkward. She wanted to like Heather for her father's sake.

'I hope your mother didn't give you a hard time about coming out with us tonight.' Her father looked at her with sympathy in his eyes. 'I meant what I said about coming to live with us. The offer's still there, isn't it, Heather?'

'Absolutely. I understand how conflicted you must be feeling at the moment, Caitlin, and we want to make the transition period as painless for you as possible.'

'Thanks, but I can't leave my mother on her own, it wouldn't be fair.'

The waiter brought the wine and opened the bottle, pouring a little in a glass for her father to try. He made all the right noises and the waiter poured the wine while the three of them watched him. Then he left and the conversation resumed.

'Is she being reasonable about it all?' her father asked.

Caitlin laughed. 'No. When has she ever been reasonable about anything?' Then Caitlin realised how disloyal that sounded and said. 'She's finding it very hard.'

'But she's not taking it out on you?' her father asked hopefully.

Caitlin couldn't lie to him. The time for deception was over. There'd been too much of it recently.

'She's hurting and I understand that completely. Remember, Brandon was having an affair when he was with me, so I know how it feels to be the wronged woman.'

The waiter brought the first course and they tucked into the mushrooms. It didn't take long for her father to resume the discussion.

'Yes, but you can't compare the two, dear. Nina has always known about Heather. At least, for a few years anyway. Brandon is a total moron with cotton wool between his ears. I doubt he understands what love is.'

Her father drank some of his wine. Heather sat quietly, listening to the exchange. Caitlin didn't want to make trouble, but she couldn't let that comment go.

'But there was a time when you were perfectly happy to see me marry that moron.'

Her father sighed and took her hand. 'There's not a day goes by when I don't regret my part in that. I was wrong to give in to Nina and let the engagement go ahead. I should have put my foot down at the beginning. I'm so sorry, Caitlin.'

'So… you never liked Brandon at all?'

'No, darling, I never liked him. But, in my defence, I did think you loved him once. Was I wrong?'

Caitlin smiled. 'I thought I loved him, but I never knew what love was, until now.'

Heather picked up on this and leaned forward. 'Are you in love, Caitlin? Real love this time?'

'It's unrequited I'm afraid. The man whose spare room I stayed in after the crash. He's a friend and a fellow paramedic. But the week after I moved out, he went speed dating and met someone who he's smitten with, apparently.'

The main courses arrived, and the smell of lobster was divine. They all declared the food to be first class and there was a long gap before the talk resumed. This time Heather led the discussion.

'It's probably on the rebound. Speed dating sounds like the kind of thing you do when you're trying to move on but instead of giving yourself time to heal, you go hell for leather into another relationship.'

'I'm not even sure he felt the same way about me though. He's the type that helps people. He's kind and sensitive as well as strong and sexy.'

'He sounds like a catch,' said Heather. 'Don't give up on him. The speed-dater may be just a flash in the pan. Not the real deal. Why don't you try to find out more about her? Or be really brave and just ask him? I mean, what have you got to lose?'

'Good advice. If you don't mind me asking, how did you two get back in touch? You were childhood sweethearts weren't you?' Caitlin realised she was really liking Heather and was enjoying the evening immensely.

Heather glanced at Alan who smiled. 'Facebook,' Heather said.

'I have a business page,' said her father, 'all the businesses seem to use them, and I didn't want our company to be overlooked. So I set one up. Then the next thing I know, there were messages for me from Heather, asking if I was the Alan Hewitt that went to the youth club we both frequented as teenagers and we started talking.'

'Then we met up and… we both realised the spark was still there.'

'And the spark became a flame?' asked Caitlin smiling.

'And the flame became a fire that nearly burnt the house down,' said Heather.

'Heather,' said her father in a warning tone.

'Oh never mind Heather, Caitlin's a woman. She's not a child any more, Alan. And a very beautiful and gracious woman if you don't mind me saying so.'

'Don't mind a bit,' said Caitlin laughing. 'Thanks for the compliment.'

'I don't say things unless I mean them,' said Heather.

Caitlin was liking Heather more and more. And not just because of the compliment, even though it made her feel warm inside. Heather was straight talking, intelligent, and confident. She was glad for her father that he had someone who could support him and also stand up to him.

'Okay,' said her father, 'who's for a dessert?'

'Well, I'm sure you can guess what I'm having,' said Heather.

'Panna cotta. Caitlin?'

'I'll have the same.'

'Great.' He turned to the waiter hovering near the table. 'Three panna cottas, please. *Grazie.*'

'Tell me more about the business,' Caitlin said.

Surprisingly, it was Heather who answered.

'Well, I went into property development soon after my divorce twenty years ago. I started small, buying a house, doing it up, selling it for a profit, then banking the money and buying another one. So now I've got property all over Leytonsfield and money to invest. I'm going into business with Alan and have enough to keep the company going for a while, with a view to expanding in the future.'

Caitlin glanced at her father, wondering how he would react to Heather being the spokesperson rather than him. He was nodding at everything she said and smiling. He was obviously proud of his new business partner.

At the end of the evening, Caitlin hugged her father,

then Heather. There were promises to have similar meals out and Caitlin must come to Heather's house for a meal as well. She left Rocco's feeling happy; for her father and for herself.

―――――――――

Caitlin put her key in the door, grateful that the locks hadn't been changed.

She found her mother in the drawing room, still drinking champagne and drunk.

'Mother? Why don't you go to bed?'

'I was waiting up for my daughter even though she's an ungrateful wretch who doesn't care if I live or die.'

'You know that's not true. I'm going to make you a coffee, then I suggest you go to bed.'

Caitlin went into the kitchen and Nina followed her. She sat at the kitchen table and watched as Caitlin made her a black coffee, no sugar or milk.

'There you go.' She put the drink on the table and turned away to leave the kitchen. 'Where are you going?'

'I'm going to bed, Mother, which is where you should go after your coffee.'

'Sit down and tell me what happened tonight.'

'No. I won't sit down because I'm going to bed. What happened tonight is that all three of us had a thoroughly enjoyable meal and we intend to do it again soon.'

'So you're going to move out and live with them, I take it?'

'No, I'm not. I'm going to stay here with you until the house is sold. I'm not leaving you.'

'Even if I want you to? If I want to be alone?'

'You hate being alone. No, I'm staying. Goodnight, Mother.'

Caitlin left the kitchen and made her way up the stairs to bed.

Chapter Thirty-One

Emma was still in bed when Jay got up the next morning. He made himself some toast and tea and tried to make as little noise as he could so he wouldn't wake her.

He was working with Matt who was excited about his impending wedding to Ben and most of their conversations centred around venues, catering, and places to go on honeymoon.

'Am I invited?' asked Jay with a grin.

'Of course and you can bring the lovely Emma as your plus one.'

Jay had been thinking about Emma a lot since the previous night. Her behaviour had been strange. Especially putting her head on his shoulder when he had been asleep. The sensible thing to do was to talk to her about it, but she was a sweet girl and he didn't want to upset her.

The morning was crazily busy and there was no time for a break. Then in the afternoon, they were called to an estate where a young boy of fifteen had sustained injuries from other teenagers. Police had been called. Instructions to wait until the area was safe before proceeding.

'Is that all the information we've got?' asked Matt.

'So far it is,' answered Jay. 'Just hope there's no knives involved. I hate treating knife wounds.'

'Me too. I hate any kind of violence.' Matt shivered.

They both knew that knife crime was on the increase and stabbings were much more commonplace these days. They needed to be prepared for anything.

When they got to the scene, they could see a body lying in the road. It was obviously the boy who had been injured.

Jay parked the ambulance an appropriate distance away from the boy. They had to assess the danger before getting out of the ambulance as the police were conspicuous by their absence.

'Can't see anyone. The other kids have probably scarpered.'

'We can't just leave him. I can't see if he's breathing from here,' said Matt.

Jay phoned the control room to see if there was any more information, but they were told not to approach until the police got there.

'Right,' Jay said as he opened the ambulance door, 'I'm going to check it out.'

'Be careful,' said Matt as Jay opened the back door of the ambulance to collect his equipment.

Jay walked swiftly to the boy lying in the road, but when he had reached shouting distance, the boy leapt up and ran hell for leather down the street. At the same time, a gang of youths appeared from behind parked cars and front gardens and started throwing rocks and bottles at Jay and the ambulance.

It was sudden and frightening. One minute Jay was

thinking about the injuries the boy could have sustained, to prepare himself to look after him. The next minute he was being pelted by hard objects thrown by people hiding from him. His first thought was to get back to the ambulance but he wasn't sure he'd make it without being seriously injured. He was too far away.

Jay tried to protect his head by holding his arm up, but with the speed that the missiles were flying at him and laden with his equipment, he couldn't get away from the bombardment, so he crouched down in the road, trying to protect his head.

He risked looking up and towards the ambulance, and his heart nearly stopped beating. The windows were smashed, including the windscreen and the front lights. He couldn't see Matt and hoped that he'd had the sense to crouch down or get in the back of the ambulance for safety.

He was hit on the cheek by a rock and felt the warm flow of blood down his face, dripping onto his uniform. The missiles were coming from all around. There must have been dozens of kids involved. There was shouting; angry, harsh voices filled with hate surrounded him.

Then a bottle was thrown that was a direct hit and everything turned black.

Caitlin and Sally were working together when they had a call from the control centre to assist another crew as they were only two minutes away. Police were on the scene.

'I wonder what that's all about?' said Sally.

'Don't know,' said Caitlin, 'we'll find out soon enough.' Caitlin switched on the sirens.

Caitlin had been riding high after her conversations

with her parents. She was free again and it had felt so good. But then, after a shift with Paul when he told her about Jay and Emma, she had come crashing back down again.

She vacillated between despair when she thought that she had lost Jay forever, and hope that his relationship with Emma wasn't serious and he did have feelings for her. Being wishy-washy and doing nothing or taking the easy way out and running away had been her choices in the past. Things had to change. She needed to be proactive. It was better to know for sure that Jay wasn't interested rather than live this half-life where she tortured herself with doubts.

Heather had recommended she talk to Jay or at least find out more about Emma. She should take her advice.

They turned the corner into the street the call-out was on and caught sight of the ambulance.

'Oh my God!' said Caitlin.

'Shit a brick,' said Sally.

The ambulance was a wreck. There was broken glass everywhere. Two police vans and three police cars were parked haphazardly. Two officers were helping a paramedic who lay in the middle of the road, blood covering his face. Matt was being helped by another officer. He looked to be in shock. The neighbours were out in force, some trying to help, some taking pictures and videos on their phones and others standing around as if they were watching outdoor entertainment.

Caitlin leapt out of the ambulance, closely followed by Sally and they grabbed their equipment from the back and walked swiftly to the paramedic in the road. She was just about to talk to the police officers and ask about the extent of the person's injuries when she realised it was Jay lying there unconscious.

'Oh my God, it's Jay,' she said, as Sally tried to steer her in Matt's direction.

'I'll handle this one, honey, go and see how Matt is.'

'No! I can manage, Sally,' said Caitlin. This time she would be professional and impartial. Unlike seeing her father and Heather together, when she had been useless. She would do her job and think about things afterwards.

'Okay, if you're sure.'

'I am. Very sure.'

Caitlin felt immense anger that a group of teenagers could callously attack people coming to help them. She spoke to the officers and got the gist of what had happened. An empty beer bottle was next to Jay and they assumed it was the object that had hit him. He was unconscious but not deeply as they had got him to open his eyes once. He was drifting in and out of consciousness.

'Right. Thanks guys.' Caitlin proceeded to check Jay's heart rate, blood pressure, oxygen saturation, and respiration rate, while talking to him constantly. She shone a light in his eyes to test for pupil size and reaction, then, after assessing the wound on his head caused by the bottle and finding it superficial, she put a sterile cover on it, while she checked him over. The A&E staff would assess if he needed stitches when they cleaned out any fragments of glass. Finally she put a cervical spine collar on him to protect his neck.

'Jay, it's me, Caitlin. Wake up for me.' She kept talking to him as she checked his vital signs and Sally came over with the stretcher. They got him onto it and took him to the ambulance. Matt was already there relatively unhurt but shaken up, so Sally drove, while Caitlin stayed in the back with Jay and Matt.

'I feel so bad that I hid in the ambulance while Jay was

out there, unprotected, taking all the abuse and having rocks and bottles chucked at him.'

'Matt don't blame yourself. You did the right thing. You weren't hiding, you were just sheltering from the attackers. Jay probably should have waited for the police, but I know what he's like and he would have wanted to help the boy. Little shit.'

Caitlin was blazing mad on behalf of these two, hard-working paramedics who only wanted to help a teenager who had been hurt.

'Thanks, Caitlin. I feel like packing this job in. It's too stressful. We never even got a break.' Matt said indignantly.

'Goes with the territory I'm afraid.'

'How's Jay?'

'Doesn't look like a serious head wound but I'd be happier if he'd wake up. All his vital signs are okay.'

Caitlin continued to monitor Jay. Halfway to the hospital, he started moaning and opened his eyes.

'Jay, hi, are you waking up?' Caitlin leaned over him so she could whisper to him. 'Jay, you're going to be okay. We're nearly at the hospital. Can you talk to me?'

'Caitlin?'

'Yes, darling, it's me. Everything's going to be fine now. Matt's okay and you will be too. Do you remember what happened?'

'No.'

'That's okay, it'll come back to you.'

'Cait?'

'Yes, my love?'

But Jay closed his eyes again and Caitlin kept monitoring him until, thankfully, they pulled into the A&E ambulance bays.

Chapter Thirty-Two

Caitlin was relieved when she found out that Casey was the consultant in charge of A&E that day.

They rushed Jay into Resus and Matt was triaged and found to be unhurt physically but was traumatised by what had happened.

Caitlin rang Dan O'Connor's GP practice to leave a message for him to call her. She didn't have any other numbers to try and didn't want to bother Casey.

Caitlin, Sally and Matt waited for news of Jay who had been sent to the scanning department for an emergency CT scan to see if he had suffered any internal injury to his head.

'Do you want to talk about it?' Caitlin asked Matt when Sally went in search of drinks.

'No. I'll probably be offered some kind of counselling, but I'd rather just be home with Ben. I've rung him and he's picking me up.'

'Good. Did you mean it when you said you were thinking of giving up the job? I wouldn't blame you.'

'I don't know Cait, I love the job, but it's long hours and we don't always get a break. I find it really tiring. By the time my days off come round, I'm too knackered to enjoy them.'

Sally came back with the drinks. 'Don't ask me if this is tea or coffee. I pushed the right buttons, but I don't think they're attached to the right drinks. I hate vending machine drinks anyway. I've put lots of sugar in yours, Matt.'

'Thanks, Sally.'

They sat, sipping the strange concoctions passing for tea, and gazing at all the people waiting to be seen.

Sally whispered, 'I'd like to bet more than half these people could have gone to their GP. Waste of NHS time and money.'

'Very true. I should try Jay's parents again. Sally, if there's any news will you come and get me?'

'Of course I will.'

Caitlin put the empty plastic cup in a bin and then went outside to phone the surgery.

'I'm afraid he's in a meeting and can't be disturbed at the moment,' said Imelda, the office manager.

'Could you give me the O'Connor's private number?'

'Oh no, dear, I couldn't possibly do that. Confidentiality you understand.'

'Then could you ring Eloise O'Connor and tell her Jay is in A&E, please? I'm a paramedic who works with him. Could you give her my number?'

'Yes, I can do that for you. Is he alright?'

Why do people ask that? Of course he wasn't alright. What they really mean is—is he alive or dead?

'He's having a CT scan. We'll know more when we get the results.'

'Oh dear, poor Jay. Yes, I'll phone her straight away.'

Caitlin waited outside and breathed deeply. It was a pleasant day, warm, with the late September sun caressing her face. Far too nice a day for all the nastiness that had gone on.

Ten minutes later, her mobile rang.

'Is that Caitlin? It's Eloise O'Connor. I'm in the taxi so should be with you soon. Tell me the full story when I arrive. Are you okay, love?'

'Yes, I'm fine. See you soon.'

Caitlin started feeling emotional for the first time since she'd seen Jay lying in the road. She'd thought she was doing well, being calm and professional, but the sound of Jay's mum's voice, so caring and loving, threw her back into the reality of the situation. Jay could have died. He could have a severe head injury which could affect his cognitive ability. He couldn't remember what had happened. What if he lost his memory altogether? She couldn't bear it if Jay sustained permanent disabilities as a result of a group of lowlife scumbags…

'Caitlin.'

A taxi had pulled up and Eloise stepped out of it. Caitlin had never been happier to see someone in her whole life.

Eloise opened her arms and Caitlin stepped closer for a hug. She couldn't stop the tears that flowed, nor did she want to. No words were spoken but the women held on to each other in an unspoken unity.

Eventually Caitlin broke away. 'Jay is still in scanning. Sally said she'd let me know when they get a result.'

'Okay, thank you, dear. Now, tell me the whole story.'

So Caitlin and Eloise sat on a bench and Caitlin told her all she knew.

'A group of teenage boys with too much time on their

hands.' Eloise spoke calmly but Caitlin could imagine the turmoil that must be going on in her mind. The O'Connors were a close family. If you hurt one of them, you hurt them all. And Jay was Eloise's baby boy. Despite the fact he was thirty and fit as a butcher's dog, Eloise still saw him as the cheeky little boy he must have been.

'Right. Let's go and see if he's back shall we?'

'Eloise?'

'Yes, dear?'

'Is it okay if I hang around for a while? I want to know he's going to be alright.'

'Of course you can.'

They went back inside just as Sally was coming to find Caitlin.

Eloise and Caitlin went straight into Resus while Sally and Matt waited in the reception area.

Casey was there talking to Jay, who was now awake and looking better. He had a clean bandage on his head, having had staples to close the wound.

'Mum,' said Casey as they gathered around Jay's bedside.

Eloise bent over the bed and kissed Jay tenderly. 'How are you, darling?'

'I'll live, Mum.'

Caitlin hung back and let Eloise talk to her sons. But she watched Jay all the time. He kept catching her eye and she wished they could be alone. If they were, she would tell him. Just come straight out with it regardless of anything else like uncertainty, pride, not wanting to be rejected or hear that he loved someone else. She'd say, "I love you, Jay O'Connor, and I always will."

Casey was watching her and she realised that he had just asked her a question.

'Sorry, Casey, I didn't hear what you said.'

'It's okay. You must still be reeling from the experience of seeing your colleagues in that state. Are you okay?'

His voice was gentle, and Caitlin felt the tears behind her eyes again. This time she was going to be strong and she nodded.

'Yes, I'm fine. Like you say, it was an unpleasant experience, but Jay is the one we need to look after.'

'Well, you'll be pleased to know that Jay's scan is clear. No internal injuries, his wound is superficial. I don't think he needs to be admitted so long as he promises to do what he's told and rests up for a week or so.'

'I'll make sure of that,' said Eloise trying to be stern but not fooling anyone. Her phone rang and she said, 'It's Dan' before stepping out of the cubicle to take the call.

'Sally and Matt are still here. Can they come and say a quick hello? I know they're both frantic with worry over you, Jay,' Caitlin said.

'Of course. Anyway, I'm indestructible. It's one of my superpowers,' said Jay.

'Bollocks,' said Casey as he left the cubicle to see to another patient.

Then Jay and Caitlin were alone. They both spoke at the same time.

'I just want…'

'Jay…'

'Ladies first,' said Jay falling silent.

'I was so worried about you. Seeing you lying in the road, with the blood over your face, it made me realise that—'

'Hi, there, gorgeous, we just wanted to see how you were before we went off duty.' Sally came in, followed by Matt.

'Jay, are you okay? I should have done more, I'm so sorry.'

'What do you mean, Matt? You did exactly the right thing by taking refuge in the ambulance. I was the idiot that thought I was invincible instead of waiting for the police.'

Caitlin stepped back and let Matt and Sally talk to Jay.

Casey and a nurse came in and then Eloise. Caitlin's moment for telling Jay she loved him had gone.

'Your father's waiting at home for you and I've phoned for a taxi, so if you're ready, we'll get you home. It was lovely seeing you again, Caitlin. And nice to meet you two.' Eloise turned to Sally and Matt and they all hugged.

Caitlin left Jay in the bosom of his family and friends, feeling that she had just lost the opportunity to tell him how she felt. Next time, if there was a next time, she'd just come out with it. She had absolutely nothing to lose.

It was only when she got home that she realised no one had phoned Emma to tell her what had happened. Her name hadn't been mentioned. If Jay had been so smitten with her, wouldn't he have wanted to go home to the cottage to be with her? Instead, he seemed perfectly happy to be taken home to his parents' house. It was the right decision, obviously, as Jay needed the care and attention that he knew he'd get from his mum. Still, it was curious.

Chapter Thirty-Three

Dan O'Connor was waiting at home to see for himself how bad Jay's injuries were. Once he had satisfied himself that his youngest son was going to be okay, he went back to work.

When he had left, Jay went straight to bed, after taking some more painkillers as he had a crashing headache and felt a bit sick. He was also aching all over and discovered more small cuts and bruises that had been inflicted by rocks and bottles thrown at him.

He still felt shaken by what had happened. Why did a group of strangers hate the ambulance service so much that they would want to stop them from doing their job? The worst thing for Jay was the boy who had pretended to be injured, lying in the road in ambush. How long would he have stayed there if Jay hadn't got out of the ambulance to help him?

The police would want to talk to him and Matt, try to identify the teenagers involved. He doubted there would have been any CCTV to assist them. Jay tried to remember what the boy looked like as he was running away, but he was just a boy with no distinguishing features to pick him out in a line-up. He was slight, wore trainers and a hoodie and could run fast. Not much to go on. Could be any teenager in Leytonsfield.

Eventually, Jay fell asleep. When he woke it was late afternoon and the sun was just beginning to set. He looked at his phone and saw that he had fifteen missed calls. Emma. He'd forgotten to phone Emma.

'Emma, hi, sorry I haven't been able to phone before now.'

'Jay! Thank goodness. I've been worried sick, especially when you weren't answering your phone. When you didn't come home I thought something must have happened, so I phoned the control centre and they told me you were in hospital. I phoned the hospital and after hours of being put through to different people who couldn't help and were, quite frankly, useless, I spoke to your brother—'

'What? You spoke to Casey?'

'I was frantic, Jay, you have no idea what it's like being told someone you care about is hurt and you can't get any information out of anyone.'

'Sorry, Emma, but—'

'Then I finally got answers from Casey. He said you'd been ambushed and had a head wound. Are you alright? You could have died!'

Jay stood up and gazed out of the window at the garden. Leaves were just starting to change colour on the deciduous trees. Soon they would litter the lawn with gold, red, yellow, and brown. He loved autumn, it was his favourite season.

'Emma, calm down, I'm fine. I'm staying with my parents for a while. I need rest and—'

'Come home, Jay, I can look after you. I had a lovely meal all prepared, and I could practice my nursing.'

'What I need is for you to look after the cottage. Can you do that?'

'I want to be with you, Jay, can't I come and stay with your parents too?'

'No!' Jay spoke too sharply but the thought horrified him. 'Emma, listen—I really need you to look after the cottage. Please. I'll be back soon. I just need a few days' rest, that's all.'

'Can I come and visit you? I could bring you some food or whatever you need.'

Jay nearly laughed out loud at the idea of someone giving food to his mother. She would be deeply offended.

'Emma, I have everything I need here. Please just stay in the cottage and look after it for me.'

'Well, okay, if you insist.'

'Oh, I do. Thanks. I'll ring you later okay?'

'Tonight?'

'No, not tonight. Maybe in a day or so.'

'I don't mind if you want to ring me later on tonight. I've got no plans. Well, I haven't now.'

'Maybe this would be a good time to get stuck into your studies.'

Jay was desperate to get off the phone, but he didn't want to upset Emma.

'Oh, Jay, I can't concentrate on work, not when I think of the nightmare you went through. I just want to be with you, to comfort you.'

'Emma, I'm fine, okay? I'm with my family. I'll see you soon. Bye.'

Jay felt mean ending the call as he did, but he couldn't talk to her anymore, she was making his headache worse.

He put on an old towelling robe that was kept for members of the family who stayed the night. He thought it may have been Riordan's as it was too long for him, but it was comforting to wear. It smelt of home.

He wandered downstairs and was greeted in the hallway by SpongeBob who hurled herself at him, jumping up and dancing on her back legs until Jay picked her up.

'Hello, gorgeous girl!'

He carried her into the kitchen where his mum was rolling pastry.

'Hi darling, how are you feeling now?'

'Okay. I forgot to phone Emma. She wasn't happy.'

'Oh dear. We should have phoned her earlier. I didn't think.'

'Me neither.' Jay was far too busy thinking about Caitlin and how she had looked like an angel when he opened his eyes and saw her lovely face. He hadn't seen her for what seemed like ages and he'd been reminded how beautiful she was and how much he loved her. If there had been the chance to talk he would have asked her about the wedding and whether it was going ahead. He still had no idea if she was getting married or not.

'Jay, are you sure you're alright, darling? You look awfully pale.'

'I think I'll have a cup of tea and then I'll go back to bed.'

'Good idea. I'll make you one.'

His mother put the pastry in a bowl with a tea towel over it, then put the kettle on.

'It was lovely seeing Caitlin again,' she said.

'Yes.'

When the tea was made and they were both sitting at the kitchen table, SpongeBob in her basket keeping her eye on them both, Jay had the urge to tell his mother everything.

'Mum?'

'Yes, love?'

'I've got a problem.'

'Tell me.'

'I love Caitlin, but I think she's going to marry a complete moron called Brandon. Emma is acting as though we're a couple and I don't know what to do about it.'

'What are your feelings for Emma?'

'I don't have any. I was pleased when I thought she could be a housemate and help with the mortgage and bills, but she's completely taken over. She cooks a three-course meal every night, even when I'm on a late.'

'Is she a good cook?' Eloise sipped her tea and smiled.

'Yes, but not as good as you.'

'Well, that goes without saying, dear.'

Eloise poured more tea for them both.

'Is that all she does?'

'No. She buys things for the house. Cushions, rugs, bath-mats, vases of flowers. Do you think I'm over reacting? It doesn't sound that bad when I say it out loud.'

Eloise sat back in her chair. 'You need to talk to her. If this is the first time she's shared a house with someone, she may not know how to act. You could gently explain that, while you appreciate everything she does, it isn't how you want the relationship to be. Maybe arrange a day a week when she can cook for the two of you if that's what she wants and the rest of the time you both follow your own timetables.'

'Sounds easy when you say it like that.'

'Emma may be more reasonable than you think she is.

Perhaps a few days apart will help her to settle into her own routine.'

Jay got up and rinsed and dried his mug and then put it away in the cupboard. Eloise was still drinking. He didn't know anyone who drank as much tea as his mother.

'There's something else.'

'Caitlin?'

'Well yes, but something else apart from Caitlin.'

'Oh?'

'I'm thinking of travelling overseas again. I've been in touch with Steve to find out if I can join him on his travels. When I feel better. I just want to get away for a bit.'

Eloise stood up and held out her arms to him. They hugged and Jay felt the tension draining away. There was nothing like a hug from his mum to make him feel better.

'I think that's a splendid idea. Travelling is a great way to put things into perspective. I wish I'd done more when I was young. Oh, my darling Jay, I'm just so grateful that you're well and it'll be lovely to have you home so I can spoil you. Don't rush back too soon, will you.'

Jay kissed his mother's cheek. 'I promise. Right, I'm going back to bed now. Are the family coming?'

'I've told them not to come until tomorrow as you need your rest.'

'Good. Thanks, Mum. I love you.'

'Love you, too, sweetheart.'

Jay dragged himself back upstairs thinking how lucky he was to have his family to support him. He would talk to Emma and Caitlin when he felt stronger. Then, whatever happened, he would go travelling.

Jay fell asleep straight away. Later, he thought he heard his father's voice and his hand stroking the hair away from his face. But it could have been a dream. He didn't wake up until the morning.

Chapter Thirty-Four

Caitlin had the weekend off. A rare occurrence that she didn't want to waste. What she really wanted to do was see Jay but before she did that, she needed to find out about Emma. And the best way was to meet the woman in person.

When she arrived at the cottage, the first things she noticed were the hanging baskets on either side of the front door. Beautiful autumn colours blended with greenery. She recognised ivy, pansies, chrysanthemums, and asters. They were tastefully arranged, and the baskets looked professional. Caitlin couldn't remember there being brackets on either side of the door before. It made the front look completely different.

Before she rang the bell, she studied the cottage. Something else was different, but she couldn't put her finger on it. Then she realised, the curtains had been replaced by blinds.

Caitlin rang the doorbell with a heavy heart. If Jay was allowing Emma to make all these changes, then she really had got her feet under the table. And in such a short time as well. It had only been a few weeks since Caitlin moved out.

'Hello, can I help you?'

Caitlin was a bit shocked at how young Emma looked. And beautiful. Her hair was what Caitlin called "carrot" and her face was covered in freckles. She had a small nose and full lips and a wide-eyed innocent look that she imagined most men would find attractive.

'I said can I help you?' Caitlin realised she had been staring at Emma.

'Sorry, I'm Caitlin, I work with Jay.'

'Yes.'

'I think I may have left some earrings somewhere in the house when I was staying here. Would it be okay if I came in and had a quick look?'

'I haven't found any earrings and I've gone through the spare bedroom and cleaned it from top to bottom. I think I would have found them if there was anything to find.'

Emma clearly didn't believe her, but Caitlin was determined to look inside the cottage now that she was here.

'I think they may have dropped down the side of the couch or under the cushions. I won't take up too much of your time. Please.'

'I'm a bit busy at the moment. I'll have a look for you and let you know.'

Emma wasn't convinced and Caitlin changed tactics. 'Those hanging baskets are gorgeous! They improve the whole look of the front. Was that your idea?'

'Yes. I made them myself.'

'Really? Oh my goodness, you are clever. I bet you've made a lot of lovely additions to the cottage. There's nothing like a woman's touch.' An ironic statement if ever there was one as Caitlin had contributed nothing to the ambience of the cottage, except a load of miscellaneous stuff that Jay had forever been tidying up.

'Yes, I have. Well, I suppose you can come in for a couple of minutes and then you'll see for yourself.'

'Oh, thank you, that is so kind of you.'

Once she stepped over the threshold, Caitlin wondered if she had come to the wrong address. It looked so different, it took Caitlin's breath away. Rugs on the floor, different pictures on the walls—the cheap prints that furniture stores sell—vases of flowers on every surface. Caitlin wondered where the original pictures were, as she hadn't seen any of the ones that were clustered together before.

'Oh, this is wonderful! Are you an interior designer?' Caitlin hated the fact that she was being two-faced, but she still hadn't gained Emma's trust and knew she didn't have long to do so.

'No, but I am quite creative.'

'Absolutely! Right, I'll just have a quick look for my earrings.'

'Would you like some tea?' asked Emma.

Thought you'd never ask. 'I'd love some, thank you so much.'

Caitlin pretended to look for her imaginary earrings while keeping an eye on Emma. She moved about the cottage with a familiarity that stabbed Caitlin in the heart.

'So, how're you getting on with Jay then?' Caitlin asked with her hand down the side of the couch. She found a pound coin and half a dog biscuit.

'Oh, we're fine. I knew the minute I saw him, that he was the one for me.'

'Right. How did you meet?'

'We were at a social event and our eyes met across the room. So romantic. Do you take sugar?'

'Yes, one please.' Paul had said they'd met speed dating. Something strange there.

'Have you met the rest of the O'Connors yet?'

'Yes, of course. They're a lovely family.'

'Yes, they are.' Caitlin didn't have any more questions. She'd learned everything she'd come to find out. Jay and Emma were an item and she was beautiful and he…

'Jay said you're getting married too.'

Too— what did she mean, too? 'No, actually, the wedding isn't going ahead after all. In fact, could you tell Jay when you see him as I haven't had the chance to talk to him. I think he'd like to know.'

'Of course. I'll be seeing him later tonight. We never let a day go by without seeing each other, or at least talking on the phone. He wanted me to come and stay at his parents with him, but I knew I'd never get any work done so we compromised, and I go to say goodnight to him.'

'Are you studying?'

'Yes. I'm going to be a nurse. Jay and I have so much in common.'

'Can I just use your bathroom?'

'Of course. You know where it is.'

Caitlin ran upstairs and shut the bathroom door. It was like walking into an Aladdin's Cave of scents, candles, bottles of products in all colours of the rainbow. Caitlin shut her eyes and tried to stop the tears. Had Jay really fallen in love with this woman in such a short time? She looked around at everything and felt as if she was in a parallel universe.

What did she do now? She was no match for Emma, and it wouldn't be fair to tell Jay how she felt about him. It was too late. Emma had won and she had lost.

When Caitlin had got herself together, she went back downstairs. She couldn't wait to get away from the cottage and the impossibly perfect woman that had stolen Jay's heart. She'd lost him. The pain was excruciating but she would continue her cheerful act until she left.

Emma was in the kitchen, cleaning the surfaces. She wore Marigolds in bright pink that clashed with her hair. She turned as Caitlin stood in the doorway.

'Thank you so much, Emma, and I'm sorry I've disturbed you. I'll leave you in peace now.'

'Did you find your earrings?'

'No, sadly. Never mind, I'll keep looking.'

Emma smiled at her and Caitlin knew she hadn't believed a word of the earring story.

'Well, goodbye then,' said Emma.

'Goodbye and give Jay my love, won't you?'

'Of course.' Caitlin knew she'd do no such thing.

It was a lovely autumn afternoon and Caitlin didn't want to go home and face her mother. She was meeting Sophie later in Mellow, but now she just wanted to be alone with her thoughts. There was something strange about Emma and she needed to think about it.

Caitlin headed for Manor Park.

It was a perfect day. Warm autumn sunshine, blue skies and the leaves just starting to change colour. She wished she had SpongeBob with her. The little dog would love tramping through the woods and chasing things she could never catch. Maybe she should ask Jay if she could take her for a walk and then call in on Betty. She'd have to ring the nursing home first to make sure it was okay. Maybe she'd do that on Sunday before she went back to work on Monday.

Caitlin found a secluded bench near some trees and sat down.

She needed to make sense of Emma and Jay. Emma had lied by saying that they'd met at a social event. It wasn't a big lie though and Caitlin could understand her reticence in telling people she'd been speed dating. Some people, especially the quiet, shy ones, would find it hard to admit that they needed help in finding their life partner.

The thing that bothered Caitlin the most was the fact that Emma seemed too good to be true. Nobody could be as perfect as she seemed to be projecting. And she didn't think she'd met the real Emma. Even when she'd thought she was breaking down barriers, Emma's smile never reached her eyes. Emma didn't trust her, that was certain. Maybe she had seen through Caitlin's act. She had been playing a role, over the top with her praise. Perhaps Emma was too clever to be taken in.

Why was she focusing on the negative? Was it a case of sour grapes? She wanted Jay to be happy as she loved him. She realised now that she'd never loved Brandon. There had been a physical attraction there at the beginning, as he was a handsome man. Then, there was the fact that their families were close friends. She had thought that meant they had something in common. Now, of course, she realised it meant nothing of the kind.

Caitlin closed her eyes and concentrated on the feeling of warmth on her face and the smell of autumn in the air. Gradually she started to relax. She had two choices; she could forget Jay, except as a colleague—she'd still have to work with him sometimes—or she could be proactive and ask Jay outright. If he said he loved Emma, then that would be that. She'd wish them both well and admit she had lost.

But if he didn't love her…? What? Would she throw herself into his arms and declare undying love? Would he believe her?

Realising she was no further on and starting to feel hungry, she stood up and headed for home.

Chapter Thirty-Five

It was Saturday night and Mellow was buzzing. There were several groups of young women who were out for a good time. They were loud and sometimes raucous, screeching with laughter at something one of them said. There were also groups of young men, eyeing up the women.

Sophie and Caitlin watched them with amusement while they drank red wine and ate bar snacks. They had managed to get a table away from the main groups and settled down for a girlie chat with two bottles of Mellow's best red wine to be going on with.

'So, what's new, Cait?'

'Jay and Matt walked into an ambush when they attended a call-out and a large group of teenagers threw bottles and rocks at them.'

'OMG! That is horrific. How are they?'

'Jay got a head injury—suspected concussion—but he had a scan and it's clear, thank goodness. He's at home with his parents for a few days. Matt had the sense to climb into the back of the ambulance. He's shaken and was very scared but isn't hurt physically. The ambulance is a write-off.'

'That is awful! Have the police got the little shitbags?'

'I don't know, to be honest. I haven't seen Jay to ask him.'

'I can't believe there are people like that. What the absolute fuck!'

'My sentiments exactly.'

They drank their wine, musing on the awful people that exist in the world. Sophie shook her head and looked as if she wanted to find them and punch their lights out. Caitlin had calmed down since the incident. She was still furious on Jay and Matt's behalf but realised that being angry wasn't going to change anything. She would take her cue from Eloise O'Connor, who she admired more than any woman she had ever met and be calm amidst the chaos of life.

'I met Emma.'

'Emma who?'

'The woman who is living with Jay.'

'OMG! *That* Emma.'

Sophie filled their glasses to the top as if the revelation she was about to hear called for strong drink and lots of it.

'She's younger than I thought she would be and didn't smile much. And she lied about how she met Jay. Paul said they met speed dating, but Emma said it was a social occasion.'

'Well, to be fair, speed dating *is* a social occasion.'

'She was intimating that it was a proper party or event.'

'Is she pretty?'

'Very.'

'Bitch.'

'Exactly.'

They drank in silence for a while, listening to the groups

of young people all around them having loud, energetic fun. Caitlin was reminded of her hen night. Which reminded her of being handcuffed to Jay. If only she'd not been hung up on Brandon and could have seen that she had the perfect man right there, beside her.

'I've made a decision,' said Sophie grandly.

'Tell me more.'

'Well, you might think this is crazy in the light of what happened, but, if you think about it logically, you'll see it makes perfect sense.'

'What are we talking about?'

'I'm going to open my own business and offer dog-walking services to the rich and famous. They would have to be rich to afford my prices,' said Sophie.

'Right. Interesting idea. I take it you won't be putting any of the dogs on Instagram?'

'Oh no, this is purely taking the little darlings for a walk once or maybe twice a day. Depending on how much time I have and how many customers I get. You see them in New York all the time, people who start small with just a few dogs, then the demand grows, and they end up with a nice little business.'

'This isn't New York, Sophie, are there enough rich and famous people in Leytonsfield to keep you going?'

'Of course. If not, I'll travel further afield.'

'What about training? You have to know what you're doing, right?'

'Training for who? Me or the dogs?'

'Both.'

'There are courses to teach people everything they need to know. And how to run a business.'

'Well… good luck, I wish you well.'

'Thanks, honey.'

'Won't this interfere with your quest to find a husband?'

'Are you kidding?' Sophie sat back and waved her wine glass for emphasis. 'Haven't you heard that the way to a man's heart is through his dog? All those professional men out there who are too busy to walk their dogs are just waiting to meet a woman like me. A woman of independent means, a businesswoman, who loves dogs. I'll be fighting them off, Cait. Maybe you should come and work for me. Being a paramedic is far too damned dangerous. Move into a safer profession.'

'Dog walking?'

'Dog walking. And it may lead to other things. I might open a pooch parlour after I've learned how to groom the little darlings.'

'You won't just have tiny dogs like SpongeBob. You could have clients with Great Danes, or Alsatians. You'll have to learn how to handle all sizes.'

'I will not be put off. I can handle all sizes. And if I can't, I'll just have to stipulate a maximum weight or something. You can't put me off, Cait, I'm going to do this.'

Caitlin was laughing now. Being with Sophie always cheered her up. She was full of bright ideas, most of which failed spectacularly. But her enthusiasm for life was infectious, and Caitlin hoped that one day, Sophie would succeed at something that changed her life for the better.

'A toast,' said Caitlin, 'to your successful venture and may you meet the man of your dreams with a tiny dog.'

Caitlin phoned the nursing home on Sunday morning to be told that Betty wasn't having a good day, so her plans to take SpongeBob to see her had to be abandoned. Caitlin was disappointed on two counts; she wouldn't get to see Betty who she was growing fond of and she wouldn't have an excuse to see Jay.

It was obvious that Jay and Emma were an item, and a close one if the things Emma had told her were true, but that didn't stop her yearning to see Jay. She still loved him and feelings as deep as hers couldn't be turned off like a tap. She kept telling herself to move on and forget him, but it wasn't as easy as that.

Caitlin mooched about the house, wondering what to do with herself. Her mother was out with friends at one of her luncheons. Her mother worried her. She seemed to be in denial and attended all the functions she had always patronised. Just without her father. One day she would meet Alan and Heather at some social do and Caitlin hated to think what would happen then. She needed to face reality and plan for the future, but she had never had to make decisions like that for herself. Someone else had always done it for her. Mainly Alan.

Of course, Caitlin herself was in the same situation. She would need to start looking for somewhere to live, once the For Sale sign went up. The future was so uncertain, and it made her feel uneasy.

Caitlin was just about to make herself yet another pot of tea when the doorbell rang. She wasn't expecting Brandon to be standing on the doorstep.

'Brandon.'

'Can I come in? It's jolly cold out here.'

'Yes, come in.'

'Kitchen, is it? I'd love a coffee.'

'Of course.' Caitlin sighed as Brandon marched off down the hall.

Brandon sat down at the kitchen table and watched her

as she busied herself making two coffees. She used the coffee machine to make an espresso for Brandon and a latte for herself. She expected him to take his phone out and check his emails or his social media posts as he always did, but instead he sat and watched her. Caitlin found it unnerving.

Caitlin wondered if she should be polite and make small talk, but Brandon detested social chit-chat and whatever she said, it would probably be the wrong thing.

She put the coffee on the table, sat down and waited.

Brandon cleared his throat, then looked out of the window at the grey sky.

'Bit awkward.'

'What is?'

Brandon sighed but didn't look at her. 'Need to tell you something and you won't like it.'

'Oh?' Then the penny dropped. He was finishing with her because of the baby.

'Fenella and I... well we've been... we've known each other for a long time.'

'Yes, like you and I, Brandon. We've known each other since childhood, our parents being in the same business. It's a small world, isn't it?'

Caitlin sipped her coffee and watched Brandon's face. He was staring at her as if he'd never seen her before in his life. Caitlin realised the truth of that statement as she'd never been able to be herself around him, he'd always intimidated her too much. Now, however, she was being one hundred percent feisty paramedic Caitlin who was ready to tackle anything and anybody.

'Quite. Well, the thing is... I know I said we hadn't been seeing each other, but, well...'

'Oh for pity's sake Brandon, stop prevaricating and spit

it out. No, on second thoughts don't bother. I know what you're going to say as I saw Fenella the other night in Mellow and she told me she was pregnant with your child. Congratulations by the way, but you might want to tell her to stop drinking alcohol, it's not good for the foetus.'

'What? You know? Why didn't you say something? I told Fenella not to tell anyone. You're right about the drinking though. So, of course, the wedding's off. Between you and me, I mean. Have to do the right thing by Fenella. It's a chap's duty. I'm sure you understand.'

Brandon looked relieved and smiled at Caitlin. She stared at him with a blank expression and his smile vanished.

'There's one other thing though, poppet—'

'Stop calling me that stupid name!'

'Sorry… of course. Caitlin. Sorry. It's the business you see. The merger. Your father is refusing to play ball and says he's going to run the business himself. Never heard anything so ridiculous. He's risking losing everything.'

Caitlin said nothing. This was why Brandon was here. Fenella being pregnant was just incidental.

'So, you want me to convince my father to go ahead with the merger, despite the fact that we are not getting married? And you intend to marry Fenella?'

'Well, yes, that's about the size of it.'

'No.'

'What? What do you mean no?'

'It's the opposite of yes, Brandon. I know it's a word that you don't hear very often as you surround yourself with yes men, and women…' Caitlin realised she used to be one of his yes women, agreeing to everything the man said. But no more. 'Today, it's a no from me.'

'I don't understand, Caitlin, you're talking nonsense. I

do hope you're not having another breakdown. Shall I call your mother?'

'No, I'm not having a breakdown, in fact, I'm thinking more clearly than I ever have. And absolutely no to phoning my mother. She has her own problems which are none of your business. But the biggest no is to your request that I persuade my father to go ahead with the merger. Now, if you don't mind, I'm busy, so would you please leave.'

'Now, Caitlin, there's no need to be like this. It's clear to me that you are suffering—'

Caitlin stood up abruptly, pushing the kitchen chair over so that it hit the tiles with a clatter.

'The only thing I'm suffering from is having to listen to your voice, but fortunately, I don't suffer fools gladly anymore, so get out!'

'There's no need to—'

'Get out!'

Brandon stood up too and started to back away. 'It's obvious you have temporarily lost control of your senses, and I have no intention of staying here a moment longer. I hope you get the help you need. Goodbye, Caitlin.'

He turned his back on her and hurried out of the kitchen. She waited until she heard the front door slam, then picked the chair up and sat down again.

Caitlin felt drained. She was shaking, so she made herself another coffee then thought of the look on Brandon's face and started laughing. She laughed until tears rolled down her cheeks. Never again would she let another person control her or tell her how to live her life.

Chapter Thirty-Six

Much as Jay loved being home with his parents, even with the rest of the family popping in periodically to see how he was doing, he soon grew bored and was eager to get back to work.

The day after the incident he woke feeling awful. His head hurt and his whole body ached where the missiles had found their target. He did as instructed by his parents and stayed in bed for a couple of days, but then slowly began to heal and got up for short periods. There were plenty of jobs to do in the house and garden, and he took SpongeBob for leisurely walks every day.

Soon, with the combination of fresh autumn air, loving care, and his mother's cooking, he began to heal physically and mentally. He would never forget the fear that had overwhelmed him as he crouched in the road, his body being pummelled by bottles, rocks, and other missiles. He wasn't going to be beaten, however, and the only way to not let the perpetrators win was to go back to work and carry on a normal life.

The police had interviewed him, but he couldn't give them much of a description of the teenagers. Matt had visited him a couple of times with Ben and they had talked it through, trying to make sense of it all. There *was* no sense in it. It was a malicious attack for no reason, and they had to put it behind them and carry on. Matt had already returned to work and now it was Jay's turn.

He arrived home to find Emma waiting for him like a Stepford wife, even down to the apron she was wearing.

Jay had texted to say he would be coming home that afternoon and Emma must have worked non-stop to ensure the cottage was as spotless as she could make it. There were additions to the ornaments and soft furnishings that she had bought in his absence. The cottage was almost becoming a caricature of itself. A typical English cottage, chock full of knickknacks. Jay was in danger of feeling claustrophobic in his own home.

'Jay, welcome home, where you belong.' She came forward and shyly kissed him on the cheek.

'Hi Emma. How are you?'

'I'm a lot better now that you're back. I've been worried sick the whole time you've been away. I know you were with your family, but I could have looked after you just as well if you'd stayed here. Anyway, like I say, you're back now, where you belong.'

'Has anyone been round to see me? Any visitors at all?'

'Visitors? No, none.'

'Right. How's the studies going?'

'Oh, I haven't been able to do any with you not here. I couldn't concentrate on anything else. I wish you'd let me come and stay, or at least visit. Your parents wouldn't have minded, would they? Especially when I explained how concerned I was.'

'Well, I'm back now, so…'

'So everything's good.' Emma smiled and Jay started walking towards the stairs.

'Don't leave, dinner is almost ready. We're having salmon salad and Eton mess. I know how much you enjoyed the first one I made for you. Can I get you a drink first?'

'I ate a big meal at my parents and couldn't eat another. Sorry.'

'Oh, go on. I'm sure you could manage something. Just come and try. I'll serve the starter and then you can see how you feel. Maybe just have starter and dessert.'

'Emma, I'm honestly not hungry.'

Emma's face fell and she looked as if he'd slapped her.

'Oh. Okay then, I'll put it all in the fridge for tomorrow. I'm sure it'll keep.'

Jay hated to see Emma so downhearted, but he had to make her realise that all this attention on him was unhealthy from someone who was simply a housemate.

'Emma, listen. I think we need to have a talk. Sit down will you?'

'What have I done wrong?'

'You've done nothing wrong, but I think we need to clear a few things up.'

Emma perched on the couch. Jay chose an adjacent armchair.

'When I agreed that you move in, I meant it to be as a housemate, to help share bills, etc.'

'Is it the money? I can pay you more if that's the problem.'

'No, Emma, it's not the money. It's you.'

Emma's face crumpled and she started crying. 'I thought you liked me. When we met, you were so kind, and we've got so much in common. I've never lived away from home before and I was just trying to do the right thing.'

Emma was crying in earnest now and Jay felt guilty at upsetting her.

'Emma, listen. It's not you. You're pretty and sweet, a good cook and a great homemaker.'

'I am all those things, aren't I?' She blew her nose and tried to smile.

'Yes, you are. And I think we could be good friends in time.'

'Do you think,' she looked at him beseechingly, 'we could ever be more than friends?'

'No, because I love someone else,' Jay said.

'Who? No, sorry, you don't have to answer that, it's none of my business.'

'She's someone I work with.'

'A paramedic?'

'Yes.'

'Oh. Does she love you?'

'No. She's going to marry someone else.'

'Oh.' Emma fell silent and Jay wondered if he'd managed to get through to her.

'Emma, listen. Why don't I put the food you've made in containers and put them in the fridge, and we can have them tomorrow? And you go and have a rest because you've obviously worked really hard to get the cottage looking nice.'

'I'll do it. The kitchen is my domain, so I'll sort the food out. Do you think you might want something later? We can eat in a few hours if you like?' She got up and went into the kitchen.

'No, Emma, sorry, I won't.'

Jay was pleased with the rapid change in Emma. She

seemed almost cheerful again as she put the food into Tupperware containers.

Jay wandered into the kitchen and saw the overflowing pedal bin in the corner. 'I'll just empty the bin.'

He tied it up and then went out to the black bin just outside the kitchen door. He was amazed at how much was in it. Even with two people in the house, the black bin hardly ever got completely full. He noticed a cardboard box that should have been put in the recycling bin, not the one for general rubbish. He took it out and saw that it had held a Waitrose Eton Mess. So, Emma hadn't made it herself after all. But if she didn't have the time, that was okay with him, why did she feel the need to lie about it?

He looked for other boxes to put in the recycling and found ready meal boxes that had contained salmon and mixed salad. He took them out and then jumped as he realised that Emma was standing in the doorway watching him.

'What are you doing, Jay?'

'You should have put these in the recycling, Emma, that's all. No worries.'

'So you know my secret now. I sometimes buy stuff ready cooked. It's not a crime. I've been so busy trying to get the house looking nice, that I ran out of time.'

'I know. It's fine. Really, I'm okay with it. I don't expect you to slave all day to produce a three-course meal. In fact, I'll cook sometimes. We'll share the load.'

'Really? I thought that, being a man, you'd want me to do all the cooking and cleaning.'

'Not at all. Is that the kind of set-up you're used to? Did your father want his dinner on the table every day at the same time?'

'Yes, my mother relied on me to help with my three

siblings, but my father never lifted a hand to help. He said it was women's work. I suppose I thought all relationships were like that.'

'What we have is just a friendship, it's not a relationship and never will be. So long as you understand that this arrangement will work, but if you don't, then we're going to have to part company.'

'Oh no, please don't tell me to go! I love it here, Jay, love living in the cottage. I promise I'll change.'

Jay put the cardboard in the bin for recycling and turned back to Emma. 'I tell you what, I'll make us a drink and then we'll write down all the major tasks and we'll split them fifty-fifty. How about that?'

'I can make the drinks if you like.'

'No, I'll make them. Tea or coffee?'

'Coffee, please.'

'Right, go and get some paper and a pen and we'll get this sorted.'

They sat together on the couch and Jay wrote a list of things to be done, daily, weekly, and monthly. He then included his rota for the week and they shared the tasks equally.

'This woman you're in love with, is it the one who lived here for a while?'

'Caitlin, yes. Why?'

'No reason, I was just wondering.'

'Right. Now, I'll cook when I'm on an early shift or maybe we can have takeout.'

Jay realised that Emma wasn't really listening, so he put the paper and pen down to deal with later. Maybe she just needed a friend to talk to.

'I'm sorry, Jay, for the misunderstanding. I'm not very experienced with things. I'll try to do better, I promise.'

'Hey, you don't need to try to be anything. Just be yourself. I like you a lot, Emma, and I think we could be good friends, but I don't expect anything from you. And if you want friends round, or a boyfriend, that's fine too.'

Emma looked at her hands, clasped together in her lap. 'I don't have many friends. I had a couple at school, but they went on to university and I hardly ever see them. I left school when my mother became ill, to look after my brothers and sisters. She's got MS and it'll only get worse.'

'That's why you're doing A levels now?'

'Yes. The kids are old enough now to help Mum, so it's my turn. But sometimes I don't know how to be myself. Do you understand?'

'Of course. You're making up for it now and making a career for yourself. That's something to be proud of.'

'I'm glad I met you, Jay, and I wish things could be different. But I understand if you love someone else. Okay, shall we finish our rota now?'

Jay picked the paper and pen up and they continued to allocate tasks. He thought of how hard it must have been for Emma, being a carer at such a young age. He would do everything he could to help her to realise her dream of becoming a nurse.

Chapter Thirty-Seven

Caitlin was determined to take SpongeBob to see Betty on her next day off. She was happy to get out of the house as the atmosphere was oppressive. Her mother still blamed her for everything that had happened.

Her father was still promising her that things would be different now and he would be a better father to her.

Caitlin had been invited to Heather's for a meal and had a thoroughly enjoyable time. Heather was charming, and Caitlin could see how much in love the couple were. It felt strange for Caitlin to watch another woman with her father when she'd only ever seen him with her mother. Seeing her father so happy made her feel sad that she didn't have that kind of love in her life.

How could she compete with a woman like Emma? A gorgeous young woman with natural beauty that didn't need make-up to enhance it. Emma obviously adored Jay and he probably felt the same way. The fact that they'd only just met was incidental. They were proof that love at first sight really did exist.

Caitlin arrived at the O'Connors' just as Eloise had returned from the shops.

'You will stay for a drink, won't you, Caitlin?' said Eloise as she let her into the house.

'Just a quick one, thanks.'

SpongeBob was doing her dance and Caitlin scooped her up in her arms and cuddled her.

'I have so missed this little one. Have you missed me, Princess?'

'I'm sure she has. I saw her Instagram posts and was impressed. Your friend is obviously artistic and has a flair for style.'

'Sophie is full of bright ideas, but somehow they never seem to amount to anything.'

Caitlin sat at the kitchen table and told Eloise all about Sophie's plans to be a professional dog walker and, in her usual way, Eloise listened but didn't criticise. She was the kindest person Caitlin had ever met and she wished she could confide her feelings for Jay. But it wouldn't be fair on Eloise. Jay loved Emma and she had no right to complicate things for them.

'And what about you, Caitlin? Are you still getting married?'

'No. We're not together anymore.'

'I'm sorry to hear that.'

'He was seeing another woman and has made her pregnant. He never loved me. I realise that now. We were pushed together by our parents and he was my first serious boyfriend.'

'Oh, Caitlin, that's awful, I'm so sorry.'

'Don't be, I'm not. That's not all,' Caitlin said, 'my father has been having an affair for the past five years. The house is up for sale, I'll have to find somewhere to live, and everything's falling apart.'

'Oh, my dear girl, come here.' Eloise held out her arms to Caitlin who stood up and moved into the embrace gladly. As she was enveloped in Eloise's arms, she wished that she were her mother. Then felt disloyal for thinking that. But her own mother had never hugged her like that, a feeling that she was being wrapped in a warm blanket of love and acceptance that she never wanted to move away from.

When the hug was over, Caitlin sat back at the kitchen table. There was no point in wishing for things that were out of reach. Being with Jay and part of the O'Connor family. She had to face reality and start looking for a flat or bedsit to rent.

'If there's anything we can do, please tell us won't you?'

'Yes, thanks, Eloise, I will. If I could come and see SpongeBob now and again, that would be good. And of course I'll take her to see Betty as often as I can.'

'Of course. Whenever you want. Just let me know when.'

———

Betty was delighted to see her little dog again. The reunion was joyous with SpongeBob wriggling with delight and desperate to get on Betty's knee and the old lady hugging and kissing her.

Caitlin was pleased to see that Betty looked a lot better. She had more movement on her left side and was having intense physio to strengthen her left arm and leg, to the point that she could walk, slowly, with support on her left side.

'Good for you, well done, Betty,' said Caitlin as she

hugged her friend. Betty had stopped being just a patient a long time ago and was now a close friend.

It was October with the days getting shorter and the weather changing. There was a definite nip in the air, so they stayed in Betty's room for the visit.

Betty spoke slowly and Caitlin sometimes had to ask her to write things down, but most of the time she could make herself understood and mentioned that there was a chance that she could go home with carers coming in each day to make sure she had everything she needed and to prepare meals if necessary.

'That's wonderful, Betty, I'm so pleased for you. I bet you're desperate to get home.'

Betty nodded and smiled. For an independent spirit like her, it must be awful to think that this was as good as it got and she might have to spend the rest of her days in a nursing home, no matter how good the home was and how caring the staff. She'd want to be in her own home, with SpongeBob and her own things around her.

Betty pointed to the top drawer in her chest of drawers and pointed to Caitlin.

'Something for me?'

Betty nodded and Caitlin opened the drawer to find a white envelope with Caitlin and Jay written on it.

Caitlin frowned. Why both their names?

'Do you want me to read it now?'

Betty nodded and said yes. She waved her hand at Caitlin to hurry up.

Caitlin sat down and opened the envelope. It was a sheet of A4 with writing on it, headed To Jay and Caitlin. There was no preamble, Betty got straight to the point.

There's a few things I want to say.

Firstly, thank you both, from the bottom of my heart, for being kind, good friends. Thank you for looking after SpongeBob so well and bringing her to see me. I wouldn't have survived this stroke if it wasn't for you two. You gave me something to look forward to in seeing you and my dear little dog. All the struggles I've been through, all the pain, the discomfort and the frustration was worth it because the end is in sight. I will go home soon.

The other thing I wanted to say concerns the two of you. Anyone can see that you love each other. Real, true love that will last.

I know life hasn't been easy for you lately, Caitlin, and you deserve some happiness. I believe you'll find it with Jay.

Jay, you have loved Caitlin for a long time, and you've been the best kind of friend to her while she sorted out her life and realised that all she needs is right there beside her.

I want you to know that I understand. I was young and in love once. But don't delay too long. Life is short and gone before you know it. Stop wasting time! Don't spend the rest of your lives regretting the things you didn't do, and the chances you didn't take.

Live life to the full. Travel. See the world while you can. Then settle down and make babies. For they are the future and one day you'll be ready to hand the baton to them. I deeply regret I couldn't have children of my own. Don't be like me.

And know that as long as you have each other, you have every-thing you need.

Love and God bless to both of you.

Betty and SpongeBob.

Caitlin was crying by the time she had read the note. Betty was watching her with a smile and eyes full of love.

'Thank you,' she said.

Chapter Thirty-Eight

'Hello, stranger, how's things?' he asked.

Jay and Caitlin were working together, the first shift for a long time, and Jay was thrilled.

'I know, it's been ages. Are you fully recovered now? You must be or you wouldn't be back at work.'

'Fit as a flea now, thanks for asking. Matt is doing well too.'

'I'm glad.'

'Did they ever find the boys who did it?'

'No. Not enough evidence. All the people standing around watching would have known who they were but...' Jay let his sentence trail off and Caitlin picked up on his meaning.

'But they weren't going to rat on their kids, or neighbours' kids.'

'Exactly. Case closed. I'm not thinking about it anymore, just getting on with my life.'

'The best way.'

'Yep.'

Caitlin was driving and Jay kept his eye out for the jobs coming through. He loved being a paramedic and always gave it one hundred percent, but today, he wished he could drive off with Caitlin somewhere where they could be alone and talk properly. About things that mattered. Usually, the banter in the ambulance was light-hearted and frivolous, something to say in between jobs. The switch to be fully on and ready to save a life, from having an emotional heart to heart would be too much.

Even so, Jay had to know if Caitlin was still marrying her Hooray Henry.

'Caitlin?'

'Yes?'

Just before he asked his question, a job came through.

'Never mind, it'll keep. What have we got? Male thirty-six, lives alone, overdose.'

'Right, let's go.'

When they pulled up outside the house, Caitlin frowned. 'I've been here before.'

'Overdose?'

'Yes, it was. He'd taken paracetamol.'

'Okay, let's go and see what we can do.'

'Hello, ambulance service,' Caitlin called as she pushed open the front door. Same as last time, Mike had conveniently left it open for them.

Mike was sitting in the same armchair as the first visit, staring into space. On the coffee table in front of him, sat a small bottle of pills.

'Hi, Mike, remember me? I came to see you a while back.'

Mike shook his head and didn't look at her.

'I'm Caitlin and this is Jay.'

'What have you taken, Mike?' said Jay as he picked up

the bottle. Fluoxetine; more commonly known as Prozac. 'Have you taken some of these?'

Mike nodded and then started crying.

Caitlin knelt down next to him and gently rubbed his shoulder. 'How many, Mike?' she asked.

'I don't know,' he sobbed.

'Okay. We need to take you to hospital. Will you come with us?'

Mike nodded and Caitlin looked at Jay who was still examining the bottle of pills. He put it in his pocket, and they helped Mike stand up and guided him into the ambulance.

'I'll drive,' Jay said. He knew Caitlin should be the one to sit with the patient as she'd seen him before and may be able to get more information from him.

'Ready, Jay,' Caitlin called, and Jay switched on the sirens and lights and pulled away from the house.

Mike had been drowsy which was a sign of fluoxetine overdose. The symptoms started out as mild but could rapidly escalate. He could hear Caitlin gently talking to Mike to get him to open up to her. He could have taken other tablets and the bottle Jay had in his pocket was three-quarters full.

If asked his opinion, Jay would have said that Mike's overdoses weren't true suicide attempts, instead they were a cry for help. He didn't want to die, he just wanted someone to listen. GPs were busy and although they did their best to help depressed patients—the fluoxetine had been prescribed by Mike's GP—it wasn't enough. He needed a mental health team referral and they needed to see him urgently.

Jay was relieved when they arrived at the hospital and could get Mike the help he desperately needed.

It was lunchtime and, although paramedics were often too busy to take their breaks, today, Caitlin and Jay signed off and said they were taking time off for lunch.

Jay suggested buying a sandwich or pie from a deli or cake shop and sitting in the ambulance to eat. Caitlin agreed. She wanted to ask him about Emma.

While they were munching sandwiches and doughnuts and sipping coffee, Caitlin was thinking of how much she had missed Jay. She loved his company. Just being in the immediate vicinity as him, even if they weren't speaking, she felt at peace, happy. No one else had ever affected her like that.

Caitlin sighed.

'Penny for them?' said Jay.

'I was just thinking how much I enjoy working with you,' she said.

'Why does that make you sad?'

'I'm not sad, Jay. Well, maybe a bit.'

'So… are you still getting married? To Brandon?'

Caitlin collected all the paper bags from their lunch and put them in a carrier bag to dispose of later. She had told two people to let him know that the wedding was off. Paul and Emma. And she had told Eloise. All this time she had thought that Jay knew and hadn't bothered contacting her.

'No, the wedding's cancelled. I told Paul but he obviously didn't tell you.'

'He never said a word. Perhaps he forgot.'

'Yes, perhaps. And I told Emma and your mother.' Caitlin watched his face to see his reaction to the mention of his new girlfriend's name.

Jay frowned and shook his head. 'I haven't seen my

family since I came back to work. Emma didn't mention it either. When did you see Emma?'

'It was when you were staying with your parents, after the attack.'

Now she would have to confess all. Admit that she only wanted to see what Emma was like. What would he think of her? A nosy bitch probably.

'I don't understand. If you knew I was at my folks, why did you go to the cottage?'

'It was Emma I wanted to meet.'

'But... why?'

'Because you two are an item and I wanted to check her out, make sure she was good enough for my bestie.' Caitlin laughed to try to keep it light-hearted, but Jay's face was a picture of bewilderment.

'We're not an item. She's renting the spare room, that's all. I needed someone to help with the bills and, fortunately, she's happy to look after the house while I go travelling.'

Caitlin was the bewildered one now.

'I don't understand. Paul told me you two were going out. You'd met speed dating and it was serious. And when I went to the cottage, Emma gave me the impression that you two were an item as well. All the things she'd done to the cottage: hanging baskets, cushions, rugs, candles. And when did you decide to go travelling?'

The radio in the ambulance alerted them to the fact that they'd been incognito for too long. Caitlin reported back to base that their break was over. Immediately they got a job. A woman with chest pains. Jay switched the sirens on, and they sped away.

'Jay, we need to talk. People are obviously not passing on accurate messages. Can we meet after work?'

'No problem. Shall I come to yours?'

'Yes, come round tonight.'

'Okay.'

Caitlin vowed that she would tell him the truth. That she loved him and wanted to spend the rest of her life with him. But she put all personal feelings to one side to concentrate solely on the patient they were rushing to help.

Chapter Thirty-Nine

Jay arrived home to find that Emma was out. She had left a note on the kitchen table that said she was speed dating again and not to wait up. A big change from the Emma who had greeted him like a 1950s housewife after the ambush. Ever since they had talked, Emma had been the perfect housemate. They were good friends, laughed and joked together, and shared the chores in the house.

Jay had a shower, put a ready meal in the microwave, then opened his emails to see if there was one from Steve. He was eager now to be off, travelling to some exotic destination. The only problem was Caitlin. Her revelation today that she was not getting married after all left the way clear for him. He had a decision to make. To stay at home and try to win Caitlin's heart, or to go travelling with Steve and leave behind all the heartache, uncertainty, and pain of the last few months. It should be a clear cut decision as he loved Caitlin more than life itself, but the truth was, he didn't know how she felt about him and he could never give her the lifestyle that Brandon, or another man from their world, could give her. She had spent her life in luxury and Jay wondered how hard it would be for Caitlin to give it up.

There was an email from Steve, but it wasn't the one he was expecting. Steve was returning to England as he felt homesick and missed his family. He apologised profusely to Jay who he knew would be disappointed by the news. Travelling was wonderful and he'd recommend it, but it could get lonely if you were doing it alone. Steve urged Jay to find someone to go with.

As Jay ate his ready meal, he thought about Caitlin. She'd be the perfect travelling companion. He pictured them strolling at midnight on a tropical beach, the moon spreading a silver path on the sea and the air warm and filled with the fragrance of exotic blooms.

Jay threw the rest of his meal in the bin and cleaned his teeth vigorously before jumping on his bike and driving round to Caitlin's parents' house.

As Jay pulled up outside the house, he felt again the sense of awe that such a beautiful property evoked. There was a For Sale sign outside and Jay wished he had a spare million pounds knocking around so he could buy the property for Caitlin and himself. Or maybe just for Caitlin if it turned out she didn't feel the same way about him as he did for her. He would still buy her the house. He would give her the moon and stars if he could.

The front door opened, and Caitlin appeared.

'Hi,' said Caitlin.

'Hi,' replied Jay, 'Is it okay to leave the bike here?'

'Yes, it'll be safe.'

Jay climbed off and put his helmet in the storage box. He followed Caitlin into the house.

The hallway was wide and spacious. Doors off to both sides were polished wood, as were the skirting boards. There was a parquet floor and the carpet on the stairs was red with a silver fleur- de-lis pattern. It was spotlessly clean and tidy. Someone had gone to a lot of trouble to clean the house thoroughly before putting it on the market. He guessed that someone wasn't Caitlin. They had obviously had professional cleaners in.

'Are your parents at home?' asked Jay. The last time he'd seen Caitlin's parents was when she was in hospital after crashing Sophie's car. They hadn't been especially friendly towards him.

'No. My father lives with Heather now and my mother's gone away for a few days.'

'Right.'

'Let's sit in the kitchen and I'll make you a drink.'

Despite the kitchen being large, it managed to be cosy as well with an island in the middle and stone flags on the floor. It had the country kitchen feel to it; homely and snug.

'Would you like tea or coffee?'

'Tea would be good, thanks.'

Caitlin made a pot of tea and Jay watched her. She still looked sad and Jay wondered if she was heartbroken at not marrying Brandon.

'I'm sorry to hear that the wedding's off. What happened?'

Caitlin carried the teapot to the table and Jay collected the mugs, then poured the tea for them.

Caitlin stared into space as she sipped her tea. She held the mug as if it was warming her hands even though the heat was on in the kitchen.

'Brandon had never stopped seeing Fenella and she got

pregnant. He felt he had to do the decent thing and they're getting married.'

'The cheating bastard,' said Jay. 'I'm sorry, Cait, you've had an awful time recently, haven't you? Your fiancé and your father both having other women.'

'Well, like you told me once, there's always two sides to every story. I've met Heather and I really like her. She's going to work with my father to make the business successful. They're in love and it's good to see. My father is like a different person. He smiles, jokes, and has done a complete U-turn in his view of the ambulance service. He can't praise paramedics enough for saving his life.'

'What about your mother? She must be cut up about your father having an affair for so long.'

'I don't really know how she feels because she won't talk to me. I do know that she never loved my father and has always known that he had other women.'

'Why did she put up with that?' Jay couldn't understand how any marriage that wasn't based on love and respect could survive. Clearly the Hewitts marriage hadn't.

'My mother used to be a model, and a successful one. Her pictures graced the covers of Vogue in her heyday. I think my father thought of her as an asset who would look good on his arm at business functions. And in return, my mother got a hard-working man who kept her in luxury and turned a blind eye to her occasional dalliances. She's gone on holiday with a friend and I wouldn't be surprised if she returns with a man in tow.'

What a way to live, thought Jay. So unlike his own parents who had always worked together for everything they had gained in their lives. They consulted each other on every decision that they made and worked as a team.

'Where will you live when the house is sold?'

'I'll probably stay at Sophie's for a while. I haven't really thought about it. Anyway, I want to hear about all the travelling you're going to be doing with Steve.'

Jay laughed. 'Steve emailed me today. He's coming back to England, so I won't be travelling with him.'

'Oh no, that's a shame. What will you do?'

'I'm still going to go travelling, Caitlin, I need to get away. So… I was wondering if you'd like to come with me? Now that you're not getting married and you'll soon be homeless, it's the perfect time.'

'Me? Oh, no… I don't think I could. I need to stay here for my parents. And Sophie is starting a new business. They need me.'

Caitlin wouldn't look him in the eye, so Jay stood up and knelt at Caitlin's feet. He took her hands in his.

'There's something I haven't told you, even though I've been longing to say it for so long. I love you, Caitlin, and I want to spend the rest of my life with you. I'm not asking you to come with me as a friend, but something more; lover, boyfriend perhaps. Imagine how good it would be getting away from Leytonsfield for a year or so, just leaving it all behind. Doesn't that sound appealing?'

'You love me. Jay, did you just say you loved me?'

'Yes, I love you. I don't know how you feel about me, so I don't expect you to say it back—'

'Oh, Jay, you have no idea how much I've wanted to tell you, too. I love you too, Jay, so much.'

'Really?'

'Yes, really.' Caitlin stood up and pulled him up onto his feet. 'Kiss me.'

Jay kissed her. At first it was gentle, then deeper and passionate. Then Jay picked her up and she wrapped her legs around his waist. He put her on the kitchen table

without their mouths breaking contact. The kiss went on...
and on until Jay knew he was going to explode if he
couldn't make love to her. He cupped her face, then moved
downwards until he was cupping one breast through her
clothes. She moaned and shivered.

'Let's go upstairs,' she whispered, and Jay didn't need
telling twice.

Jay picked Caitlin up in a fireman's lift, throwing her
over his shoulder and making for the stairs.

Caitlin squealed and giggled all the way up to the next
floor.

'Which way?' he gasped when he got to the top.

'Left, third door.'

Luckily, the door to Caitlin's bedroom was open and he
dropped her onto her bed and fell on top of her, making
sure he didn't squash her. He kissed her again, this time
with even more passion. He slid his hand under her blouse
and found her breast, playing with the nipple that was
standing erect. Caitlin moaned and Jay helped her off with
her blouse, then unclipped her bra.

He kissed her breasts. They were small and beautiful,
with rosy pink nipples that he loved. Even though Jay had
only ever seen Caitlin naked once before, he remembered
every second of the encounter and had often dreamed that
they were together again.

'I've got no condoms,' he said wishing he'd had the fore-
sight to bring some with him, but he had never dreamed the
day would end like this. He still couldn't believe that Caitlin
had told him she loved him.

'My father's left some in his bathroom cabinet. I'll get
them,' said Caitlin as she scrambled off the bed and hurried
out of the room.

Jay pulled his T-shirt off, then sat on the bed and waited

for her to return, which she did a minute later. She handed the condoms to him.

Caitlin straddled him. Her breasts pushing against him were sending messages to his groin and he lay down. Caitlin slowly unzipped his jeans and caressed his erection. He was desperate for her but wanted to make it last, so he moved her gently onto the bed and removed her jeans, so she was just wearing her panties.

Jay put his face between her legs, breathing in the sweet, musky scent of her. He nuzzled her through the material until she writhed on the bed. Then he slipped off her pants to find her wet and ready for him. But he wanted to make her come first as he suspected that when he entered her, he would go off like a rocket as he was so aroused. So he used his tongue to tease her and he caressed her inner thighs and Caitlin groaned and wriggled until she gasped out his name.

Jay licked her clitoris until he brought her to orgasm, and she clung to him and cried out loud, and he held her until her climax was over. He loved the way she climaxed, with her eyes shut and her head thrown back, crying out with complete abandon. The thought he could bring her to such ecstasy made him feel good.

'I want to feel you inside me,' said Caitlin.

Jay quickly sheathed himself and gently entered her. She was perfect and they fitted together as if they were made for each other. He moved slowly at first, hoping Caitlin would have another orgasm, but he didn't know how long he could wait. Fortunately, Caitlin was still aroused, and she wrapped her legs around his waist and clung to him, moving in time to his thrusts. Jay watched her face. Her eyes were shut and her mouth open as she got closer and closer to a climax.

They moved together as one and reached orgasm at the

same time. Caitlin cried out, louder this time and Jay also let go with cries of his own.

He lay beside her, spent and happy.

'That was…'

'Yes, it was so…'

'Amazing!' they said together.

After Jay disposed of the condom, they lay together, wrapped in each other's arms, and fell asleep.

Chapter Forty

It didn't take long for the Hewitts house to sell, and, as the new owners wanted to take possession as soon as possible, Caitlin had moved in with Sophie.

It was Friday night, the end of another long, arduous week and Sophie and Caitlin had gone to Mellow for their usual wine and catch up. It had become a ritual that neither wanted to break, even though they were now living in the same house.

Sophie was upbeat, full of news of her new business which was starting to take off.

'I've got three dogs to walk now, and if I do a good job, hopefully, by word of mouth, I'll get more customers.'

'That's great, Soph.'

'Of course, I'll advertise as well. I'll put posters in shops and I'm thinking of a small ad in *Leytonsfield Life*. What do you think?'

'Yes, go for it.'

Sophie sat back in her seat and folded her arms.

'If I'd told you I was walking two elephants and a tyrannosaurus rex, you wouldn't have turned a hair, would you? You haven't heard a word I've just said.'

Caitlin put her hands over her face and groaned. 'I'm sorry, Sophie, but all I can think about right now is Jay. He's leaving the UK tonight.'

'Tonight? I didn't know it was as soon as that.'

'He brought the date forward as he couldn't wait to get away. He's not happy with me at the moment. He said that if I loved him, really loved him, I would go with him.'

'Well, he has got a point. I've never really understood why you won't. I mean… your father's with Heather now and happy. And your mother… well, let's face it, she'll never be happy, but that's not your problem is it?'

'She needs me. It's a big upheaval for her, losing her home and her husband. I want to be there for her when it all gets too much.'

Sophie sipped her wine slowly. She had decided to cut down on the alcohol as she had to get up early to do dog walking and getting plastered every night wasn't conducive to a six o'clock start.

'Can I say something, and you won't get upset?'

'Depends what it is.' Caitlin felt that anything would upset her at the moment.

'Well, I'm going to say it anyway. Your parents don't need you, Caitlin. You have always needed them, and at the crucial times of your life when you needed them the most, they haven't been there for you. Even now, with all the changes going on, they're not thinking of you. Oh, I know your father and Heather asked you if you wanted to live with them, but it was obvious they'd rather be alone.'

'They're in love and I didn't want to play gooseberry.'

'And what about your mother? When has she ever thought about your needs?'

Caitlin stared at the table, not wanting to see the anger in Sophie's eyes.

'My mother needs me. She may not acknowledge it, but she does.' Even as Caitlin said it, she didn't believe it herself.

'Really? Since when? And has she apologised to you for forcing Brandon on you?'

Caitlin looked up then and laughed. 'The word "apology" is not in my mother's vocabulary. My father apologised though.'

'Well, at least that's something.'

Sophie sipped some more wine. 'Okay, level with me now. I'm your bestie and I have nothing but your welfare at heart. And, in my view, you're extremely unhappy. You love Jay but you won't go with him. Why?'

Caitlin sat forward and lowered her voice, even though, as the wine bar was full with the usual Friday night crowd, nobody could have heard her.

'I'm scared.' She looked at Sophie and saw the puzzled frown on her face. 'I've never been in love before. Not like this. The way I feel about Jay is scaring me to death.'

'For goodness sake, why?'

'Brandon was my only real boyfriend. He called the shots and I just followed. He told me he loved me but…'

'But?'

'Brandon said things because he thought they were the right things to say. There was never any emotion there. When Jay told me he loved me, it was like every romantic novel I've ever read, every film I've ever seen. I felt as if I was walking on air, flying… oh God, I don't know.'

'And that scares you?'

'Losing it does. What if we get to some foreign country and Jay realises he's made a mistake? What if he dumps me because he meets someone else?'

'What if *you* realise *you've* made a mistake or meet someone else?'

Caitlin shook her head. 'That would never happen, never in a million years. I love Jay so much, it hurts, and I want to be with him.'

Sophie leant forward, smiling. 'And I bet if you asked Jay the same question, you'd get the exact same answer. He's loved you for a long time, Caitlin. On your hen night, he was knocking back shots as if they were going out of fashion just for the privilege of being handcuffed to you. A man who doesn't drink that much allowed himself to get drunk for you. That's love, girlfriend.'

Caitlin remembered her hen night and smiled. 'Did Jay really win?'

Sophie grinned. 'Put it this way—I wasn't going to allow you to be stuck with the FBB bitch all night when Jay was champing at the bit.'

Caitlin searched the pockets of her jacket for a tissue to wipe away the tears that had fallen at the thought of losing Jay forever. She found one and pulled out a folded piece of paper with it. She frowned and opened it out.

'What've you got there?' asked Sophie.

When Caitlin realised what it was, she put her hand to her mouth. 'Oh no! I'd forgotten all about it.'

'What? What is it? Tell me!'

'It's a letter that Betty wrote to me and Jay. I promised I'd pass it to Jay and I completely forgot about it.' Caitlin handed the note to Sophie and she read it quickly. 'What shall I do?'

'What time's his flight?'

'Eleven.'

'So, he'll need to be at the airport a couple of hours beforehand. We've got time. Come on!'

'Sophie! We won't have enough time.'

'Bags of time. I have a new car, remember. It can do nought to eighty in seconds.'

'Okay, but don't forget the speed limit's seventy.'

Jay had arrived at the airport three hours before his flight, but hadn't checked in. He wanted to give Caitlin enough time to get there. Even though she'd said no to waving him off, he hoped she'd change her mind.

Jay had been ecstatic when Caitlin had said she'd loved him too. Being with her, making love, and then lying in her bed, naked and satiated, was the best feeling he'd ever had.

He'd spoken to Josie and asked her opinion. As twins, they told each other everything and she was always capable of getting to the heart of the matter. She had told him that if Caitlin needed more time, then he should give it to her. Caitlin had been through a lot over the last few months and he should be supporting her, not giving her ultimatums.

Jay bought himself a coffee and sat and people-watched. Couples, young and old, families and people on their own, moved through the airport like a constant breeze. Some were obviously veteran travellers, some were not and looked bewildered as if they had no idea what they were doing or which queue to join. Jay watched them disinterestedly. Usually he was entertained by people but today all he could think about was Caitlin.

He realised that he needed proof that Caitlin loved him, and he had thought that by agreeing to travel with him, she would be proving her love. But she said no to the travelling. Then he had asked her to come to see him off. Again she'd said no.

Now Jay didn't know what to think. Caitlin had thought she'd been in love with Brandon and she'd happily gone along with everything he suggested. She'd sworn that she loved him but refused to go with him. Perhaps Caitlin didn't love him at all.

Determined to give her the benefit of the doubt, Jay bought himself another coffee and waited.

Chapter Forty-One

Sophie's new Toyota RAV4 flew down the motorway on the way to Manchester airport. She was going for practical this time as the car had plenty of space for the dogs.

Caitlin realised she was biting her nails again and pulled the sleeves of her sweatshirt over her hands to stop herself.

'We'll get there, stop panicking.'

'He wanted me to see him off, but I thought it would be too upsetting, so I said no. I wish I'd said yes now.'

'Caitlin, stop stressing. We'll get there, don't worry.'

'What if he's changed his mind? I'm no good at relationships.'

'That's because you've never had a proper one,' said Sophie, changing lanes to overtake a slow-moving lorry.

'What about Brandon?'

'What about him? Your relationship with Brandon was all about him telling you what to do. Relationships should be about sharing, respecting each other, and compromise.'

'I should have compromised, shouldn't I?'

'No, I think Jay should have. You didn't tell him you

wouldn't go travelling, you just said you couldn't leave now. That's fair enough with everything you've got going on in your life.'

Caitlin had started chewing the cuff of her sweatshirt and folded her arms to stop herself.

'You think I should have gone with him?'

'It doesn't matter what I think. It isn't right for you at the moment.'

Caitlin groaned. 'Why is life so hard?'

Sophie grinned. 'It'd be too boring if it were easy. Right, we're here, there's the turn-off for terminal two.'

It was time to join the queue for security for the flight to Hong Kong. Jay had drunk so many coffees he was buzzing. He had been hoping to sleep on the eleven-hour flight but suspected he'd be awake for most of it, regretting the things he'd done.

She wasn't coming. He had to face it. Maybe she didn't love him after all. He stood up and picked up his hand luggage, then heard his name being called.

'Jay! Wait!'

Jay turned around and saw Caitlin and Sophie running towards him. They were both out of breath and must have run all the way.

He waited until they reached him then opened his arms and Caitlin flung herself into them. They held each other tightly and Jay buried his face in her hair. He daren't hope that she was coming with him as she had no luggage and no ticket, but she had come to say goodbye and that meant a lot.

'You came. I knew you would.'

'I came to tell you I love you and to give you this.'
Caitlin handed him a piece of paper.

'What's this?'

'Betty wrote us a note and I promised I'd give it to you
after I read it, but I forgot. I'm really sorry, Jay.'

'Can I read it now?'

'No, read it on the plane. And know that I wasn't saying
no to travelling, just not right now. And I'll wait for you to
come home. I'll be here waiting. I love you Jay, more than I
can express.'

'I love you, Caitlin. Thank you for coming to wave me
off, it means a lot.'

'You better go.'

'Right. A last hug?'

They had a quick hug and then Jay walked away. He
turned and waved and felt like a complete bastard as he saw
that Caitlin was crying and Sophie was trying to comfort
her. But he kept going, got himself through security and
then made his way to the gate to board the plane. When he
got there, they were still boarding the first-class passengers,
so he had time to read the note. He sat down, opened the
folded paper up and started reading.

'He's gone,' sobbed Caitlin and I should be with him. Why
do I keep screwing everything up?'

'Let's go and get a coffee and have a sit down.'

Caitlin allowed herself to be guided to the nearest coffee
shop. Sophie pushed her gently into a chair and joined the
queue.

Caitlin had never felt so bad. It was worse than when
she found out that Brandon was still bonking Fenella. Much

worse than when she found out Fenella was pregnant with Brandon's child. The only thing she could compare it to was when she had seen Jay lying in the road, blood pouring from his head. That was worse, but only marginally.

'Right, get this down you.' Sophie returned with two lattes and two slices of carrot cake.

'Sophie, I want to thank you for being a good friend. I don't know what I'd have done without you. Let me pay for these.'

'No way. I have more money in the bank than you could earn in a lifetime. I'm not boasting, but I just want you to stop worrying about everything. You need a friend right now, and I'm it. In fact, if you want to help me you could do some dog walking. Now that you'll have more time on your hands.'

Caitlin smiled. 'I'd love to help you.' It would help her too; stop her obsessing about Jay morning, noon, and night. He had promised to post photos on Facebook and to direct message her whenever he could.

They ate their cake and Caitlin was sipping her coffee when Sophie started laughing. Caitlin couldn't see outside the coffee shop so had no idea what she was laughing at.

'What's so funny?'

'Life, hon, that's what's so funny.'

'Well, it's not making me laugh at the moment I can promise you.'

'Well maybe this will,' Sophie said as she stood up and held her chair out for someone behind Caitlin. 'Just going to… powder my nose.'

Before Caitlin could ask her what the hell was going on, Jay sat down and smiled.

'Jay! What the…? Have you missed your flight?'

'Yep,' he said with a big grin.

'That's awful. How? I thought you had plenty of time to board.'

Jay waved the letter from Betty. 'This made me see sense. ...*as long as you have each other, you have everything you need.* That's what she said. It made me realise that I don't need to go travelling when I've got paradise right here.'

'Oh, Jay.'

'Too cheesy?' he asked.

'Maybe, but lovely. Like you.'

'I'm sorry, Caitlin, for ever thinking I could leave you. Whatever I do in my life from now on, I want you by my side, and if that means my travelling days are over, then so be it.'

Caitlin leaned across the table and took Jay's hands.

'Your travelling days are not over. I want to go travelling, at the right time. I want to do everything you want to do. But more than anything, I want to fall asleep next to you, and wake up the next morning, with you beside me. If I could do that for the rest of my life, I'd be happy.'

'That's what I want, too. But... you will come with me to see all the places we've not seen yet?'

'Yes, of course, I will. Maybe after Christmas. Then, like Betty's letter says, we'll settle down in Leytonsfield and make babies.'

'I love the sound of that.' Jay grinned. 'Would you do something for me?'

'Of course, anything.'

'Spend Christmas Day with my family. You'll love it. We can go and see your parents on Christmas Eve or Boxing Day if you like, but Christmas Day at my parents' house is pretty special.'

'I wouldn't miss it for the world. And I'm sure my parents will be fine without me on Christmas Day.' And every other day, thought Caitlin. But joining Jay's family made up for that.

'So, what now?' asked Jay.

'Now, we go home. If we can find Sophie. Then tomorrow, when Betty is home, we take SpongeBob back.'

'That's going to hurt,' said Jay, 'but in a good way. When we settle down, we can fill our home with dogs. And babies.'

'But before that, we go travelling. We can spend lots of time together planning our itinerary for next year,' Caitlin said.

'And when we're not doing that, we can be having hot sex.'

'Oh, yes, lover boy, lots and lots of hot sex.'

'Betty didn't put that in her letter.'

'I think it was implied.'

Jay gazed at her with such a look in his eyes that she nearly melted.

'I do love you so much, Caitlin.'

'And I love you. Always will.'

They sat, gazing into each other's eyes then realised that Sophie had joined them at the table.

'So,' she said, looking from one to the other, 'Are we sorted now? No more misunderstandings? Can we go home then?'

'Yes, let's go home.'

Epilogue

Six months later

Jay and Caitlin sat on the sand, holding hands, and watching the sun begin to set. It had been a perfect Bali day. Hot with a cloudless sky.

Sophie had flown out especially so she could be a witness. Caitlin had bought a white, floaty dress to wear. She hadn't needed to buy shoes as they both went bare-footed. It's the best way to dress for a beach wedding, to feel the sand between your toes. She wore flowers in her hair. Jay dressed in white jeans and a white shirt, worn loose.

Sophie wore a baby blue chiffon dress with a large, white camellia in her hair, and cried during the ceremony. Sophie hardly ever cried.

They'd been in Sydney, Australia, enjoying a meal in one of the best restaurants in the city at Darling Harbour. They'd spent an idyllic day, having visited Sea Life, the Opera House and had completed the bridge walk. The views of Sydney from the top of the harbour bridge were amazing.

After their meal, Jay had got down on one knee and proposed, to the delight of the customers and staff alike. Caitlin had been ecstatic but neither of them wanted a long engagement. Caitlin had been there, done that and had no intention of repeating the experience.

So, they'd talked about it and both agreed that Bali would be the best place for a beach wedding. They'd spent the happiest day of their lives. It had been perfect, from the arch covered in flowers, the meal the three of them shared afterwards and the laid-back, easy-going way the ceremony had gone. No stress, no awkward relatives, no expense. Just the three of them and the civil celebrant.

Sophie, of course, had met a man and she was sharing cocktails with him at the beach bar. She'd declared it the best wedding she'd ever been to.

And now, at the end of a perfect day, they sat together on the sand and watched the glory of an Indonesian sunset. The colours were like brushstrokes in the sky. The clouds looked as if they were on fire with the myriad shades; from yellow, to orange and red.

Caitlin rested her head on Jay's shoulder, and every now and then he kissed her gently on the forehead.

'I love you, Mrs O'Connor.'

'And I love you, Mr O'Connor.'

'Do you want to go yet?'

Caitlin sighed. 'I never want to leave here, it's been the most wonderful day of my life. I never thought I could ever be this happy.'

'There'll be more days like this, Cait, I promise.' said Jay, 'This is only the beginning.'

'The first day of the rest of our lives.'

He kissed her again and they stayed, sitting together, holding hands, watching the sun sink lower until it dropped into the ocean and disappeared from view.

Next in The O'Connors Series

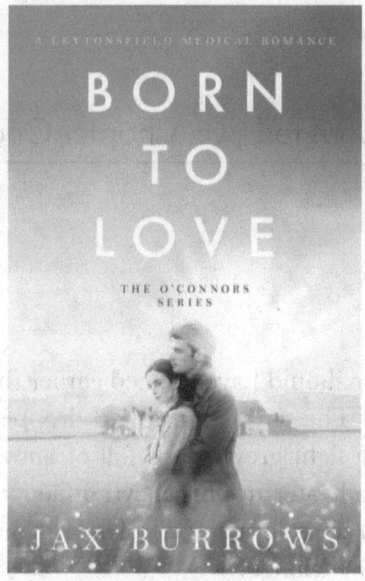

vinci-books.com/borntolove

Two strangers. One snowstorm. A chance neither expected.

Midwife Josie O'Connor is tired of delivering everyone else's happy endings. Stranded in a snowstorm, she's rescued by grumpy doctor Charles Atkins. As their hearts thaw, they must decide if their connection is a fleeting moment—or the start of forever.

Turn the page for a free preview…

Born to Love: Chapter One

Josie O'Connor should have noticed earlier that the weather was closing in. The temperature had dropped, and the sky was heavy with light grey clouds full of snow. She shivered and turned the heater up in her Mini Cooper, then turned the radio up to sing along to one of her favourite Christmas carols: Away in a Manger.

Her mind had been elsewhere when she had left the South Yorkshire home of Harriet, a midwife Josie used to work with before Harriet took maternity leave.

Josie had hugged Harriet, congratulated her, and given her all the Christmas presents she had bought for Harriet, her husband Frank, and Chloe, the latest arrival. Her new baby was adorable, and Josie felt mixed emotions as she held the tiny, soft, wriggling human in her arms. She was happy for Harriet, of course, she was, but jealous of her too. She had everything Josie wanted. A loving husband, a gorgeous baby and a future as a wife and mother.

Josie was determined to get home that night. Her twin brother, Jay, and his new wife, Caitlin, were returning from their overseas travels and, much as she wanted to see her beloved twin again, she had a bone to pick with him. Jay and Caitlin had married on a beach in Bali with two witnesses. Josie hadn't been invited. She was hurt but understood the reasoning behind it. She would never have done that to him though. When she married, all the family would be there to celebrate with her. First, of course, she had to meet the right man.

Josie turned the windscreen wipers on to their highest speed and looked up at the sky which had decided to shed its load. It was getting dark already and Josie knew she'd have to put her foot down if she was going to beat the weather. The wind had increased, and snow swirled and danced in front of the car. The wind pushed at the car as if trying to knock it over, so Josie decreased her speed, despite her anxiety to get home to Leytonsfield as quickly as she could.

Josie had two choices: she could head to the motorway which would probably be the best option or take the Woodhead Pass route, which was scenic and would take longer but was Josie's preference. She loathed driving on the motorway, feeling safer on the A roads.

In fine weather, the surrounding moors looked beautiful and Josie loved the drive to Harriet's, but in bad weather, they were dark and dangerous. At present, she could hardly see them through the snow which was building up to become a blizzard.

She was still trying to decide which way to go when she saw a man step into the road in front of her car. If she hadn't been driving so slowly she might have hit him. He had a dark jacket on and wasn't wearing anything reflective. He was waving his hands for her to stop, and his face was white in the light from the headlights.

Josie moved into the side of the road and pulled on the handbrake but left her headlights on and the engine running. She had heard of scams where people stopped cars in such a way then either robbed the driver or stole the car. Sometimes both. Josie was aware of being alone and no match for a man if one attacked her. Maybe it was time she invested in self-defence classes.

She lowered the window slightly, but not enough that the man could put his hand through. He bent forward and Josie could see the desperation in his eyes.

'Please... we need help. My wife's in labour and the baby's coming. Can you help?'

Josie forgot her fears immediately and got out of the car.

'Have you phoned an ambulance?' she asked.

'Yes, but since then the baby's head... well, I think I can see the head. Can you help her?'

So, the baby's crowning. Josie left her headlights on as they might give her precious light to work with and moved swiftly to the car where a woman was writhing and crying in pain. Her partner had pushed the front seat of the car as far back as it would go, and the woman was reclining on it with her hands resting on her belly. There was fluid on the seat and the floor of the car, indicating that the woman's waters had broken.

'What's your name, love?' asked Josie.

'Brenda,' the woman gasped. 'Is Mike there?'

'Yes, but I'm a midwife and can help you deliver the baby. There's not enough room for both of us in here.' Josie laughed but the woman was too busy breathing through another contraction to join in.

'May I examine you?'

Josie took the woman's groan as a yes and, kneeling in

front of her, pulled her patient's maternity leggings and panties, which were at her knees, further down and took them off, handing them to Mike who had clambered into the driver's seat and was watching Josie's every move anxiously.

The car was a Nissan but surprisingly spacious and Josie was confident that she could help Brenda deliver her baby safely, provided the cord wasn't around the baby's neck or they weren't dealing with a breech or brow presentation.

Josie felt Brenda's belly and was relieved to feel that the baby was in a good position; head down facing Brenda's back. She then examined the business end as one of the consultants she worked with called it, and the baby was definitely on its way.

'Is she alright?' asked Mike with a tremor in his voice.

'She's fine,' said Josie.

'Arghh!' said Brenda as another contraction twisted her inside out.

'Push, Brenda, that's it—you're doing well.'

Josie was aware that this poor woman was delivering a baby in a blizzard with no pain relief. She felt overwhelming admiration for her. Women were so strong when they had to be. Mike, however, looked as if he was about to pass out. He needed something to do.

'Why don't you ring the ambulance service again and tell them things have progressed since your first call?'

'Right, I'm on it.' Mike climbed out of the car and Josie breathed a sigh of relief. Now she could concentrate fully on Brenda.

Mr Charles Atkins was spending Christmas alone in his brother's cottage in the Peak District. An isolated, lonely place that suited Charles's mood perfectly. He had swallowed his pride when Andrew offered him the retreat and forgot the animosity he felt at the obscene amount of money Andrew earned in his private practice in London. He was desperate to get away and the offer of the cottage was exactly what he needed.

The plan was to pretend Christmas wasn't happening and drown his sorrows in copious amounts of whisky. To that end, he would need more of the stuff as well as essentials such as bread, milk, baked beans, and coffee. If he needed to eat he could exist on beans on toast; he'd done it before as a medical student. Then it wasn't lack of money that forced him to eat frugally, but the long hours he had spent on the wards, studying for exams, and trying to keep body and soul together. He had never had the time to eat properly.

Charles stocked up with provisions and booze in the small supermarket in the village. He ignored the Christmas music being played, the brightly coloured tree in the corner, and the tinsel strewn over everything in sight. Christmas. Bah humbug!

The snow was falling heavily now, and the pavements were already becoming treacherous. He glanced over to the pub on the other side of the road. Andrew had told him all about the village and its inhabitants and the pub sounded as if it was worth a visit. As it was the only one in the centre of the village, it was a warm, friendly place apparently, where everyone knew everyone else in the typical intimacy of village life. He would have liked to have ordered a pint and sat in front of the roaring fire that Andrew had assured him burned merrily all winter, but in his present mood, he wasn't up for making small talk and being cheerful. He was better off alone in the cottage.

Charles drove his four-wheel-drive Subaru carefully down the winding road that led out of the village. Moorland Cottage, as Andrew had named it, was conveniently within walking distance, which was useful in good weather, Andrew had told him. Now, however, with visibility at almost zero and the temperature falling, Charles was glad of his car.

He was nearly back at the cottage when he passed two parked cars, both with headlights blazing. The Mini had no one in it, but the Nissan, which had the interior light on, contained two women who looked to be engaged in a sexual act in the front. One woman was bare from the waist down and the other woman was kneeling in front of her, and… at the long, drawn-out cry of the first woman, Charles realised his mistake. He would recognise the agony in that cry anywhere; he'd heard countless women in labour emit the same sound.

Charles parked up ahead of the Nissan and got out. He noticed the man next to the car on his mobile.

'Can I help at all?' asked Charles.

'Uh, I don't know. I've phoned the ambulance and it's on the way. The lady says she's a midwife.'

'Right. I'll just see if there's anything I can do.'

Charles put his head around the open door. 'Need any help?'

The midwife who was encouraging the pregnant woman to push, frowned and glared at him. 'There's nothing to see here. You could talk to the husband if you want to do something to help.'

Charles was taken aback by her abrupt manner but considering the unusual circumstances and the fact that she didn't know he was an obstetrician, Charles decided not to take umbrage.

'Okay, if you're sure.'

'Push, Brenda, the baby's nearly out. Push down into your bottom. Yes, that's right, good girl.'

'Be careful that the cord isn't around the baby's neck.' Charles couldn't move away despite the midwife's orders. He was ready if she needed him to step in.

The midwife glared at him. 'I've checked.'

'Good. Be ready to catch her; once her head and shoulders are clear, she'll come out like a cork out of a bottle.' The midwife ignored him.

'Come on, Brenda, that's it… you're doing great, just one more big push.'

'Aaarrrgggh!'

'She's here. You've done it. Oh, she's beautiful, Brenda.'

The baby let out a lusty cry and waved her tiny hands at the world, as Josie deftly lifted her and put her on Brenda's chest.

Charles had a lump in his throat as he beckoned the man to come forward. He did, with tears streaming down his face.

'Come and meet your daughter,' said Charles.

'Oh my goodness, Bren, you did it. Oh, I love you so much. Can I see her?'

Mike came forward and kissed his wife then stared at the baby in awe.

Charles removed his woollen jacket and took off his Aran sweater, then put his jacket back on. 'Here, take this to wrap her in. It's warm and soft.'

'Thank you.' They wrapped the tiny girl in the sweater and stared at her in rapture.

The midwife had got out of the car and was bending

and stretching to ease her aching muscles. Charles recognised the signs of fatigue in her face, something he'd experienced himself after attending a long labour. She'd been squashed into the footwell of the car which can't have been comfortable for any length of time. He felt a surge of admiration for the midwife and the new mother.

'Congratulations. Lucky for them you came by.'

'Thanks,' she said. 'I wish the ambulance would turn up, I'd be happier if the cord could be cut and she was checked over by the experts.'

A siren in the distance getting closer made them both look up in the direction of the sound.

'Looks as if your wish is granted,' said Charles.

Fifteen minutes later, Brenda, Mike and the baby were safely in the ambulance and on their way to the hospital, and Charles and the midwife were huddled together in an increasingly violent snowstorm.

Charles felt cold without his favourite Aran sweater and was eager to get back to the cottage to start on the first bottle of whisky.

'Right, I'll be on my way. Have you got far to go?' he asked.

'I live in Leytonsfield in Cheshire.' Now there's a coincidence, thought Charles.

'Be careful on the motorway in this weather.'

'I'm thinking of taking the A628. I avoid motorways if I can, especially in weather like this.'

'The Woodhead Pass would be worse—if they haven't closed it already.'

Charles wasn't happy about this. She was in a Mini Cooper, a car not built for serious weather conditions. She'd be tired after delivering a baby in difficult circumstances. It was his duty to try and dissuade her.

'Why not come back to the cottage for a while and see if the blizzard eases. You can stay the night and leave in the morning.' It would only delay his date with the whisky bottle by one night.

'I need to get home tonight. It's Christmas Eve tomorrow and I don't want to be stuck here over the festive season.'

Charles fumbled in his inside pocket and produced one of his cards. 'Here, take this and ring me if you get stuck. Don't take risks, it isn't worth it.'

The midwife squinted at the card in the dim light and then looked at him. 'Mr Charles Atkins. Obstetrician and Gynaecologist.'

'And you are?'

'Josie O'Connor.'

'Midwife extraordinaire.'

She smiled. It was the first time he had seen her smile and Charles realised she was extremely attractive with her hazel eyes and long dark hair.

'Right. I'll be off. Nice to meet you.' Josie got into her car and started the engine. Charles watched her drive away with mixed feelings. The last thing he wanted this Christmas was company, especially that of a beautiful woman. He wanted to be a miserable so and so on his own and forget his problems for a while. But, on the other hand, he hated the thought of anything happening to Josie because she'd stopped to help a complete stranger.

Charles hoped that, if the road was closed, she'd ring him. Perhaps he'd postpone his binge drinking until later just in case.

Born to Love: Chapter Two

An obstetrician. Of course, he had to be an obstetrician, didn't he? No wonder he knew all about the dangers of birth, such as the cord around the baby's neck. Only someone who delivered babies for a living would be able to retain such a cool, self-assured demeanour when faced with a woman in labour. He must have delivered hundreds of babies. Well, so had she and the baby was safe and well, as was the mother. Because of her. She should be proud of herself.

Josie tried to concentrate on the road, which was proving harder with each mile she drove. The weather was getting worse the further she travelled.

By the time Josie had reached the turnoff for Manchester and the A628, she was too late. The familiar red metal sign telling motorists that the road ahead was closed sat firmly in the middle of the lane. She had no choice but to turn around and go back.

Josie took her phone out of her pocket to let her mother

know that she may be delayed, but there was no signal. Sighing with frustration she turned her car around and headed for the motorway. She'd drive slowly and carefully. It was fine. She could do this.

Driving back the way she had come was harder as she was heading into the wind and the blizzard was obliterating her view of the road. She knew she should stop and ring the doctor to help her. It was madness to drive in these conditions and common sense told her she was putting her life— and other people's—in danger. But Josie was stubborn and desperate to get home. She wanted to see Jay again.

She drove on, slowly crawling along the narrow country road. She could only see a few feet ahead of her in the full beam of the headlights; large snowflakes hit the windscreen and were angrily swept away by the wipers. She could see nothing on either side but a white swirling mass. She knew there were fields, dry stone walls, copses, hills, and streams. The Peak District was a beautiful place in summer. Now it was the stuff of nightmares.

Hypnotised by the white world she was enclosed in, Josie didn't notice that she was drifting into the middle of the road until a car coming in the other direction sounded its horn to warn her. She pulled the steering wheel over to the left as hard as she could and skidded on an icy patch of road, the Mini ending up in the ditch with the wheels spinning uselessly.

No, oh, bugger! I don't believe this. Josie thumped the steering wheel in temper. Then broke down and cried.

When her hissy fit was over, she wiped her tears away with the back of her hand and listened.

The engine had stalled but the radio was still playing. A children's choir was singing *In the Bleak Mid-Winter,* their voices pure and sweet. Josie joined in. She loved singing and had always been in choirs from schooldays to university and then the hospital choir at Leytonsfield General, and it distracted her from the predicament she was in.

The blizzard was as fierce as ever and Josie felt the first stirrings of panic. Whenever she was in a tricky situation or had a difficult decision to make, she thought of her gran, her mother's mum, a lady of infinite common sense and wit. When she'd died at the age of ninety-two, Josie didn't think she would ever get over it. Her mum had told her that Gran was watching over her and she could talk to her at any time. So she did.

Okay, Gran, I need your help. She knew what her gran would say. Phone the doctor, he didn't give you his phone number for nothing. Ring him.

Josie took her phone out of her pocket, forgetting there was no signal, and stared at the blank screen. Okay, so find a public phone box. To do that, however, she would probably have to walk to the nearest village as she hadn't noticed one on the drive to where she was now. Where was she? She didn't know. She'd kept on the same winding road, except for turning around at the junction to the Woodhead Pass, so if she kept walking, she'd surely end up back in the village.

Josie had a choice—she could stay in the car and hope another motorist came by who she could flag down. Or she could get out of the car and start walking back to the village. She was warm where she was but how long would that last? It was freezing out there and what if she wandered off the road and lost her way? She could get stuck in a snowdrift and then what? Death from hypothermia?

Okay, Gran, what's plan B?

Josie waited for inspiration. Then she peered out of the

windscreen as she thought she spotted light. Yes… there were headlights coming towards her. She quickly opened the driver's door and gasped for breath at the cold and the strength of the wind. She had no thoughts now of serial killers or people trying to rob her. Her gran had sent this person to rescue her.

'Are you okay?'

Josie recognised the voice. Then she felt relief when she saw his face. She had never been so grateful to see anyone before. It was the doctor, and he was sensibly carrying a torch.

'I had to pull the wheel over with some force and skidded on a patch of ice.'

'Right. Get your things and get in the car. There's nothing we can do about the Mini until the snow melts. It looks as if it's stuck fast.'

When Josie clambered out of her car, she saw what he meant. Her little motor was almost completely buried in a snowdrift with more snow covering the top and side. If she'd stayed in the car much longer, she would have been buried too.

She did as the doctor said and relished the warm interior of the four-wheel drive. She bet he had snow tyres as well. There were no carols playing on the radio though.

'Have you got a suitcase or overnight bag?'

'No. I wasn't planning on staying the night. I've only got the clothes I'm wearing.'

'Right.'

The doctor climbed in, put his seat belt on and proceeded to perform a perfect three-point turn.

'Thanks for coming. How did you find me?'

'Process of elimination. I knew you had to be somewhere between the village and the turn off for the Wood-head Pass. It wasn't difficult.'

'How did you know I needed help?'

'I made a lucky guess. The blizzard is getting worse, the forecast is dire. A Mini Cooper is no match for these conditions. I shouldn't have let you go. I blame myself.'

Josie bristled at that. 'It was my decision, not yours. You can't blame yourself. I'm a grown woman.'

'You may be a grown woman, but you weren't thinking straight. You were desperate to get home and nothing was going to stand in your way. Common sense had flown out of the window. No, I should have insisted you stay overnight or at least until the roads had been gritted.'

'I'm glad you didn't try insisting. I'm grateful for your help but no one tells me what to do.'

The doctor gave her a sideways look with the hint of a smile. 'Would you like me to stop and let you out? Or take you back to your Mini? Or would you prefer to accept my help?'

Chastened, Josie realised the truth of what he said. She needed his help and she'd have to accept it, at least until the roads were open again.

'I'm sorry. I'm grateful and, of course, you're right.' Josie hated to admit it, but she needed this man, at least for the next twenty-four hours.

'Apology accepted.'

Josie kept quiet and stared ahead at the snow. It was mesmerising watching it dance in the headlights.

They turned right off the road and the doctor pulled up outside a stone cottage. The side of the cottage faced the road and the front looked out over the moors. The views would be spectacular in daylight.

'Right. Let's get inside,' said the doctor.

They were glad to move from the freezing cold into the warmth and light of the cottage.

'Oh, this is lovely,' said Josie gazing around her. The living room was small with low ceilings and exposed wooden beams. There was a three-piece suite in brown leather, adorned with brightly coloured cushions, that looked comfy and inviting. A television sat on an oak stand, and there was a bookcase and a coffee table. But the thing that drew Josie's attention was the cast iron wood burning stove in the corner of the room.

'Oh, I love these,' she said moving towards it and holding her hands out to the blaze.

'Careful, you'll get chilblains if your hands are cold,' said the doctor who was standing in the doorway watching her.

Josie moved away. How long would she have to stay here with Dr Grumpy? Nice as the cottage was, she wanted to be at home with her family. But he was putting himself out to help her and she needed to be more gracious.

'I just wanted to say again how much I appreciate your help.' That came out all wrong. It sounded stiff and too formal.

'You're welcome. I wasn't going to leave you out in the snow.'

'No, but still… Dr…?'

'Atkins, but you can call me Charles seeing as we're going to be sleeping under the same roof.'

'Right. I'm Josie.'

'Yes, I remember. Would you like me to show you to your bedroom?'

'Yes, please.' She hoped he wasn't expecting her to go to bed yet, it was far too early, and she hadn't eaten for hours.

Josie followed Charles up the narrow stairs, the wood creaking with nearly every step. You couldn't sneak home in the early hours in this cottage, thought Josie, the house itself would give you away.

'Sorry it's only a single bed, and the room's quite small. The wardrobe is minute too, but I imagine you won't mind that. At least you can hang your coat up.'

'You're not selling me this room, Charles.'

Charles laughed and his face lit up. His eyes sparkled and laughter lines appeared. He looked completely different when he smiled. It was a shame his default setting was miserable.

'Sorry. I'm not used to the idea of a visitor yet. I had planned to spend Christmas here on my own.'

'Really? Whatever for?' Josie was amazed that someone would choose to be alone at Christmas. 'Don't you like Christmas?'

'Normally I don't mind it, but this year... it's complicated. Anyway, how about a drink? Tea or coffee? I'll make it while you settle in and have a look around. I'll lend you a T-shirt to sleep in if you want.'

'Yes, thank you. Yes to the T-shirt and either, I drink tea and coffee. Anything really. Whatever you're having.'

'Right. Okay then. There should be a new toothbrush in the bathroom and a flannel. I'll hunt out some towels. Use whatever's there.'

'Yes, I will, and thank you again.'

'No need to keep thanking me. Right. Come down whenever you're ready.'

'I will.'

Charles left and Josie listened to his footsteps running lightly down the stairs. She sat on the edge of the bed and closed her eyes. This wasn't on the agenda. She had taken some annual leave to welcome Jay and Caitlin home and spend some quality time with her family. She was looking forward to a normal O'Connor Christmas at her parents' house. For the last few years, she had been on duty so felt she had earned Christmas and New Year off.

Not only was she away from her family but she was disturbing Charles's plans. But why on earth would anyone choose to spend Christmas alone? Whatever the reason, he must be annoyed to have an unwelcome guest drop in. No wonder he was grumpy, she would be too if her plans had been scuppered in such a way.

Josie sighed and looked around the bedroom. The bed was comfortable enough even though she hadn't slept in a single bed since she was a teenager. The room was tidy, and the bed linen smelled fresh. She stood up and gazed out of the window but all she could see was snow still swirling around. Visibility was almost nil.

Time to go downstairs and join Charles. She took off her coat and hung it in the wardrobe. It looked lonely hanging there on its own. She closed the wardrobe door and made her way to the kitchen.

'You said anything, so I decided hot chocolate would be a good drink for this weather.'

'Fantastic, I love hot chocolate. And you've got marshmallows as well. Thank you.'

Josie sat at the kitchen table, sipping her hot chocolate. Charles sat opposite her. The wind howled around the cottage. It could be worse, she could still be stuck in her car in a snowdrift. Or out on the moors, lost and alone.

'I know you said not to keep thanking you, but... I am grateful.'

Charles smiled and nodded.

They sat in silence, both lost in their own thoughts. The

blizzard continued to howl, and Josie wondered how long she would have to stay here, in an isolated cottage with Dr Grumpy. Then, as if she heard her gran's voice, the words appeared in her mind; Angels come in many forms.

Grab your copy...
vinci-books.com/borntolove

About the Author

Jax lives in the NW of England with two cats - George and Cloud. She spent the last twenty years working in a cancer hospital as a secretary and retired in the middle of the pandemic. Her colleagues still managed to give her a decent send off.

Jax writes contemporary romance novels set in a small fictional town in Cheshire. All her stories have a happy ending which is hard won. She doesn't shy away from serious subjects - her characters have a lot to cope with! But that makes their happy ever after all the sweeter.

When Jax isn't writing or plotting a new series, she listens to music or reads. She can sometimes be found doing a sneaky cross-stitch whilst listening to an audio book.

www.ingramcontent.com/pod-product-compliance
Lightning Source LLC
Chambersburg PA
CBHW011422010726
47494CB00011B/2463